# YANOMAMI

*A novel*

## Marc André Meyers

ISBN: 1530457858
ISBN 13: 9781530457854

"Hay que endurecerse, pero sin perder la ternura jamás."

Ernesto Guevara de la Serna

# CHAPTER ONE

Comandante Paulo lifted himself from his hammock and walked out of the wooden hut. The sides were made out of woven bamboo and the top of palm leaves. His blue eyes blinked as he stared out, momentarily blinded by the sun. He felt tired and a little dizzy. The night had not been easy, with the malaria monkeys harassing him – every time he had a malaria attack he would invariably dream about monkeys and sloths. They whistled at him as they dangled around, fierce and somewhat aggressive. He gazed for one moment at the yard, rubbing his face where a beard blended with the long curly hair, the black softened by the first white strands. Celeste was washing clothes by the water and came to him excitedly as soon as she saw him. "Coffee, Comandante?"

He waved yes, and in a few minutes she brought him his tin can with coffee and sugar. She uttered a little sigh as he caressed her black shiny hair and sipped on the coffee. Her loose dress, which hung almost to her bare feet, bulged in front, and she was visibly pregnant. Celeste was almost pure Indian and her quiet demeanor and effacing presence were clearly learned from childhood. Indians had to be subservient.

He walked back inside and sat at a simple table, made with rough planks. He opened a book and briefly leafed through it, reading at random.

*Ocamo Mission, Venezuela, July 2001.*

*Rested at the Ocamo Salesian mission yesterday, already 100 km inside Venezuela; government troops from Bogotá have been pursuing us to the border. We need time to recover strength due to long march through forest, carrying Denilson in hammock. He has a punctured lung and is receiving medical help at the mission. Yesterday night met Louis Bonaparte, anthropologist from Berkeley. He has been studying the Yanomami for the past thirty-five years. He loaned me his famous book,* Fierce Yanomami, *which I am reading while we wait for Denilson's recovery. It is very poor, dialectically speaking, but it contains good ideas. Father Antoine Ibernegaray, Professor Bonaparte, and I talked into the early hours of the morning. The scotch brought by Bonaparte helped to lift our spirits. It is a very capitalistic beverage, but we all indulged in it. It was one of the most interesting evenings of my life. We used three radically different approaches and yet converged, at the end, on the same common points. Father Antoine is a Christian Socialist. Bonaparte can be described as a Darwinian Capitalist, and I am the Marxist par excellence. We represent different ideologies, different concepts of life. No need to expand on this. We all recognize that the native populations of Latin America have been the great losers in these five hundred years. It is imperative to preserve whatever is left, at whatever cost. Bonaparte is resigned that, in the end, Darwinian Capitalism will crush them. Father Antoine, that they will become eventually exemplary Christians, devoid as they are of the vices of civilization. And I argued that they have a primitive communist society, with little concern for individual property. Tomorrow, Bonaparte will take us to the village of Bisaasi-Teri.*

He looked up and reflected for a moment. The visit had caused a deep impression within him.

"Here are some fried eggs and manioc flower," Celeste said, handing him a plate. "Comandante, you've been in the hammock for three weeks."

He shook his head, which felt painful and hollow, then looked lovingly at Celeste, thanking her. Putting the plate on the table, he took another sip of his coffee. His hand shook slightly as he lifted the cup to his mouth. He took a pen, thought for a minute, then wrote:

*August 2002, Caguan*

*The past combat in Los Pozos in which my troops joined forces with Col. Soto Mayor's FARC was a total and cruel farce. We were supposed to fight paramilitary units from Bogotá. Captain Mendoza lured us into attacking a group of peasants that had barricaded themselves in a village. I ordered the compañeros to stop when I saw that FARC was massacring the peasants. I even threatened Mendoza with my compañeros.*

*They are a bunch of cowards and we cannot continue to co-operate with them. Fourteen peasants were killed because they refused to deliver their crop of coca paste to FARC. And we took part in such an operation. I ordered my compañeros to retreat to the border with Venezuela. They marched on to the Esperanza camp. I was too weakened by malaria to go.*

After closing his diary, he looked, once more, at his tremulous hand. He had barely been able to write. A bittersweet taste filled his mouth. It was the malaria flavor; he knew it. He turned around and yelled, "Celeste, get a pot of warm water. I am going to shave."

"To shave, Comandante?" she exclaimed in surprise as she wobbled to the kitchen to heat up some water.

She set it up outside and brought scissors and a mirror. "Let me cut the hair off before you shave, Comandante. Then we'll put the hot water on your face. I also got a razor blade."

She proceeded to work quietly and diligently. Gradually, the features emerged from under the beard. The well-shaped chin, the sunken cheeks and the scar that cut from the lower lip to close to the ear. Celeste's scissors moved to the hair, which she sculpted with precision. As she did this, she stroked his hair with love and admiration.

Paulo grunted somewhat sadly, as he watched his face re-emerge. "*Le ravage des années,*" he murmured, quoting some famous French writer that he had read umpteen years ago.

"What, Comandante?"

"I look ravaged."

"You look very handsome. If our little child is half as beautiful, I'll be happy. If he could only have your eyes."

In the mirror, Paulo saw the sharp blue eyes, where fire still burned. The skin was dark and wrinkled by the years of sun, rain, mosquito bites, and hardship. He struggled with the razor, holding it in his left hand and trying, in vain, to remove the stubble. His frail body trembled a little. The arm had a deep scar and was mauled.

"Let me do this for you, Comandante. Your elbow does not bend enough." She gazed at him quizzically. "You're looking very good."

"Celeste, you're being kind. The last time I shaved was twenty years back and now I see in the mirror the father of that young man."

"You're young for me, Comandante." He patted her on her head again, caressing her like a dog. He was a little awkward at that; it was a gesture he was not accustomed to.

"Celeste, I could be your father." But the handsome features were still there, in the mirror, carved in deep wrinkles. He grinned and analyzed his teeth. Decay, a broken molar, and the dark yellow and brown color from many years of jungle. Thanks to Natasha he still had a few teeth left. She had been enormously patient with him, taking him to the Berkeley doctors and dentists, getting his mangled elbow operated on, installing several crowns on his teeth. There they were, shiny gold nuggets in a deep red hole.

"Yes Celeste, I'm an old horse."

"And old horses need fresh hay," she said, smiling.

"You're better than hay, you're pure honey." Then, suddenly turning serious, he added, "Celeste, we go to town today."

Her expression darkened. "Watch it, Comandante, they might recognize you. You know that the government put a bounty on your head!"

"Celeste, we've lost the revolution. Or the revolution has lost us. I'm a dinosaur, and there are other issues that drive the young guerrillas."

"They want money and power, Comandante. They just want to reap the profits of cocaine and spend it on whores and parties."

"It's not as simple as that, Celeste. I should've seen the change earlier."

"You'll always be our hero, our Comandante."

"Well, we're going to town. Get me some different clothes. Let me take these fatigues off."

They walked for two hours through a narrow trail in the thick jungle. The eggs and manioc had strengthened him, and he gradually regained his legendary stamina. Celeste walked behind Paulo, and Antonio, his faithful adjutant, closed the column. He carried a rifle. The trail gradually descended and disembogued into a small river. From there, the town was only one mile downstream. This is where Antonio stayed. He had been instructed to wait for them. They would return the next day.

San Vicente del Caguan consisted of a reasonably old masonry church and perhaps thirty wooden houses. A few grocery stores, bars, even a cabaret. Most houses had some kind of shop. The river was sufficiently wide to provide transportation for small boats. A pile of oil drums and several wooden boats tied side-by-side marked the harbor. The water was dark green, since the rainy season had not yet arrived. Any day now it would turn murky and acquire a light brown coloration. An airstrip at the edge of town doubled as soccer field and pasture. It was enough for the occasional Cessna that transported government officials and drug traffickers. The town lay on the Caguan River, in southeast Colombia. It was in a disputed zone, claimed by both the FARC guerrillas and the government. Thus, there was no police, and the citizenry kept the law, helped by the local *alcaide* and by the close-by FARC camp.

Father Antoine Ibernegaray had been at the confessional for over one hour, and was sweating profusely. There was no way the light breeze coming in through the church door could reach him, and the heat generated by his huge Basque body was intense. He felt caged and uncomfortable. He would have to have a bigger confessional made. In spite of the discomfort, this was a monthly chore that he secretly enjoyed. Taking score of his new flock, getting to know their little and not so little sins. For such a small town, there was a lot to reveal in the secret of the confessional. He had gone through several kids that confessed their usual fights, thefts, cursing, lying, and the euphemism "I sinned against myself." He had heard it for many years, and there was nothing he could do to stop them. They would probably leave in contrition, pray their Holy Marys and try very hard, for a couple of days. Then, it would be back to normal again. No, he was looking out for more serious stuff, for assassinations, betrayals. And for sins that he could correct.

"Father forgive me, for I've sinned. I've broken all the commandments."

An electric shock ran through Father Antoine's spine. Yes, he remembered this clear voice, eloquent even in the whisper of the confessionary. But from where? And a great sinner he was! He would find out soon. In his unmistakable French accent, he replied, "Confess my son, and repent. I will listen to you, but only God can forgive."

"I've broken all commandments, from the first to the last. Pride was at the bottom of it all."

"My son, you're being very hard on yourself." Father Antoine suddenly remembered the elegant voice, the Brazilian accent. Through the reticulated wood separation, he could capture a glimpse of the blue eyes. It had to be Comandante Paulo; it had to be him.

"Proceed my son," he said, as their meeting at the Salesian mission in Ocamo came back to him. Yes, it was in the upper Orinoco River, before he had been transferred to Caguan. Professor Bonaparte was with them. They drank into the night, into that wonderful night. They argued fiercely for hours, three orators, and three fiery souls. Father Antoine knew that it was not pride that had inspired the Comandante; it was his love and dedication for the destitute of Latin America. His pride had been satisfied much earlier, after the first combats, the first acts of courage. Thus, it had to be all love.

As Paulo continued his confession, logical and sequential, on how he had broken each and every commandment, Father Antoine's ears moved closer to the wooden screen. He wouldn't, he *couldn't* miss one word of this. This was a momentous decision for Paulo, to give himself back to the Holy Catholic and Apostolic Church, to his former archenemy.

"And my wife, the mother of my children Natasha and Ernesto, was the companion of one of my lieutenants in Nicaragua. I pursued her, sending her man to missions far away, to dangerous missions."

"David and Bet Sheba," murmured Father Antoine.

"Yes, Father, David and Bet Sheba. In one of these missions, he was killed. And she became mine."

"A mortal sin, two mortal sins."

"And this is how I came to Colombia, to these jungles that have sapped my strength, that have drenched my ideal."

Father Antoine had forgotten the heat, the darkness. His entire body was tensely leaning against the wooden screen. For one brief moment he remembered that he, too, was here to expiate his sins. Sins of the flesh, that was weak, even in his strong body, built like a tree. Sins that he had committed in the seminary at Arles. Sins that the older boys had taught him, and that he had passed on to younger boys. This was many years ago, and remorse still pursued him. Twenty years of jungle, one thousand years of jungle would not erase the memory.

"And your other sins, my son?"

"I openly accused my father of being an exploiter of the poor, of being a corrupt capitalist. It broke his heart. And he died not having seen me for twenty years. All his love I turned into hate!"

"Yes, my son, this is a capital sin."

"I attacked the Church relentlessly for years."

"So did Saint Paul, my son."

He continued and systematically revealed his actions over the past twenty years.

Then, it was the turn of Father Antoine. He presented the Church's position on his sins. He summarized by saying, "You have to be totally and completely convinced that you will not commit these sins again. And your absolution, which is given by God, will not be easily granted. You have to redress your bad deeds with good deeds. What can you do?"

For one moment, Paulo reflected. Then, he spoke, sadly but with that same determination and strength with which he had led student marches in his undergraduate days, with which he had led countless troops into battle and danger.

"I'll dedicate myself to the protection of the very life and culture of the native tribes of this forest. I'll be the protector of the Yanomami. Is this acceptable, Father?"

"My son, all your sins will be forgiven, for you have committed them in the name of love. Love for the poor, for the destitute. Your love manifested itself through Marxism-Leninism, to which you adhered rigidly for over twenty years. And this doctrine became your master, your god. And a cruel and demanding god it was, asking for crimes from you and for all of those that surrounded you. How many died, how many wounded? And look what is happening around you. Your god has failed you."

"Yes, Father, I'll do this. And as a sign of humility, a sign of atonement, I'd like to ask you to take the communion tomorrow, the communion that I rejected one year ago, when we first met."

"Go my son. And if you're truly committed to this deed, God forgives you through me, his humble shepherd. I'll give you the Host tomorrow."

Paulo got up and left. Behind him the line of women, children and a few men were patiently waiting. They, too, had their sins, but they realized that the blue-eyed gentleman must have had a truckload of them. The length of stay in the confessional was a measure of the gravity of sins. The old spinsters knew this so well. From the corner of their eyes, they looked in awe as he kneeled down, made the sign of the cross, and prayed, tears running down his eyes. Celeste knelt at his side.

On Sunday morning, people came from all around for mass. Several horses were tied down around the large mango tree in front of the church. The little grocery stores were transformed into bars, in preparation for a day of drinking. The children had decorated the plaza with paper farandoles. Red, green, and yellow. There was an air of excitement in the town. It was the feast of the Assumption. The procession circled the plaza and ten dignitaries carried the Virgin, placed on a palanquin. Behind the platform, six children dressed as angels. The tall figure of Father Antoine in resplendent garments of gold and light blue, a gift from the townspeople, followed them. He towered over all. The girls wore satin dresses with white wings attached to the back. The boys had red satin outfits, shields made out of turtle shells, and carried swords: the Archangels Michael and Raphael. Their long and pointed wings were yellow and blue: the colors of Colombia. Father Antoine looked at the procession proudly. A few egrets and macaws had to be shot for the occasion, but the forest was full of them. The kids were duly forgiven. He was happy that the statue had finally arrived from France, after many months of waiting. Notre Dame de Lourdes looked magnificent. Her pale and peaceful features spread harmony throughout the town. Inside, the crowd pushed into the nave. He hoped that she would protect Caguan from the throes of sin.

The procession finally entered the church, where it was awaited by the children's excited looks and the solemn ladies of the Congregation of Mary, with their light blue banners and veils. The men stood at the back, ready to walk out at the first opportunity. They needed to smoke, spit, and urinate.

In his baritone voice, Father Antoine paid a beautiful homage to Mary in an inspirational homily. His prose was poetic as he asked for her intercession. The crowd prayed to her, asking for her blessing. "She is the path through which we, imperfect beings, can reach God. She will, with her infinite ability to love, be the bridge between God Almighty and us. Being our mother, she will protect us. Being our mother, she will guide us. Being our mother, she will always love us. But we need to be in touch with her."

He finished his homily by repeating Paul's words to the Corinthians: "'And in the end, there will be no pride, there will be no knowledge, there will only be love.'"

At communion time the townspeople lined up to receive the Host. Among them was Comandante Paulo, thin and taut, followed by his pregnant wife. He could not keep from analyzing. His mind always pressed the limits of thought, of perception. As he waited in line, he equated the worship of Mary to old rituals in which the goddess represented fertility, protection, and love. He remembered the fertility goddesses unearthed all the way from Western Europe to Eastern Siberia. This worship, transposed to Catholicism was, strangely, still alive. As if the primordial spiritual tone in the universe was a female force; as if the woman, the womb, embodied eternity and renewal. As if a male God had to be balanced by a female force. He also knew that in South America Marianism, the cult of Mary had taken hold in a strong, almost incontrollable fashion. It was a matter of worry for Rome, but these things were not easy to regulate.

As he continued his mental analysis, he shook his head momentarily. He had seen, in his past twenty years of struggles in America and Africa, that dedicated priests and nuns, in the smallest of the villages, carried out a far greater task than his fellow revolutionaries. The Revolution was lost. All the bitter fighting, all the struggles, were in vain. Wherever the Left won, it established, in its turn, a repressive government. The FARC in Colombia collected the cocaine from the peasants and exported it to get cash. In Angola, where he had struggled along with Cuban troops, a retrograde Communist dictatorship had been implanted in the name of socialism. The poor people were now under the yoke of new masters. Yes, communism with its parades and highly recognized collective displays was also a religion. And what gods it had: Lenin, Stalin, and Mao. Each one of them claimed millions of lives. Of these, only the Che was pure. Che, the quixotic lover. Che the romantic. He had admired him beyond reason. He had emulated him. But El Che also had flaws.

This morning, in this small town of San Vicente del Caguan, he, Comandante Paulo laid down his arms. The singing in the church and the music were hauntingly familiar. He remembered his childhood in Monlevade, where priests and Dutch nuns had raised him. It seemed that life was closing its circle, that he was returning to these strong beliefs, to that faith. And his next task was to redress his wrongs, to help save the last Indians in the Amazon, to protect them from predatory interests, from nationalistic eruptions.

He would seek to correct all the excesses of youth. At his side was Celeste, and he petted her head with his left hand, moving his stiff elbow up. She looked at him and smiled. Her inscrutable Indian eyes had a childlike glimmer and he realized, at that moment, that he loved her, and that their love would produce a child of European and Indian ascent. He whispered into her ear, "Now, we need to get married, Celeste."

"You're already my man, Comandante."

"We'll make you a new white dress."

"But no wings, Comandante, please," she smiled.

"We killed enough egrets."

At this, she commanded him to be quiet. She took his hand and pressed it.

They took the Host, given by Father Antoine. Paulo felt the same emotion with which he would receive it, as a child, in Monlevade. The mysterious Host in his mouth, as it dissolved away, transporting him to another universe. On his knees, he made a solemn vow to carry out his mission, to his utmost ability. Also, to be a good and loving husband and father. To conduct whatever is left of his life with dignity, honor, and love. And to abandon the arms with which he has caused so much havoc.

Outside the church, Father Antoine greeted his flock, with a big smile and warm hugs. He was hungry and thirsty. Pilar had prepared a good meal of turtle, rice, and manioc. And, preciosity of preciosities, a couple bottles of white Muscadet wine awaited him, cool in the kerosene refrigerator. The Salesian priests had sent him a case from Lourdes, together with the statue. As Paulo approached him, he opened his arms in a broad embrace and hugged him.

"The return of the prodigal son. Come join me for lunch. And who is the charming lady?" he asked, with a wink.

At that moment, Paulo heard popping noises, from the forest. Then, the burning pain. He knew he had been shot. It was a familiar burn, and he did not panic. Instinctively, he dropped to the ground. In horror, he watched Father Antoine twist in pain. *He's also hurt.* More shots. Paulo felt more stings, as two, three bullets penetrated his body. Father Antoine fell on the ground, blood gurgling from his mouth. The townspeople ran in disarray. Celeste, terrified, threw herself on him, crying.

"My beloved Comandante. What are they doing to you?"

He looked at her, and there was a smile in his mouth. Blood trickled from the corner. He knew his hour had come.

The church bells tolled. He looked at the blue sky, and everything was peaceful. The pain was there, everywhere throughout his body. The blue turned lighter and lighter and merged with the sun. He was back in Monlevade, and felt the warm hand of Alaide, his beloved nanny, holding him. His head rested on her soft and tender lap. He was a little scared, but everything will be fine. She smiled at him.

# CHAPTER TWO

Natasha Chauny lay on her futon and looked at the pictures that she had pinned on the wall of her tiny Berkeley room. At her feet, Tonto, a black and furry mutt, looked at her with infinite admiration. She could feel his insecurity. No wonder, she had left him for a week and had just returned from Florida. Separation anxiety, she thought. She stroked his head, her hand burying deep into the silky black hair, as her eyes moved between two photographs. One, in faded black and white, showed a man in uniform holding an automatic rifle. The other showed a younger man embracing her, a Mayan pyramid in the background. It was Aaron, in Uxmal. They had crossed the Yucatan together, on motorcycle. She had loved him, she still loved him beyond measure. But he had graduated and moved away. He said that he resented the loss of freedom. He just left, happy and go-lucky as when he had entered her life. After having broken her heart.

The flight, originating in San Francisco, had been half empty, and Natasha had been able to sleep for a couple of hours. She was exhausted from finals and was looking forward to the break. The Delta Airlines Boeing 777 taxied along the runway, after circling once over the beautiful south Florida coastline. She gazed out with excitement, seeing Key Biscayne and Crandon Park carved in the blue ocean. Memories of her childhood ran through her mind.

As soon as the jet stopped, she stood impatiently. She grabbed her REI backpack and threw it over one of her muscular shoulders, a remnant of her crew days at Berkeley. Tall and attractive, her blonde hair and blue eyes made her look German or Scandinavian. Her olive skin and the slight elongation of her eyes proved that assumption false and gave her an exotic appearance. Her clothes were casual, 501 jeans and Birkenstocks. Yet, she walked with elegance and grace as she trotted out of the plane, and anxiously looked for Ernesto. For a brief moment, before entering into the air-conditioned airport, she felt a whiff of hot air. She could almost cut through the moisture. Familiar smells and a balmy breeze came from the Caribbean.

She was anxious to spend some time with her younger brother. They had both been busy, she trying to finish her studies, he with his new job as Novartis sales manager. She needed to get away from Berkeley, where memories of Aaron haunted her at every corner. Her cell phone rang. Ernesto said that he was held up at a meeting and that she should wait for him outside, at the curb. She felt disappointed and walked to the arrival section of the airport. She waited at the curb for a good fifteen minutes, before she heard honking coming from behind her. Ernesto, in a brand new Land Rover SUV, stopped at the curb. He waved from inside.

"Sis, you're looking really good." He pulled his sunglasses back and studied her, as he flipped open the passenger door to the car and motioned her in.

"You're the expert, Ernesto," she said.

"Please call me Ernie. That's what everybody calls me here."

"Do you know who you were named after?"

"Yeah, I heard the story. It's Che Guevara's first name. And it's embarrassing."

Natasha knew that Ernesto was sensitive about his background. He tried hard to be an all American and to fit in. His name, Ernesto Chauny de Betancourt, did not help. He was a good-looking, athletic young man. He had not finished college, opting instead to go into sales. He was a good talker and had few inhibitions. In the fast moving world of pharmaceuticals, he was making a name for himself. Although twenty-two, he had already proven himself.

They chatted excitedly as they drove past downtown and crossed Rickenbacker causeway into Key Biscayne. Natasha looked at the familiar beaches filled with sunbathers, at the blue ocean crisscrossed by peaceful sailboats and aggressive cigarette boats.

"They represent two cultures, Ernie. The sailboats are the Anglo and the cigarette boats the new Latinos."

"Yeah, they're lots of fun. I've arranged for us to party in Many's boat on Sunday."

"I'd rather go sailing," she said, hoping for a more peaceful outing.

"No chance, Sis. In Rome, do as the Romans."

"Have you forgotten our little sailboat? I would drag you behind, tied to a rope. You'd wear your snorkeling mask."

"It was a lot of fun. I saw several big turtles and a shark once."

"I remember that you totally panicked."

"I just wanted to give you a demonstration of how fast I could swim. There! Look at all these new buildings."

Natasha could see the transformation of Key Biscayne from a peaceful island into a plush community. Mercedes Benzes, BMWs, Jaguars, Bentleys, and Ferraris were everywhere. It had become a millionaire haven. They turned left on Ocean Lane Drive and entered the luxurious Commodore Club condominium.

"My new place," he announced proudly, as they passed the guard gate.

"And what happened to Mom's house?" She was shocked.

"Oh, I convinced her to sell it and trade it for a condo. It's so much more convenient. Our house was falling apart, Sasha."

"How could you have done this without checking with me, Ernie? It's the place where we grew up."

"And who would take care of it? I had to change the entire plumbing. I had a flood and we had mold all over. Give me a break, Sis, it's only a house."

"I bet you got rid of all our furniture too."

"Of course, that old stuff didn't go with my lifestyle. But I kept all your trinkets."

"Thank you, Ernie. You're so caring."

She only had herself and her mother to blame for Ernesto's attitude. He had been spoiled rotten since he was in the crib. Her grandmother Concepcion, their mother's mother, did not help either. She doted on every wish of the boy. She had lived with them for a few years. *"Tienes que ser hombre, Ernesto,"* she would always say, when he complained about being roughed up by other boys. *"Deles duro."* The next day, Ernesto would come home, proudly displaying the scars of his fights. Concepcion would listen to his exploits in awe, as he described the punches that he had unloaded on his adversaries. *"Son unos flojos,"* she would say. *"Tienes que pegarles bien asi, en la nariz."* She would throw an imaginary punch. She had lived her life through the men that she had married, raised, or grown up with. She justified her actions by saying that the poor boy's father was absent and that they had to do everything to avoid Ernesto becoming a *maricon. "Con tres mujeres en la casa, es muy peligroso."*

There was a tradition in Latin America to let boys get away with murder and to be strict with girls. This created spoiled machos and submissive women. But Natasha had changed in Berkeley. She had changed a lot. She would not become somebody's pet. She had her own dreams and aspirations.

They spent the afternoon visiting the sites where they had spent a wonderful childhood. The Catholic School, the parks, the little nooks and crannies of the island that they had explored together. Natasha felt that Ernesto was genuinely excited about her visit. He was proud of his apartment, which had a gorgeous view to the ocean. It was a typical bachelor pad, with state-of-the-art electronic equipment. A widescreen TV with surround sound, DVD, everything. This was all in stark contrast to her Spartan quarters at Berkeley. She prided herself in her simplicity, in being free of the temptations of a consumerist society. She wanted to continue her studies and get a PhD. But that was the way Ernesto was. He always wanted the latest equipment, the trendiest clothes. Their mom used to comment that Natasha had taken after her father and that Ernesto was like his Brazilian uncle, Clayton. "And I gave you two a little common sense and some good looks," she would say, laughing.

That evening they decided to go to the Silver Fox, an old upgraded joint in Miami Beach. The painted fox at the top of the entrance had a brand new shiny coat and his sly eyes and inviting smile attracted a disparate crowd of old local alcoholics and younger "Me Generation" types that wanted to be different. As Ernesto walked in with Natasha, the local crowd greeted them. He was a regular customer. Proudly, he introduced his sister to his buddies, an eclectic group, all united in their love of partying. Lining the back of the bar was the older crowd, consisting of sun-wrinkled and cigarette-smelling folks.

"Hey, Ernie, your sister's cute," one friend said.

"Keep your paws off her."

Ernie ordered beers and tequila shooters. They toasted her.

"To my dear sister Sasha, who will purge the world of all evil."

She felt the burn in her throat and the fire in her soul as she licked the salt, downed the tequila, and chewed on the lemon.

A couple of rounds later, she felt relaxed and on top of the world. She loved to drink and had to control herself.

"You know, Ernie, the appreciation for booze comes from the French part of our family. From the Indian part comes the fact that we can't handle it." The buddies roared. Ernesto was embarrassed.

"But we don't have any Indian blood."

"Just one drop, Ernie, enough to get us into trouble." They roared again. Natasha was embarrassing Ernesto, the quintessential chauvinist. He got some of his own medicine and it stung.

By the time they left for Tremores, a classy Latin disco, they were all high. Natasha and Ernesto stood by the bar and chatted while the others fanned out in search of companionship. Emboldened by the tequilas, she asked him, " Why don't we go to Colombia to visit Mom?"

" I've been so busy here, I don't know if I can break away."

Natasha knew that the timing was not right and decided not to press the issue. Tomorrow, when they were sober.

The next morning, Ernesto took Natasha surfing. They had to drive north for a couple of hours and she fought off the hangover with several cups of strong coffee from a thermos. She enjoyed surfing, but failed miserably at first.

"You'll get it, Sasha. You have my genes, my precision."

Inspired by her brother, she did not give up until she finally caught a small wave with the longboard and rode it for nearly one hundred yards. She was elated and so was her instructor.

Resting on the beach, they talked about their childhood in Miami, about Colombia.

"You're too young to remember, Ernesto. I was seven and you four when we left."

"Do you remember Papa?"

"I only saw him only before he left for Angola. I was five."

"He was in Angola?"

"Fighting with the Cuban forces. Our father is a hero in Cuba."

"I only remember him from the trip to the US last year. He was so weird."

"He is different, Ernesto. He spent twenty years fighting in the jungle, for a cause that he really believed in."

"Communism is all hogwash, Sasha. We wiped it out from the face of the earth."

Natasha patiently presented her father's point of view, based on the reality of Latin America that was so different from the affluence in America. Ernesto was not convinced.

"Why doesn't he come to the US and get a job, like everybody else?" he asked. "We have thousands of Cubans here, all former Commies. Ask any of them to return to Cuba!"

"Maybe, Ernie. I'd love to try," she said, pensively. "I saw so much goodness in him."

"The poor man. He was really mauled. The face, the arm, everything was a mess."

"I remember how he became fascinated with the story of the last Yahi."

"The *what?*"

"There was an Indian named Ishi who appeared mysteriously in a stockyard in California, in 1911. Apparently settlers and miners had massacred his entire tribe. A Berkeley professor brought him to campus and he spent the rest of his days as a display at the Phoebe Hearst Anthropology Museum, on campus."

"The first Berkeley radical," he said, with a wide grin on his face. "That's the type of story Papa would appreciate. He is the defender of lost causes."

"Don't be so critical, *Ernie*. Our father is a sensitive and bright person. He is a legend among the communist countries."

"Oh, just call me Che, Sis. I get your point. I also admire him, but in a different way. I realize that his cause is lost. Now, you..."

"Yes, I'm also a dreamer. But what can I say? I love anthropology, I love plants and flowers, organic things... things that grow."

"That's why it's taking you six years to graduate."

"Yes, *Che.*"

He suddenly jumped on her and wrestled her to the ground, while she screamed in feigned panic. They were children again, for a brief and fleeting moment. In spite, and maybe because of their differences, they were and would always be very close.

On Sunday, Many took them out on his large boat. They chatted some more, Natasha trying to convince Ernesto to come with her to Colombia. "I wouldn't mind returning to Brazil. Uncle Clayton was a great host. But Colombia..."

"Mom is expecting us for Christmas. You should see the ranch. It's fabulous!"

"Perhaps you can take it over later on…"

"Who knows, Ernie? I'd love to set up a biological reserve. Perhaps, after all this fighting is over."

"Those Colombians just love shooting each other up. Look what they did to Grandpa. They assassinated him on the ranch."

"That's true. There are deep social problems there and the drug cartels have made things worse."

"With guys like Pablo Escobar there'll never be peace in Colombia. They can kiss my ass."

"And who fuels the drug trade? Guys like your friends."

"Easy, Sasha. Just because guys like some recreational stuff doesn't mean a country has to go bonkers."

Poor Ernesto, she thought. Some things never change.

Lying there now, Natasha reminisced about their differences. They had to fend for themselves since their high school days, when their mother returned to Colombia to run the family ranch. Ernesto loved the Miami scene and embraced American consumerism with all his heart. In contrast, she was more of a dreamer and found herself fitting perfectly into Berkeley. She had always been attached to her childhood dreams through the memories of her father and followed his exploits through the leftist newspapers that abounded in Berkeley. But they loved each other dearly. She felt very close to him. Especially now that Aaron was gone.

The phone rang. It was her mother. "Natasha, I have terrible news." Natasha felt instantly dizzy. She was barely able to utter a word, while she leaned on the wall.

"Your father is dead." She could hear her mother's tears as she delivered the painful message. She did not have many details. Just some contradictory accounts that she had gotten from the story. All the papers in Colombia carried the news. "The Paladin of the Poor, of the Disenfranchised is Martyred," said the leftist newspapers, whereas the right-wing ones stated: "Government Executes Legendary Terrorist." She walked out of the apartment in shock. Her father was dead. The unexpected reality hit her and she was numb and confused.

She automatically turned toward Telegraph Avenue and to her favorite bookstore, Cody's. She needed to talk to somebody, to put her feelings in place. The street was normal; everything moved as it if nothing had happened. Nevertheless, her father was no longer there. She had some memories of him, but they were few and far apart. She tried to organize the thoughts in her mind, but could not. She tried to remember every picture, every moment she had with her father. She could not let the moment go like this.

Her friend Adalgisa was working at Cody's when Natasha entered. She looked at her for a moment and then broke in tears as she told her about her father.

"Oh, my God! Comandante Paulo? How did this happen? I'm so sorry Natasha." Adalgisa hugged her for a long time as tears rolled down Natasha's face and her body shook.

"This is so sudden and strange. I... can't explain. I'm here, in a different world, as if he never existed. And yet he is my father, he spent his life and health struggling in the jungle!"

Adalgisa held her as Natasha continued to cry.

"What should I do? Should I go there? But I don't even know where he is. I need to call Ernesto."

Adalgisa accompanied her to the apartment and she was able to reach Ernesto. He had already been informed by their mother. His reaction was quite different.

"But we hardly knew Papa, Sasha. What can we do?"

"I feel so helpless."

"Sasha, he found the end that he expected. He'd been a guerrilla fighter since we were born. What do you think?"

"I begged him to stay here when he visited us last year."

"He was so different. My friends thought he was half crazy."

"Don't say that, Ernesto. He was our father!"

"What do you expect me to do? I told Mom that I might be able to come for Christmas."

"Nothing Ernesto, I just want to share my pain with you."

"And where was he when we needed him, when we needed money for college?"

She paused for one moment. It had been Ernesto's decision not to go to college. Their mother was willing and anxious to support him. She did not reply to him, however. This would only start an argument.

"He lived in a different world. He was saving the poor."

"And losing his children. In any case, I'm extremely busy with the launching of the new product and can't take any time out."

"I am not asking you for anything. I'll call Mom again."

She hung up with a sense of loss and despair that had only gotten worse with the callous reaction of her brother. He was more concerned about his future at Novartis and his social life. The loss of his distant father was a nuisance for which he did not have much time. Surf was up and this was a most inconvenient time to pass away.

Adalgisa made Natasha some tea and went on to the Internet, where she found more news.

"I checked with the FARC site. He died in San Vicente del Caguan, in front of the church. Apparently a French priest was killed with him. The FARC is accusing the government of having masterminded his assassination. The government is saying that the Army won a significant victory over the most extremist guerrilla group and that civil unrest will now disappear in Colombia. Other newspapers have an entire retrospective on his life. You and Ernesto are mentioned in one of them. I didn't know that your mother was a guerrilla also, and that she belonged to a wealthy Colombian family, the Betancourts. And that she was married to Paco Quevedo, a drug dealer."

"It only lasted six months."

Natasha hardly slept that night. She could not just sit there after her father had passed away. She could not believe that this distant but loving being was no longer there. That far, far away in the jungle, he had fallen without her help.

Then, in the early hours of the morning, she decided. She would go there, to be by his side, one last time.

# CHAPTER THREE

Clayton Chauny looked out at the bustling city through the window of his office, in the twenty-fourth floor of a high-rise. He was in the heart of the city, where all financial decisions were made, and could feel the pulsating giant. On the horizon, the high mountains of the Atlantic sierra framed Rio de Janeiro and gave it an unequaled beauty. In the folds of the green hills the city slithered like a beast, restless and lunging. Clayton loved this feeling. He took a *cafézinho* from the subservient employee and lit a cigarette, savoring the smoke.

It had been a good year. As Vice President for Sales of the Sociedade Anonima de Mineração e Transporte, SAMITRA, he had increased exports of iron ore by twenty percent. It had taken many trips to China, Taiwan, Korea, Bahrain, and Germany. It had also taken negotiations and bribes. But he loved it, and they had set up an efficient operation. However, he felt sad. The disquieting news about the assassination of his brother in Colombia was true. First, there had been a brief article in the newspaper. He bought the Communist Party paper, which contained the full coverage and true identity of Comandante Paulo. He called Ana Maria and she confirmed that he had been assassinated in Caguan. At first, he was somehow numb and indifferent. He had not seen his brother for many years. But then he thought more and more about him, about how their paths diverged. He needed to mourn, to do something. He just did not know how. The wheeling and dealing of his job consumed him, and there was little emotion left at the end of the day. On top of everything, his autocratic German boss Dr. Breiterhof was increasingly demanding.

Clayton was an urban animal. He moved with grace through the streets of Rio in his custom-tailored gray suit. The well-cropped white hair and little stomach completed the executive image. He exuded a sense of seriousness and commitment that always impressed the customers. He had a long hooked nose and his dark eyes were too close, but his face was otherwise attractive and pleasant. It was only in his restless eyes that one could see he was a calculating individual, ready to cut the deal, at whatever cost. His impeccable credentials, which included an MBA from a top U.S. university, strengthened his position. He was one of the three key men at SAMITRA.

He closed the door of his office and opened a hard leather attaché case. Smiling, he played for a moment with the big wads of $100 bills. He had $200,000 in the briefcase.

"They should make $500 dollar bills," he murmured. "It would make my life easier." At that moment the phone rang. His secretary announced that the president was on the line.

"Good morning, Dr. Breiterhof," he said.

"Good morning, Mr. Chauny. We've got some interesting news. Could you come to my office?"

"I'll be right up. Do you want me to bring those reports?"

"The ones from Belo Horizonte? Yes."

He grabbed his attaché and walked out, giving a sly and hungry look at the secretary's thick legs, all exposed by one ultra-short skirt. She noticed his interest with some pleasure.

A minute later, he presented the report to Breiterhof with a big grin that accentuated his long nose. His dark eyes squinted, as he reached instinctively for another cigarette.

"Please, Mr. Chauny, no smoking here," Breiterhof said. "How was the meeting in Belo Horizonte?"

"Well, very well. They accepted our offer of jacking up the price of the ore from 16 to 17 dollars per ton. They are splitting the difference with us. Here is the result: 400,000 tons, to be shipped next week. We get $.50 per ton."

"My share is, as usual, two-thirds, Mr. Chauny."

"I know. I'm the junior partner." Clayton started counting the wads. "Here it is."

Breiterhof watched him carefully, then nodded.

"Tomorrow we can go to the *doleiro* (illegal money transfer operator). Have you set up your account in Liechtenstein already?"

"I still have my old account at the Banque Générale de Luxembourg."

"I'll teach you some new methods later. It's very important to be careful. Don't put all your eggs in one basket."

Clayton asked about another deal, in Romania.

"It's going well, Mr. Chauny. Our agent from France has already talked to their purchasing department. So, we'll get a cut for the purchase and one for the sale. But SAMITRA has to make a profit first. Our stockholders have to be satisfied. But they are sitting comfortably in Europe, while we are risking our necks in the streets of Rio."

Clayton shrugged. "I just had my Rolex stolen yesterday. At gunpoint."

"Haven't I been telling you not to parade around with that watch? Mr. Chauny, sometimes I get the impression that you enjoy trouble."

Clayton laughed. Yes, sometimes trouble was fun. He got back to the Romania deal. "We don't want to kill the chicken with the golden eggs,"

"We've put fifteen years of our lives into SAMITRA. It grew from a second-rate mining operation to a major producer and exporter of iron ore. We'll always defend its interests first. But I've got some exciting new business opportunities. This time, we can strike on our own."

Clayton reached instinctively for a cigarette, but restrained himself.

Breiterhof picked up the phone. "Hanna, is our chief geologist here?"

"Yes sir, he's waiting."

"Please let him in."

A few minutes later, a sunburned fellow walked in, introduced by the tall blue-eyed secretary. He was in his thirties, considerably younger than both Clayton and Breiterhof.

Dressed casually in khaki pants and shirt, his shoes had some reddish dust from the mine. Clayton noticed Breiterhof's look of disdain.

In contrast, Breiterhof wore an expensive English blazer, straight from Saville Road. He snobbishly left the last gold buttons, emblazoned with the coat-of-arms of his family, unbuttoned to show that the suit was handmade.

"Mr. Tavares, what news do you bring?"

Then he turned to Clayton. "Mr. Tavares just returned from a geological prospecting trip in the upper Amazon."

He walked to the world map that comprised one entire wall of the office and indicated the spot.

"Right here, at the border of Venezuela and Colombia. Here are the ears, and this is the mouth. The border resembles an animal's head. A dog's head."

"Yes, one of the most remote places on this planet," Tavares said. "I've got thousands of mosquito bites to prove it. But it was worth the trip. Dr. Breiterhof, you had a good nose when you sent me to look closer at that mountain."

"Yes, I suspected that the lack of vegetation could be an indication of highly mineralized soil. I have a doctorate in Mineral Economics. Go ahead, Mr. Tavares, tell Mr. Chauny what you found."

*You're always in control, always trying to show that you are better than anyone else. But I'm the one that has to do the dirty job, like collecting bribes.* Clayton's nervous fingers played with a pen.

"A large concentration of cassiterite."

"Cassiterite?" Clayton asked, suddenly alert. "I knew that there was a lot of tin in the Amazon basin, especially in Rondonia and Acre. But in that godforsaken place?"

"Yes. My preliminary calculations show that the exploitable resources could amount to four hundred thousand tons."

Clayton's mind was in overdrive. He quickly calculated. At $1,000 a ton of tin, this would be about two hundred million dollars of profit, accounting for all expenses.

Breiterhof said, "I'd like to propose that we form a corporation to exploit this mine. Our *own* corporation."

"There are a few problems, Dr. Breiterhof..."

"There are numerous problems, Mr. Tavares, but all can be overcome. Mr. Chauny, are you in?"

"We've always worked well together, Dr. Breiterhof. I believe that this could be the break we've been waiting for."

"Mr. Tavares, I hope you've followed my instructions. I don't want any report of this... or better, I want an informal report describing your dangerous and exhausting trip, but excluding any findings."

"The report has already been prepared. It states that no significant discoveries were made. I already have a draft here, which I'd like to submit to you, before we send it to our headquarters in Frankfurt."

"We go into this venture with myself as president and you two as vice-presidents, one for operations, one for finance. Are we in agreement?" He gazed intently at his subordinates, trying to see any sign of weakness.

"And what portion of the stock will each person have?" Clayton asked, already knowing the answer.

"50-25-25. I'll be the primary investor and my money will count up front. Then, we split the profits as I propose."

Clayton thought for a moment. He would have preferred a one-third cut and mentioned this. Breiterhof answered, somewhat impatiently, "I'm the senior person and should receive more. Additionally, I'm taking the major financial risk. I'm looking forward to a comfortable retirement in France."

"How boring," Clayton interrupted. He knew that Breiterhof had a little chateau close to Paris, where his wife and daughter lived. He also knew that the old man had a mistress in Rio, a former Lufthansa stewardess.

"Yes, yes it'll be boring in France. But it'll be safe. I'm sticking my neck out. And we need my high level contacts in the mining world."

Clayton quickly calculated that the difference between 33 and 25 percent was not that great. "Okay, I agree."

"Now, tell us about the many problems, Mr. Tavares."

The man had been quiet up to this point. He was clearly the subordinate and it was a privilege and opportunity to be included in the operation.

"There are three major difficulties, and I will start with the smallest," he said. "First, the Macava Mountains are remote and access is very difficult. We have to go upriver on the Auapés River. The mineral deposit is six hundred kilometers north of Manaus and two hundred kilometers from the closest town, São Gabriel da Cachoeira. Part of it can be done by river and the other part, at least one hundred kilometers, has to be done by land.

"Second, Brazil has a large tin refining company, Parapanema. They will be less than excited about the prospect of internal competition and will do anything they can to put a damper on the project."

"Mr. Tavares, you're a good geologist."

"Mining engineer, Mr. Breiterhof," he corrected.

"You're an excellent mining engineer and can take care of difficulty number one."

"Yes, I can. I've formulated a preliminary plan."

"I can take care of difficulty number two," Breiterhof said. "We'll officially produce only a small tonnage, and smuggle the greatest portion out through Venezuela, down the Orinoco River. My contacts in the National Department of Mineral Production can be very valuable. All of this will require well-placed bribes, to oil the gears of the governmental machine. If our production is officially low, Parapanema won't bother us. You know, they're well connected and supported by senators and governors."

Breiterhof paused for a minute. "And what's difficulty number three, Mr. Tavares?"

"This is the tough one. You know that the National Department of Mineral Production will only grant mineral rights to a company if the National Indian Foundation can officially certify that there no Indians in the area."

"And?"

"And, I found a small tribe, only a few families living in the mountains. They're totally backward, almost animal-like, and avoid all contact with whites. They are, I believe, Yananani or something like that. A few lost souls."

Breiterhof turned to Clayton. "This is the problem that you will resolve, Mr. Chauny."

Clayton felt a chill running down his spine. He knew the old stories and understood what Breiterhof meant. They would have to get the Indians out of there. And since they were totally wild, it was not possible to bribe them out of there. But no, he wasn't ready for the other alternative.

"Yes, Mr. Chauny, you have to obtain the clear title from FUNAI, the Indian protection foundation."

Clayton felt like running out into the street. He needed a stiff drink and a cigarette.

"I want some time to think this over. This is a tough one."

"This is why I left it for last," Tavares said. "This might be the one that breaks us."

"Let's meet in my office tomorrow afternoon," Breiterhof said. "Each of us will develop a plan for his part. Remember, this will mean seventy million dollars apiece."

"For *you*, Mr. Breiterhof, one hundred," Clayton said. "For us, it's only fifty million."

"Oh, yes, I'd forgotten." He smiled.

As Clayton drove home through the traffic of Rio, he was both excited and worried. In his middle forties, he had already amassed a few million dollars through various schemes. Not bad for an executive, but peanuts compared to the potential profit from the project in the Dog's Head. Between twenty and fifty million dollars would put him in an entirely different league. The super-league, to which belonged the biggest crooks in Brazil: presidents of large state-owned corporations, a few senators, and of course, the heads of the large road construction companies. The Guerras, Andrades, Mahfus, Colores. But the price was high. His expertise involved working out kickback schemes. At this he was the best. He knew how to approach buyers and sellers of ore, how to arrange money transfers, how to leave no trace. But getting rid of a small tribe of Indians...

Clayton felt that he needed some physical exercise to calm his nerves. He parked the car in his apartment's garage, called his wife and told her that he would work out. He walked down the street to Ipanema, passed Praça da Paz, and stopped in front of Garota de Ipanema, a popular bar. Without waiting for approval, he sat down at the best table and yelled:

"An ice-cold *chopp* with a good head, Francisco."

Within minutes the subservient and efficient waiter brought him the beer.

"Antártica, *doutor*, as you like."

Soon he was sipping on the ice-cold beer, the head covering his upper lip. He wiped it with the back of his hand, watching two girls walk by, their derrières floating in a uniquely Brazilian way, a wavy motion intended to attract the attention, a sensuous dance that was delicately inviting without being vulgar. The tension in him still churned but the caress to his soul brought by the girls soothed him. He reached for a cigarette and, before he could light it, Francisco stood by him with a burning match. He took a deep puff but it did not have an effect. His lungs already burned from too many cigarettes and the nicotine was saturated in his system. He flicked out the cigarette into the street.

He unbuttoned his shirt and ran his fingers over his chest. Karin used to belittle him saying that his body resembled a sun-tanned sausage. Taking a deep sip, he looked at the sky, smiled, and thought about beautiful forests, about his childhood in Monlevade, about him and Marco Aurelio hunting in the forest. He was still hurting from the loss of his brother. Lately, his mind flowed to his childhood memories.

And then, suddenly, the idea came to him. He grinned. Yes, he had found a solution. He would go to the Amazon and recapture Marco Aurelio's - Paulo's - last days. It would take work, lots of it. But he had a plan.

Soon after, he was at home kissing his wife and kids. It had been a good day. Karin was preoccupied with the new fashion show coming from Paris. Sabrina was ecstatic about the afternoon's birthday party. "They had three clowns, Daddy, three clowns!" Karina was busy with her collection of 150 dolls, and was ordering the nanny around, reorganizing the entire doll room.

The next morning he spent several hours developing his plan. He moved excitedly about the office, sipping *cafézinhos* and smoking cigarettes at a faster-than-usual pace.

Then, he put his thoughts on paper. At two o'clock sharp, he was in Breiterhof's office. Tavares was also there, carrying a collection of maps and reports. Breiterhof received them cordially. Dressed impeccably in a dark gray suit, he cut an impressive figure. In fifteen years, this Swiss economist had transformed an ailing company into the third-largest mining operation in Brazil. He had developed an extensive array of connections and kept abreast of all economic changes impacting the mining activity.

"Gentlemen, let me start. First, as I said, we need to set up a corporation. It has to be established in Uruguay, so that the owners remain anonymous. Our names can't appear anywhere. Second, we request permission to carry out a mineral exploration project in the region. Then, we *officially* discover the mineral deposit and lay claim to it. Brazilian Mineral Law states that we have five years to develop an industrial operation. If nothing is done for five years, we lose the mineral rights. I'll personally invest up to ten million dollars into the corporation," he said. Then, he presented the details of the plan, financial operations necessary, and timetable.

Tavares had done his homework. The cassiterite ore was rich and did not require a great deal of mineral refining before smelting. The bare operations required one crusher and one grinder, a cyclone separator, and a pilot-scale smelter. The entire investment was within the budget cited by Breiterhof. The construction would take approximately one year. The operation would be set up along the upper Auapés River. A hundred-kilometer road would need to be built between the river and the mine. The entire production facility would require approximately eighty people.

"Once I get the go ahead from the National Mineral Production Department, I can start delivering tin in sixteen months." Tavares finished his report.

"Excellent," Breiterhof said. "Mr. Chauny, what about you?"

Clayton swallowed; his throat was dry. He asked for the coffee jar and served himself a *cafézinho*. Then, he pulled his courage together and presented his plan.

# CHAPTER FOUR

Ana Maria waited at the airstrip. She felt guilty and moved at the same time. Guilty that she had let Natasha stay in the U.S. and allowed her to grow away from her. Moved that she would soon see her again, after almost two years. It was sad that the circumstances were so tragic. She understood that Natasha yearned to know her father better. A turmoil of thoughts galloped through her mind as she nervously waited for the hum of the Cessna.

Ana Maria had left Paulo when Ernesto was still a toddler. She could not put up with the guerrilla life any longer, and other priorities filled her mind. She had been drawn into the Left by her fiancé, Arnaldo, and followed him to Nicaragua. Those were the glorious days of the Left in Latin America. It seemed that this movement would take over the entire continent. Were it not for the covert CIA actions and the repressive military dictatorships, the Left would probably have won. But the killing of Che Guevara, the assassination of Allende, the ruthless Operation Condor implemented by Pinochet, the massive support of the Contras by US Special Forces in Nicaragua, the Iran-Contra supply exchange commandeered by Colonel North, were victories for the Right.

After Arnaldo's death in Nicaragua, she had fallen in love with Paulo. She desperately needed a man, and Paulo was kind and considerate. And he loved her beyond reason. So she stayed on, and soon was pregnant with Natasha, then with Ernesto. Her family in Colombia finally convinced her to leave the armed struggle and stay at the family ranch. She was hurt and disillusioned when Leftist guerrillas assassinated her father, the Betancourt y Hannaford patriarch, in his ranch. She also had the survival and future of her two kids at stake, and one day she left a long letter for Paulo, who was in Angola fighting with the Cuban forces, and disappeared from the camp. Natasha had been sick, with diarrhea, for over a month, and she feared for her life. They moved continuously under the immense canopy that covered Eastern Colombia, the province of Caquetá. Under constant attack from mosquitoes and occasional government troops, they also suffered with the torrential rains.

Ana Maria knew that Paulo was totally devoted to the Revolution and that the struggle would consume his entire life. She also knew that she and the children could not survive one more rainy season under the harsh circumstances of guerrilla warfare. Her parents were part of the old *Criollo* aristocracy and she was considered by the government as somewhat of a hostage. So, the Colombian government left her and her kids alone, at least for a while. Then came rumors of a possible incarceration, of a trial, when Paulo returned from Angola to lead the guerrilla effort in Colombia.

She was able to leave for the U.S. with the children. Natasha was then in her early teens. Miami was the first stop, and they stayed in Key Biscayne, where the family had an apartment. The organized discipline and peaceful existence of American life gradually enveloped them, and they resided there for several years. Ana Maria was restless, however, and she still needed a man in her life. All Latino men that she met would end up being chauvinists, demanding her subservience in exchange for the luxuries of an ostentatious life. She had experienced the difference with Arnaldo and then Paulo, fierce combatants, but somewhat visionary in their treatment of women. They were kind, in their own ways, and were in any case married to the Revolution. Ana Maria was an exemplary fighter, in the best tradition of the Cuban revolution. These shared experiences in the jungles of Nicaragua and Colombia had vaccinated her against macho men. And these macho men were constantly cheating on her, as if by cheating they would gain an enhanced stature among their peers.

So she had not found a lasting and meaningful relationship. A brief marriage to Paco Quevedo had not made matters any better. Like many Miami Colombians he was involved in the cocaine trade, as she soon found out. He was insanely jealous and forced her to wear a beeper at all times. In the meantime, he spent his days with his buddies and their bimbo friends. The marriage fell apart, with lots of animosity. After that, there were only flings and brief encounters that left, in their aftermath, a bitter taste, but satisfied her temporary needs.

She was totally lost in these melancholic thoughts when she heard the distant hum, barely perceptible. It gradually became a roar, as the shadow of the plane grew against the evening sky.

When the Cessna landed and she saw Natasha jumping down, she ran along the tarmac and gave her a warm embrace. They stayed like this for the longest time, tears running down their cheeks. It was the first time Natasha was back in Pasto after three years.

"Mom, how are you? You look wonderful."

"Natasha, are you all right?"

"No, Mom, I'm not fine. I want to know my father better."

"You can always be proud of him, Natasha. He lived his dream to the end, and died like a hero, mowed down by criminals."

While a servant grabbed Natasha's bag, Ana Maria led her to the Toyota SUV parked in front of the airfield.

"In forty minutes we'll be at the ranch. There, you can rest and relax. And then I have to tell you everything I heard. Oh, Natasha, it is so tragic that your father died. I never stopped loving him."

"I know. You always kept that picture of him in his guerrilla outfit in your room. He'll always be with us."

"There was always a little hope, like a little flame warming my heart. It was the hope that one day he would return and that we would be reunited."

"Oh, Mom, I miss him so much."

Less than an hour later, they entered a beautiful colonial *estancia*. The gate was covered with bougainvillea. Three maids waited for them.

"And you, Nazaré, I will never forget you!" Natasha cried when she saw her old nanny and ran towards her, embracing her. "Do you still remember me?"

Nazaré was in her fifties. She was white, had straight hair and prided herself in being the descendant of an old aristocratic family. Her surname was Villas Buenas and Natasha remembered how she always looked down on the other servants, *cholos* and *negritos*. Ernesto was always teasing the servants, playing one against the other. Natasha would watch them fight fiercely, instigated by her devilish little brother. Now she was back, and she finally felt at peace. She needed to heal from the shock, from the lies and betrayal surrounding her father's death, and there was no place like this ranch. If she only could have Tonto with her. She missed his long ears, his silky fur, his gentle eyes and quiet disposition.

"Take a nice warm bath, Natasha. I gave orders for the servants to kill the fattest chicken and to prepare nice soup, your favorite. Then you can go to sleep, to rest until tomorrow. I've lots of activities planned for us."

Ana Maria took Natasha to her quarters. She looked at the wide hallways, high ceilings, old walls, and her childhood came back to her. But, somehow, the building looked smaller. She and Ernesto would run through these same corridors and hide in the rooms. The familiar surroundings were strangely soothing.

At dinner, served by the loyal Felizmundo, they chatted excitedly, catching up with their lives.

"I hope Ernesto can come for Christmas. This is great, Natasha. We'll all be reunited."

"Not quite all, Mom."

"Yes, Paulo won't be here. But let's invite his brother, Clayton."

"Clayton? Have you been in touch with him? I would like to meet him. Ernesto said that he had a great time in Rio."

"Clayton reminds me in some ways of Paulo. However, he's such a sleaze bag! He turned into this urban animal, slick and sly. He's on his way to the ranch."

"How come, Mom?"

"He mentioned that he's involved in some mining operation in the Amazon."

Natasha then told her mother about her desire to visit Caguan, where her father had been killed.

"Don't tell me that you are joining the guerrillas!"

"No, Mom. But I have this feeling that I need to get closer to my father, to see the places where he lived, breathe the same air. I'm also fascinated by the Yanomami. Papa had told me that he had visited them. And we studied them in the anthropology class."

Ana Maria told Natasha about rumors that she had heard. That her father had a lover in the jungle. And that she was pregnant. "I hoped that he would find somebody. He was a loyal, faithful man. Loyal and faithful to his women, to his troops, to his ideals. And he paid a high price."

Natasha was hurt by this revelation. As if this was a weakness in the man she most admired. She remembered now that he had bought some childish gifts for somebody when he visited her and Ernesto. He never mentioned for who they were. "It could have been for her, Natasha, "Ana Maria said. "Apparently she is half his age."

After dinner they sat outside, and Ana Maria could, for the first time, see Paulo's fire burn inside her daughter. She spoke with heart and eloquence about the fate of these last Indians, hidden in the deep recesses of the Amazon. Natasha described their customs, their history, and their nature. Outside, they could hear the noises of the forest: crickets, cicadas, bullfrogs, and other animals that seemed to provide a chorus for Natasha's fiery speech

Ana Maria could not dissuade Natasha from visiting Caguan. She warned her about their treacherous ways and told her, once more, about the assassination of her father. The next morning, she asked a mutual friend to contact Colonel Soto Mayor. As soon as she got his OK, she made arrangements for Natasha to fly over there. She would never talk to these people again. Not after what they did to her father. Before she left, Ana Maria came to her with a small Longchamps bag.

"Take this with you. You might need it. It's a Beretta 9 mm. The best. Do you know how to handle a gun?"

Ana Maria led her to the backyard, where she showed her how to load the gun and change clips. They fired a number of rounds at bottles and makeshift targets. She was surprised at Natasha's firm and professional grip on the pistol and by how she popped bottle after bottle, at thirty yards.

"You have your father's precision."

"I used to infuriate Ernesto when I beat him at target practice."

"Let's hope that you won't have to use it."

"But you'll be left without a handgun, *mamá*."

"I have three, darling. One under the seat, in the car. One under my bed. And this one."

The Cessna circled once around the airstrip to warn the townspeople and to check for animals on the ground. As it tilted sharply to the left Natasha could see the plaza and church. This was the place where her father lost his life. This was also her hometown. The irony of life. The palm roofs of the houses blended with the dusty streets. The plane landed on the bumpy strip and moved to the end, kicking up a cloud of dust. Close to the shed that passed for an airport, a military Jeep was waiting. As she stepped out, a handsome man in fatigues took a few steps forward and introduced himself.

"Captain Mendoza of FARC. My sincere condolences, Miss Chauny. We all knew and respected your father. A terrible loss…"

Natasha felt a wave of emotion as she breathed in the thick, hot air. This was the land for which he lost his life. This sad and poor place. In Spanish, with a tinge of American accent, she replied, "Thank you, Captain Mendoza."

"I'll first take you to a place where you can refresh yourself and stay for a night. Then, we can go to the cemetery and pay homage to your father."

"I want to go there right away," she replied. "I came here for my father."

"As you wish, Miss Chauny."

They drove to the outskirts of town. The cemetery was touchingly simple. Some tombs were made of masonry. Natasha remembered, with disgust, that this was done to protect them from giant armadillos that fed on corpses.

Mendoza did not have to lead her. The two fresh tombs stood there, side by side. Painted in light blue, the color of Our Lady. Flowers from the gardens and forest had been placed on them, and the letters were written on the cement.

> Comandante Paulo Silva
> *Heroe y Martyr*
> *1952 Brasil
> +2002 San Vicente

On the other:

> Padre Antoine Ibernegaray
> *Pescador de Almas*
> *1955 Pyreneus de Francia
> +2002 San Vicente

Natasha could no longer contain her tears and cried uncontrollably. Mendoza put a strong and hairy arm around her and comforted her.

"He was a brave man, a legend among all of us. Your father died as he wished: a fighter to the end."

"I wish I had seen him once more."

"This struggle has claimed many lives."

She stood there for the longest time, thinking about the few but precious moments that she had spent with her father. Most of her recollections of him were from newspaper clips that her friend Adalgisa brought her, or from books on guerrilla fighters that Cody's, a radical bookstore, specialized in. She knew that he loved them, Ernesto and Natasha. She also knew that the struggle to free Latin America from oppression had cost him his personal happiness; he had sacrificed every-thing he had, for all these years. As Natasha recollected the few precious moments she had spent with him, she cried even harder. At last, Captain Mendoza took her back to the Jeep.

"We have arranged for you to stay at the parish house. Tomorrow I'll show you the FARC camp, half an hour from here by Jeep."

"Did my father live in Caguan?"

"No, Father Antoine lived here. Your father was part of another group, and preferred to live deep in the jungle. He spent his last weeks close to here, though. Should I make the arrangements for your return to Bogotá? There isn't much to do here."

"Let me decide this later, Captain. Please take me to the parish house. I need to collect my thoughts."

Drained from the emotion of seeing her father's tomb, she slept deeply in the small but comfortable room arranged by Pilar, the faithful helper of Father Antoine. When she awoke, it was already dark. Pilar had prepared a simple but healthy meal of rice, beans, manioc, fried plantains, and meat stew. As she ate, distracting herself by trying the vari-ous plates, Pilar stood nearby.

"*Señorita*, I remember you as a child. You and Ernesto were very sick and you stayed here. My son, Evaristo, used to play with you."

"And where is he now, Pilar?"

"He joined FARC, *señorita*. He is a sergeant. How do you still know Spanish?"

"I was born in this town." She paused for a moment. "Our mother spoke it at home, when we moved to Miami. And we had lots of Latino friends there."

"Father Antoine, God bless his soul, had a stronger accent than you."

"The priest buried by my father?"

"He was wonderful. A saint. Lost his life for our sake."

"It must have been hard on all of you."

"Yes, we miss him a lot. It was his destiny. He received your father in the confessional, and he had communion before he died."

"Communion?" Natasha exclaimed. "My father was one hundred percent communist."

"I saw him with these eyes that the earth will eat one day. Last Sunday, he had communion with his wife Celeste."

"Celeste?"

"He lived with her in the jungle. She returned yesterday. Poor man, he'll never see his child."

"Child? Then, she is pregnant?"

"That's what they say."

Her mother's rumors were correct. She felt that she had to stay longer to discover who her father was. By meeting the people close to him she would recreate him in her mind. Pilar went on and told her the stories about their childhood, stories that she had forgotten a long time ago.

At last, Natasha asked, "Could I meet this woman?"

"She lives three hours from here, past the ruins and up the mountain. One of the Indians who help us here in the parish knows where it is. But it's dangerous, *señorita*, and your white skin is not used to these hardships. Mosquitoes, snakes, all the dangers."

"I want to see where my father lived. I want to see his wife."

"The FARC people might not like it. They want to know and control everything here."

"Pilar, can you get me in touch with the Indian... what's his name?"

"Anselmo."

"Yes, get me in touch with Anselmo."

The next morning, at seven a.m., Natasha heard the Jeep stop by the house. Out jumped Captain Mendoza, freshly shaven and perfumed, in an elegant uniform. His boots were polished and he sported a thick gold chain tucked into his black hairy chest. He gave her a hug and two kisses on the cheeks, and she could smell the French cologne. "Some guerrilla fighter," she muttered, as he opened the canvas door of the Jeep and helped her in.

"Did you bring sun block lotion, Natasha?" he asked, as he offered her a tube of Coppertone SPF34. "It's very important here, especially for us whites. She looked at his face. The overall impression was white. He was handsome and well built. The eyes were a bit slanted, Indian. The hair was a little curly and the thick lips showed a trace of black blood.

He flashed his white teeth and grinned as he drove off. Clearly, he was exuberant over taking her around. "I hope you slept well." He placed his right hand on top of her left hand, in a patronizing manner. She felt the warmth and slowly disengaged it, without appearing rude.

"Tell me more about my father, Captain. How do you see him? What were his dreams?"

"I was one of his soldiers, six years ago. Then I joined FARC, *Forzas Armadas Revolucionarias de Colombia*. Your father was a believer in the pure revolution, like Che Guevara. He followed the *Handbook of Guerrilla Warfare* written by Che. But things have changed, Natasha. Things have changed a lot." He drove the Jeep through a narrow dirt road out into the forest.

"FARC prides itself in being a very efficient organization. It has roots in the revolt of the '50s, the *Violencia* days. Our camp is well organized, as you'll see. We have invested our resources well. The entire territory of Meta is controlled by FARC. You'll see that we have educational and health programs for the peasants, and that we are agents of economic development in the jungle."

As he spoke, she looked behind her and stared at the red cloud of dust kicked up in the air.

"In some ways, we are continuing the work started by your father and his *compañeros*. But we're more realistic, more pragmatic."

After crossing two bridges made of thick trunks cut in half lengthwise and laid over creeks, they entered a compound. Inside, there was order and discipline. The men walking around fell into two categories – soldiers or peasants. After stopping at the control office, Mendoza said, "I'll introduce you to Colonel Soto Mayor, our Commanding Officer."

They entered the building and a uniformed girl received them at the door.

"These are our *Farquettes*," Mendoza explained. "They are our military corps of women providing support for the troops."

"Aren't you afraid of airplane raids here? This camp is well organized but is in the open."

"Good thinking, Miss Chauny. We have an agreement with the Colombian government. We don't carry out operations in their area and they leave us alone."

A funny guerrilla war, thought Natasha. They are at peace with each other. What about the basic precepts of revolutionary combat? However, she refrained from asking any question that could embarrass her host.

They met Colonel Soto Mayor briefly. He was a tall and lanky middle-aged man, nearly bald. He had a small nose and big ears that gave him a simian look. He could have passed for a businessman in Bogotá. In his office, decorated with an old Che Guevara poster with the word *Venceremos* under it, was an assortment of modern technological paraphernalia, computers, printers, and scanners.

"We're connected to the world by satellite," he said after introducing himself and offering his condolences to Natasha.

He invited her to have lunch with him in the officer's mess, after the tour. From his desk, he pulled out a photograph of Comandante Paulo and showed it to Natasha.

"We're making a print of your father for you. After lunch, we want you to uncover his photograph in the officer's mess. This is our small way of paying tribute to a revolutionary hero."

As she looked at the thin frame and resolute face with the crystal-clear eyes in the photo, she was moved. There he was, simple and poor to the extreme, like a modern monk, determined to liberate the poorest of Latin America, of the world, from the tyranny of ignorance, disease, and misery.

In a patronizing gesture, Mendoza offered her a handkerchief, and she smelled the perfume on it.

They spent a couple of hours touring the facilities. They passed buildings that Mendoza described only as industrial processing facilities. She could not contain herself any longer. "Is it true what I read in the U.S. papers," she asked, "that you process the coca to finance your operations?"

"Is this what they say? We have to finance our cause."

"At this cost? And to what extent do the means justify the end?"

She could feel the heat rising to her face. The memories of junkies living on the streets of Berkeley, Oakland, and San Francisco were still fresh in her mind.

"The capitalist system demands drugs and somebody has to provide them. You Yankees are financing the revolution."

"The poor homeless of Berkeley are not the capitalist system. They are victims, just as the poor peasants that are being exploited in the large Latin American latifundia."

"I can see that you are Comandante Paulo's daughter. The same fire in your blue eyes."

"Let's move on. This makes me sick."

At lunch, Farquettes served them. The irony of it all did not escape Natasha. Although she was being treated with all the honor of a foreign dignitary, she felt that something was terribly wrong with the entire concept. Colonel Soto Mayor and Captain Mendoza joyfully drank ice-cold beer and the sumptuous meal contained several imported items: sweet peas from the US, chocolates from Godiva, Swiss cheeses.

"We're supplied by plane," Soto Mayor said. "This is greatly different from your father's days."

After lunch, Soto Mayor got up and eloquently eulogized Comandante Paulo, describing his dedicated life and heroic end. Natasha, moved again, thanked all the people present. She noticed that Mendoza was looking at her in a strange way, a mixture of lust and admiration, she determined.

"You have your father's blue eyes and his elegance, so totally natural, without one drop of pretension," he said.

He explained that Paulo always had the same graceful demeanor, even in moments of great fatigue and stress, when everyone around him was falling apart.

"It's strange. Ernesto and I realized the same when we took him to nice restaurants and receptions in the US."

"You're right. There was something aristocratic about him that he tried but couldn't shake off."

"Most people try to look distinguished. Father always tried to identify with the poor and destitute."

Natasha felt that he was acting strange. She realized that he was attracted to her in a dangerous manner. This feeling was being exacerbated by the heat of the jungle and by the beers ingested. When he walked out of the bathroom, he had a strange look in his face. She had seen it before, on people that had snorted cocaine.

Instructed by Soto Mayor, Natasha walked to the front of the hall and pulled the curtain from the wall. There he stood, proud and determined in his frail frame, the fatigue shirt opened, his favorite FAL rifle hanging from his shoulder, his left arm bandaged. Comandante Paulo in his finest hour, a few weeks after the 1994 combats of San Vicente del Caguan, in which his troops had outmaneuvered the government forces, broken the siege, and counterattacked them from the back. No, these days would never be forgotten, not by the government, not by FARC.

Pride filled Natasha's entire being; she felt at that moment his soul floating in the air, his spirit coming alive in her. The officers in the mess realized that her voice carried the same eloquence as her father.

"Who killed my father?" she suddenly asked in the Jeep, on the way back to San Vicente del Caguan.

Mendoza shrugged. "Nobody knows, Natasha. Probably some government agents. We are investigating."

She needed to know; she was determined to know. As they arrived in the parish house, Mendoza stopped the Jeep and again placed his hands on hers. She felt the sweat and hot, viscous warmth of his hand and pulled away. He then approached her. She moved her head and avoided being kissed on the mouth. Nevertheless, she felt his breath at the corner of her lips.

"Captain," she said, "don't you think that you're being too bold?"

"Forgive me, Natasha. I'm being taken by the moment."

"I want to stay in Caguan a little longer, and would like to have your help."

"It's very dangerous here, and we're concerned about your well being. Soto Mayor asked me to arrange for you to fly back to Pasto tomorrow. We have a plane coming to Caguan at three o'clock."

Natasha perceived an opportunity. He could help her.

"I'd like to know this place where my father died a little better. This is also my birthplace. And we've just met, Captain..."

"I'll talk to him. This territory is under our jurisdiction. Perhaps one week. I have to travel tomorrow to visit three peasant communities. How about if we see each other on Thursday evening?"

"That sounds good. And it will give me a chance to absorb all this."

"Good night."

This time, she took the initiative and kissed his cheeks, where the thick stubble of the beard was already coming out. She felt attracted to his strength, but it was a strange feeling that she could not comprehend.

The next day, Natasha left Caguan with the Indian Anselmo. Pilar had been able to convince him to arrange the trip. A few dollars of enticement and a few good words helped. The trail leading to Celeste's house was well traveled. It also led to other isolated houses in the forest. As Natasha walked, she looked - for the first time since her childhood - at the immense variety of trees in the forest in awe. She remembered the shapes of the leaves, the different types of lianas and trees, and related them mentally to her botany studies. A band of small monkeys had been following them. Anselmo explained to her the different trees. He walked at a brisk pace, unimpeded by the primitive wooden backpack in which he carried Natasha's belongings. It was a basket, tied to a wooden frame that he strapped to his forehead. As she walked, she imagined her father, who spent years of his life crisscrossing the forests of Latin America. How did he feel? Did he have time to appreciate the strange beauty surrounding him, or was he totally absorbed in fostering the Revolution? And the variegated array of human beings populating these areas? The animals, the plants?

It was already late afternoon and they were still walking. The forest gradually filled with sounds, as if it acquired a new soul. Cries, huffs, shrieks came from close and far.

Natasha was near panic. She was only vaguely familiar with the multitude of noises that come from the tropical forest as dusk approaches. It was as if each and every creature uttered a scream of despair. The *Autan* mosquito repellent that she had gotten from her mother was ineffective. The mosquitoes were relentless, and the occasional diurnal minuscule insect was now being replaced by a multitude of larger, more painful creatures; she now remembered this changing of the guard. Her arms and legs were being bitten mercilessly and she realized the mistake she had made. Instead of a T-shirt and shorts, she should have worn long pants and sleeves. Her skin was covered in a sticky mixture of sweat and moisture; her clothes were damp and hot.

Exhaustion and fear entered her soul as she wondered why she had embarked on this journey. Anselmo's pace, already brisk at the beginning, was increasing. She had trouble keeping up. Every now and then he would turn back and say, "*Ya ya llegamos, señora.*"

The forest was now darkening rapidly. Natasha uttered a sign of relief when they entered a clearing. She was both worried and anxious to meet her father's new wife. How was she? How would she receive her? The forest was already dark and the light from the clearing was yellow, almost orange. Standing in front of the house was a pregnant woman wearing a simple hand made cotton dress, white with faded flowers barely visible. She had black hair cut straight above her eyes and longer in the back; it was utterly simple. Her skin was brown, her features round, almost Asian. She waved her hand with a shy smile, then approached them and gave Anselmo and Natasha a furtive handshake, barely pressing her hand. She stared at the ground as she did that, avoiding Natasha's eyes. Natasha wanted to hug her, but held back. This Indian was the companion of her father in his last days. Why had he returned to her, rather than joining her and Ernesto in the US?

Anselmo explained to Celeste, in an Indian dialect, that Natasha was the Comandante's daughter. She had already noticed, and commented on the similarity. Then she said, as a welcome, "We all liked your father very much. He told me about you, that you studied in the United States."

Natasha felt moved by the mention of her father. Celeste motioned them in and asked them to hang up the hammocks. They climbed up to the wooden platform and Celeste left for the kitchen to prepare a meal. Anselmo set up the hammocks for them by tying the ropes at the ends to the beams in the roof. Then, he covered it with the mosquito net that went all the way to the wooden floor. They hid under them, since this was the worst time of day for mosquitoes. Within an hour they would be gone, especially the malaria mosquitoes. Exhausted, she fell asleep.

Celeste, informing her that dinner was ready, woke her up. She had prepared roasted manioc and a monkey stew. Natasha and Anselmo sat at the table while Celeste stood behind, quiet as always. Natasha fished through the stew and pulled out a little hand like a baby's. The monkey's hand. She dropped it back and concentrated on the manioc as she asked Celeste to tell her a little about her father, about his last days.

"He was a very good man, always worried about us. He had just decided to stop fighting. He couldn't any longer. The malaria, his mauled arm. Most of his troops were dead or wounded."

"Where are they?"

"Ten days' walk from here, close to the Esperanza mining camp, past Mitu."

"And what are they doing there?"

"They are hiding and waiting for his orders. They can't come to Caguan because of the FARC."

"Why not?"

"Your father did not agree with the growing of coca to support the fight."

As Celeste talked, always staring at the ground, Natasha observed her. What could her father have seen in her? They did not seem to have anything in common. She noticed the cavities that had already formed between her teeth, eating away at them.

Celeste continued: "But FARC is now much richer. All the young fighters are joining in, and your father's old fighting *compañeros* have no support from anybody."

Natasha knew that Cuba and Russia were in no condition to support political movements in Latin America any longer. In the past, Paulo had been supported and supplied by Cuba in Nicaragua, Angola, and Colombia. At one point, he had commanded several thousand troops. Communism was retreating all over the world. How could they fight, without weapons, supplies, support, and lines of communication?

"And they cannot go to northern Colombia or Bogotá because the government will arrest them. So, they're hiding there in the Dog's Head and waiting for orders."

"The dog's head?"

"This is the region between Colombia, Venezuela and Brazil."

She retrieved a map, Paulo's map. She unfolded it carefully, stroking it pensively as she did.

"Here, do you see the dog's head?"

Natasha could see clearly the border between Brazil and Colombia, and Brazil and Venezuela. There was the Neblina Peak, the highest mountain of Brazil. And indeed, the region on the southeast border of Colombia resembled a head, with two triangular ears and two wide rectangular jaws, biting into Colombia. These were arbitrary lines drawn through the thick mountainous jungle. To the northeast was the Orinoco River in Venezuela, flowing to the Atlantic. To the south, the Negro River in Brazil, flowing all the way south to the Amazon. This was the most rugged and remote area of the Amazon. Natasha now remembered her anthropology classes. The Yanomami territory was east of there, closer to Venezuela. She had read Louis Bonaparte's *The Fierce Yanomami* and followed the controversy through newspapers. She had also been reading Patrick Tierny's book, *Darkness in El Dorado.* "The land of the Yanomami," she murmured.

"Yes, your father and I have been there, we've lived close to one of their villages. The Indians are very interesting."

For one moment, Natasha was tempted to ask Celeste if she was an Indian. But she restrained herself, knowing that they were considered inferior by the whites in Latin America. There was a complex pecking order, starting with the pure descendants of the Spanish and finishing with the blacks, *los negritos.* Natasha did not know where Celeste saw herself. She knew that her father had spent his life in the struggle to free Latin America of its colonial and exploitative past. But she also knew that the sensitivities of people had to be respected. Her own mother would every now and then utter a disdainful comment about the *cholos* or *negros*. This, in spite of the fact that she had in her youth joined the armed struggle. Natasha always felt that her mother had been swept up by the events and by the university comrades. But the aristocratic *criollo* and English blood of the Betancourts and Hannafords would surface every so often. So, she was careful when she asked, "And where are you from, Celeste?"

"I came from around here, two days down the Caguan River. My father was Portuguese and he had a grocery store in Mitu. He died when I was twelve and my older brother, Manuel, joined Comandante Paulo's forces. This is how I met Comandante Paulo," she said, still looking at the floor.

Natasha perceived a drop of emotion in her voice, as if saying his name and remembering him were painful.

"I started helping them, cooking for them and getting information. That was ten years ago." She passed her hand through the thick black hair and pulled it back.

Natasha felt sorry for her. She had lost a father and lover. Out of respect she did not want to ask about Manuel.

"I also have two sisters in Auapés, but I am afraid of going there. The Brazilian government has chased out all guerrillas from their towns and people know about Manuel and Comandante Paulo."

"So, this is a good place."

"Yes, if it weren't for the FARC."

The next morning, Celeste asked her to stay a few days. Natasha was surprised by the offer. Did she do it out of politeness? Did she have an agenda? In any case, she accepted. She was eager to know more about her father. Now that she had survived the march from Caguan, she deserved a few days of rest. Antonio, Comandante Paulo's trusted adjutant, had just arrived and would protect them.

"I'd like to show you our ways, our cooking. But you are a beautiful city girl and there is nothing here for you."

"Celeste, you're wrong. I always longed to see where I was born, to return to my roots. It is very sad that I do this after my father is gone."

Moved by the moment, she hugged Celeste, feeling her protruding stomach. Shyly, Celeste put her arms around her for a moment and embraced her. Natasha noticed that they were short and could not reach completely around her.

"We must be the same age, Celeste. I'm twenty-four."

"And I'm twenty-three."

How could he have fallen for a woman half his age? And for a woman that had lived all her years under the forest canopy? What would they talk about? On what level would they communicate?

"I've known your father for over ten years," Celeste said, and Natasha heard the pride in her voice. So, she must have been twelve or thirteen when she met him.

"He was so happy when he returned from the United States. He brought beautiful gifts."

She took Natasha by the hand to her *room*, a cubicle created by walls of woven bamboo. Opening a wooden box, she showed Natasha a book on California, a stuffed Mickey Mouse, a sweatshirt with the Berkeley insignia, and a Polaroid camera. They were all neatly kept, like relics. Celeste pulled them out carefully, and looked for a long time at each one. She seemed to remember the past with each object, as if each one had its own life. Natasha understood that they were links to Paulo and to a faraway, mysterious country.

"I remember, Celeste. Dad and I bought the shirt together at the campus store."

Celeste put it on and Natasha could not help thinking that it appeared totally ridiculous and out of place. Nevertheless, she said that it looked good on her.

"He described all the places he saw, in San Francisco, Los Angeles, and San Diego."

Natasha remembered those hectic three months one year ago. She and Ernesto had shown California to their father. Ernesto had driven up the coast for three days, and they had initially planned to do the standard California tour: Disneyland, Universal Studios, Hollywood, Hearst Castle, etc. However, after one day, their father was bored. He asked them to show him cultural places, special places. He wanted to know the people, to understand the American psyche. So, they showed him the LA barrios, the millionaire enclaves, and the ethnic neighborhoods. They even introduced him to West Hollywood, "Gayland South" as Ernesto called it. They also stopped at Yosemite. For Natasha and Ernesto it was fascinating to see how their father related his observations with his preconceived ideas about the US. He had been educated under strong Soviet influence and his entire mind frame was negative in the beginning. But he was an intelligent man, and absorbed the information rapidly. He immediately saw that the diversity of the American ethnic and cultural mix was also strength. He was fascinated with everything, bombarding them with questions. He was so bubbly, so alive, and it was refreshing to see how rapidly he absorbed the essence of the US. He would ask them all kinds of questions about politics, and continuously demanded help in translating newspaper articles and TV news. His surgeries and dental treatment had gone well and he left invigorated, renewed.

"Yes, Celeste, it was wonderful having our father with us for those months. He should have stayed there. But I don't know how he would have adapted."

"I was afraid he wouldn't return. I prayed every day for him to come back." At this, she pointed to the rosary tied to her hammock. "He treated me like a little girl, as you can see from the gifts. But I was already deeply in love with him, all the way from the first time I saw him, I was twelve. I kept my love secret for many years. Every time I brought him coffee, my heart would jump. When he would casually caress my head and pet me like a little dog, I would feel the warmth filling my entire body. But I never let him know about my feelings."

"So, you loved him for over ten years."

"For over ten years. And when he became wounded in the battle of Santa Marta, I took care of him for several weeks. The wounds were infected and he almost lost his arm." Then, with a little grin, she revealed, "I just took him." Her elongated Indian eyes almost closed, and through a narrow slit Natasha could see, for an instant, the deep love that united them.

"Poor Comandante," she said at last. "I didn't give him a chance. But I also made him very happy. He had somebody to return to after his battles, jungle marches, and expeditions."

Then she turned to Natasha, took her hand and put it on her stomach, exclaiming proudly, "You'll have a little brother soon."

Natasha tried to act surprised. It was obvious to everyone except Celeste that she was pregnant.

"And how do you know it's a little boy?"

"I can tell it. Little boys cling closer to their moms. Little girls stick out. They want to leave mom."

"And what will be the name of my little brother?"

"Paulo, of course."

"But my father's real name was Marco Aurelio Chauny."

"To us, he was Paulo. And he had explained to me why he chose Paulo. He admired Saint Paul and his numerous struggles for Christianity. He told me that he would be the Paul of the Revolution, taking it to all regions, preaching it, converting everyone and everybody. And Paul was killed by the Romans, do you know?"

"I think I remember this," Natasha said, puzzled at Celeste's cunning. She was starting to understand Paulo's attachment to the girl. Paulo had been the centerpiece of her little world. Her father had left her a gift that would always be with her: Paulo, her son.

# CHAPTER FIVE

"Shaki, we have less than a day left," the Indian said. He walked at a brisk pace, at the head of the group. Short and light, he had the demure of a teenager. Only the pensive face and wrinkles on his forehead gave away his age. He was in his mid-fifties.

Following him, Louis Bonaparte sweated profusely. His body showed mosquito bites all over the exposed areas. The khaki pants were dirty from numerous slips and falls on the trail and the shirt had huge wet patches under his armpits from sweat. He looked every day of his sixty years. Yet, he had a heroic demeanor about him, like Teddy Roosevelt.

"Shaki, you're not used to this type of travel any longer," the Indian continued. "Remember the helicopter? We could have been there in one hour instead of all these days."

"Kaobawa, I told you before that we couldn't use the Venezuelan government."

Bonaparte had embarked on this adventure to help a lost group of Yanomami that lived beyond Venezuela, close to the Colombian border. He knew about this distant Haximu village, beyond the extreme southwest of the Yanomami territory, through Kaobawa's grapevine. Information traveled fast through the jungle, often in mysterious ways, and he knew of a group that had splintered from the main territory and moved west, in search of better hunting The Haximu-Teri Yanomami needed to be inoculated against measles and smallpox before the rubber tappers or gold miners got to them. He had asked the Brazilian government for permission to visit them, but this was denied several times. His enemies at FUNAI, the Brazilian Indian Foundation, had a say in this. So, he decided to strike on his own. It was typical, vintage Bonaparte.

Kaobawa, the chief of Bisaasi-Teri village, had agreed to come with him. Kaobawa had been his ally for over thirty years, since his first visit to the village, in 1967. He, Louis Bonaparte, had become a famous and controversial anthropologist. His vision of Yanomami society matched the new science of Evolutionary Biology. E. O. Wilson, the famous Harvard professor and father of Sociobiology, had found rich material in Bonaparte's findings: an isolated group of people with an inherently aggressive conduct. A group of approximately twenty thousand Indians living in one hundred and twenty villages hidden in the folds of the mountains of the upper Amazon. This last glimpse at the Neolithic was precious and important. It could mold our image of ourselves, humans, by providing a look at the psychological buildup of our ancestors. And what was the logic behind the aggressive behavior? Reproduction, of course.

Bonaparte had returned, time and time again, over the three decades, to his beloved Yanomami. He had spent a total of seven years among them. At first, his scientific research was the main goal. Slowly, gradually, he developed deep bonds with his subjects. He felt more and more out of place in Berkeley, the academic jungle. His enemies were ferocious and relentless, but he fought valiantly. The call of the other jungle, the Amazon, became stronger every year. This personal, biological bond that he had forged over the years now impelled him to this dangerous march through the forest. His aging body sent pain messages. This would be his last jungle march. But he had to carry on. There were wrongs to redress, there was hidden remorse, that he only confessed to himself, and even so, only after he had ingested half a bottle of scotch: *the inoculation controversy.*

They had left the Bisaasi-Teri village by motor boat, going up the Mavaca River as far as they could. Then, they walked. Kaobawa had brought with him ten of his most trusted warriors. They had to arrive at Haximu-Teri with a respectable force. The Yanomami were opportunistic and he would not discount the possibility of being massacred by them, if it were feasible, convenient, and profitable. Sociobiology at work.

He was incredibly tired after the long march. In past years, with support of his friends in the Venezuelan government, he had used a helicopter to ferry groups of reporters and cameramen around. A lot of this interest was due to the book that he had written, *The Fierce Yanomami.* The book, intended as a text, had sold over a million copies. Along the way, he had lost track of his original goals. Power corrupts, and he was not immune. So, this journey was also a return to his roots. His body had lost its youthful springiness. Although he was not much taller than the Yanomami, who averaged five feet, he had acquired a considerable girth. It was painful carrying this extra weight around, and his tired legs and sore feet were a reminder. Nevertheless, he had realized that his fat melted away during the trip, and he moved with much greater ease now.

He abhorred these Yanomami trails. They would simply go in a straight line, without consideration of the topography. The Yanomami were ideally suited for this type of travel. They weighed, on the average, a little over one hundred pounds. They could move, at a slow trot, for several hours.

He calculated that they covered forty kilometers per day. So, they must have advanced four hundred kilometers and, somewhere under the thick canopy, had crossed the forbidden border into Brazil. The Brazilian authorities would have detected a trip by helicopter. Brazil was becoming a powerful and ambitious nation, and its territorial integrity was a matter of great pride for the military. The government had embarked on an ambitious project, protecting its borders with satellite information, radar stations and airplanes that patrolled the vast Amazon basin. The specter of the internationalization of the Amazon and the creation of a Yanomami territory or nation was anathema in government circles. The Amazon had riches, oil, gold, and minerals, and these belonged, by some divine decree, to the spoiled inhabitants of Rio de Janeiro beaches. And to the brothers and cousins of the rich politicians. The Indians were savages and needed to be incorporated into the progressive Brazilian society. The process of integration was almost complete. A few pockets remained in the Upper Amazon.

Kaobawa ordered two of his warriors to move ahead of the group and contact the village. Although geographically distant, the village of Haximu-Teri had no history of warfare with Bisaasi-Teri. Neither had they allied themselves with the Patanowa-Teri, Bisaasi's archenemies. One of the Bisaasi-Teri girls had been traded to the Haximu-Teri several years ago, and she had an offspring. Nevertheless, Kaobawa knew the law of the jungle: never arrive unannounced unless you want to raid a village. They left trotting, leaving their bows and arrows with the others. They would return by nightfall, to let them know if they were welcome. If they did not return, trouble was looming.

"I hope we have enough medicine for the entire village," Bonaparte said, inspecting one of the baskets carried by the Indians to ensure that its contents were well preserved. He was fluent in Yanomami, and the knowledge of the language and all its nuances had been extremely valuable. He remembered well his first experiences at Bisaasi-Teri, when he was doing his doctoral dissertation work. After one year, he had to throw away all his data on kinship relationships. He learned, at great cost, that the Yanomami keep their names secret. Upon visiting a neighboring village, he checked the names of the chief and his family, as given to him by the Bisaasi-Teri "friends." He only understood the roars that he created with his names when they were translated to him. The chief was supposed to be "long dong," his wife, "hairy cunt," and his brother "eagle shit." Supremely embarrassed, he realized that he had been taken. They had made him look *mahode,* stupid. All kinship information given to him was false, and he had to start from scratch after one year. He realized that Yanomami had strict name taboos. But this had been over thirty years now, and now he knew all the names, although he never used them. The Yanomami feared that revealing the name brought about the evil spirits. He was much wiser now, and was as cunning as his friends.

The Eskimos have thirty names for snow. The Yanomami, on the other hand, had many names for their sexual appendages, and it took Bonaparte a long time before he would no longer be ridiculed. Now, after thirty years, he could dish out insults, and they had given up making a *mahode* of him.

They had already settled into a makeshift camp alongside the trail when Walaharia and Rerebawa returned. They would be welcome, but there was tension among the Haximu -Teri. They brought roasted meat and plantains from the village as a sign of good will from the hosts. They were expected the next day.

The next morning before entering the village, they groomed themselves. Bonaparte took off his shirt and pants and fixed up his penis loin like all the others. Yanomami etiquette required the foreskin of the penis to be tied to a cotton string, which was pulled up and tied around the waist. An untied penis was considered poor manners. Fortunately, Bonaparte was uncircumcised and managed to look professionally attired. They cleansed themselves at the creek, applied red *onato* paint and black charcoal on their bodies. They glued white feathers to their armbands. Kaobawa, the chief, wore a black monkey-tail headband covered with white buzzard down. He also put on a new red loincloth, which clearly set him apart from the rest of the group. They hid part of their supplies close by. They knew that they would have to share everything, once in the village.

Their entrance, after they removed the branches that closed the opening to the wooden palisade, was spectacular. Each one of them carried the bow and arrow upright, and they had a peculiar expression and mouth puckering that Bonaparte imitated as well as he could. He felt the renewed emotion of discovery, the same feeling he had thirty years ago, when he entered Bisaasi-Teri for the first time. He vowed at that moment, to himself, that he would do everything in his power to help them. They stood there, in the middle of the inner *shabono* yard, for a few minutes. Curious eyes observed them from under the *shabono*, which Bonaparte assessed with his experienced eyes. The *shabono* was new and smelled fresh. In a few months it would have a decomposed look and the tribe would move on.

The Bisaasi then began an elaborate dance; each warrior danced with his own style and sang his song. This was an opportunity to display skills. Bonaparte knew that the attention of the hosts was focused on him. He was the *nabu*, the foreigner. He proceeded with his dance, a mixture of sixties rock with some Yanomami steps that he had learned over the years. The Haximu Indians approved with shrill screams and enthusiastic shouts. After each dancer had a chance to display his individual skills, the entire group danced single file at the center of the clearing.

At last they gathered in the center and stood there, motionless, for a few minutes, holding their bows and arrows upright. This was a way of saying that they did not have any aggressive intentions. It was only then that the hosts exited the *shabono* and entered the inner courtyard. Each one of them took a guest and invited him to his hammock. The Bisaasi sat comfortably at the hammocks, holding their shin with one of their hands, while being curiously observed by the hosts. This was also the recommended etiquette, and Bonaparte followed suit. However, he was the star of the show. They had never seen a white foreigner dressed as one of them, and could see that he was uncomfortable with his penis string, which he adjusted continuously as the hosts rolled around in laughter. They inspected every inch of his body in great detail, feigning fear, revulsion, and a range of other feelings ranging from hilarious laughter to terror. They pulled at his pubic hair and poked at his skin, stopping every now and then to roar.

"What a sight I am, Kaobawa," he said at last, looking at himself. His red face and tanned arms contrasted with the white stomach. The cotton string holding up his penis had rubbed into it, and the foreskin was red and swollen. Not that he was a stranger to these customs. He even had a picture of himself having the hallucinogenic drug *ebene* being blown into his nostrils published in his book. But then he was a young graduate student, not an aging professor marked by decades of smoking, drinking, and subjecting the body to the many perils and maladies of the jungle.

"Don't worry, Shaki," Kaobawa said. "They are liking you and this is good for us."

They were served plantain soup in gourds and pieces of roasted monkey. The Haximu then reciprocated and put on their own display of dancing.

As night fell, the chanting started. It continued, at varying levels of intensity, until dawn. Bonaparte took the time to inspect the village and noticed that a young girl was sick with a high fever. The Haximu-Teri chief, Bakotawa, told Kaobawa that she had fallen sick after some white gold diggers had camped a couple of kilometers from there and that a few of his tribe's people had gone down and traded with them. This alarmed Bonaparte. "It can be an outbreak of measles," he said. "We need to inoculate the rest of the tribe immediately."

He asked Kaobawa to request permission to see the sick. Permission being granted, he went to the section of the *shabono* from where some wailing was coming. He saw a woman holding a little girl, her father nearby. The parents of the girl were livid. A shaman was chanting and blowing smoke at the sick girl, in a desperate attempt to expel the evil spirits causing her harm. They all looked exhausted.

"Measles," he said, as Kaobawa held a torch by her face. He saw the characteristic pustules and was shocked. Something had to be done, and fast.

"Kaobawa, we need to get permission right away to inoculate the village," he said. "Get in touch with the *tushaua*."

Moments later, Kaobawa returned with Bakotawa. They negotiated for a long time, while Bonaparte convinced the parents of the girl to accept the antibiotics that he had with him. The parents finally accepted Shaki's medicine. The girl was delirious. Bonaparte discovered three more children in the surrounding hammocks with signs of the dreaded disease. He recalled the '60s, when a measles epidemic had wrought havoc among the Yanomami, killing as many as half of the people in some villages. He had directed a biomedical study funded by the US Atomic Energy Commission in which the blood of many Indians was investigated. In this study it was discovered that they did not have any antibodies against measles, mumps, or smallpox. He also directed a vast inoculation program, but the Brazilian

Yanomami were excluded because he had been prohibited from entering the country.

"Shaki, Bakotawa has agreed," Kaobawa said.

"What's the price?"

"Three machetes." Then, with some concern, he added, "Shaki, are you sure we got the good vaccines? Remember the ones we gave on the Orinoco?"

"These ones were provided by the Ministry of Health, in Caracas The other ones were from the Yankees."

The remorse over the actions had not ceased to gnaw at him for all these years. This inoculation program became highly controversial because of the live vaccine used. Later, he was accused of spreading the disease. Many Yanomami believed, right or wrong, that the vaccine had infected them. In any case, he had done his work with the best of intentions. Apparently, the Atomic Energy Commission had provided an extremely strong vaccine, the Edmonston B, with live viruses. James O'Neal, a famous geneticist, had brought this vaccine. Upon inoculating the Yanomami in the villages around the Ocamo Salesian Mission, where they thought that a measles outbreak was starting, large numbers became severely ill, with fevers running as high as 107°F. He never could resolve whether they had created or contained the outbreak. The Edmonston vaccine was much too strong for the Yanomami, which had a very low antibody response. It appeared that the vaccine had infected many Indians. At least, that is what they said he had done. Of trading research support for Yanomami blood samples and for allowing the AEC to conduct a vast biological experiment in the confines of the Amazon forest. These were the same people that had experimented with Pacific Islands populations, subjecting them to radiation. Something to make Dr. Mengele chuckle; Mengele was the pioneer, but had left a following behind. He would have to carry this weight on his shoulders until the end of his life. His trip through the jungle was part of an inner need to redress whatever wrongs he had been involved in.

To make matters worse, a huge club fight broke out in the middle of the night and Bonaparte, exhausted as he was, could not sleep. He had witnessed many club fights before, and they usually occurred when there was some animosity between two people. This often escalated, others taking sides. When they pulled the beams from the *shabono* and held them upright, hitting each other in the head, Bonaparte was not surprised. He tried to sleep but could not avoid witnessing the screams and blood spilled. He knew well that the head bleeds profusely and was not unduly alarmed. Many Yanomami proudly displayed the immense gashes on their head as proof that they were *waiteri*, fierce.

Kaobawa, lying on an adjacent hammock, told him, chuckling, "Bakotawa has been screwing one of Ushubiriwa's wives and he just found out."

"Why can't they wait until we're gone?"

"You know, Shaki, it's not a pleasant experience."

"You should know, Kaobawa. What are your three wives doing right now?"

"I got rid of the horny one."

The ruckus slowly abated. Bonaparte was worried about the spread of measles. A few bloody heads over cuckoldry was only a minor affair. He tried hard to rest for the couple of hours left before dawn. He would need all the energy he could gather for the next day.

As soon as the sun broke out, Bonaparte went to work. Bakotawa was the first in line, and proudly displayed a huge gash on his skull. His wives, children, and brothers followed him. Then came the rest of the tribe, about eighty. Several had to be bought again, and a couple dozen hooks, beads, and mirrors were distributed. Shaki knew that the Yanomami expected payment for every action. All for the sake of reproduction, as E. O. Wilson would say.

After the inoculation was complete, Bonaparte passed out in the hammock that he had been offered. His dreams were restless and haunting. Images of the Ocama Mission inoculation campaign and of horribly distorted figures populated the nightmare, as a mysterious scientist in a white laboratory apron and mask observed the scene.

Bonaparte woke up after dark, from the desperate wailing that approached his hammock. The parents of Koamashima held her frail and rigid body in their arms. The rash and eruptions of measles had gotten worse. She had stopped breathing. The father screamed accusingly at him, and grabbed a stone ax, gyrating it around his head as he showered him with insults.

Alerted, Kaobawa immediately came to the rescue, placing himself between Bonaparte and the grief-stricken father. Bonaparte understood that he was being accused of having killed the girl with his medicine. The entire village now surrounded them, screaming madly.

"Shaki brings *xawara* (illness)," the father said. He suddenly attacked with his ax, aiming at Bonaparte's head. With an agile movement, Kaobawa grabbed the arm before it could strike and twisted it. He was partially able to deflect the blow, but was hit on the shoulder. At this the Bisaasi-Teri

Yanomami surrounded their injured leader, aiming their long arrows at the angry mob. Bakotawa defused the situation by stepping forward and announcing, "We'll have a chest pounding duel. The best from Haximu against the best from Bisaasi. Shaki will be first."

It was an intelligent intervention. He allowed conflict to escalate without going into an open war. He had judged, correctly, that a direct fight with the fierce Bisaasi-Teri Yanomami could have become an ugly affair. Haximu -Teri had many women and children and perhaps no more than fifteen able-bodied fighters. They did not have the experience of Kaobawa's group, which had been hand picked among the fiercest of Bisaasi-Teri. Although outnumbered, Bakotawa knew that the Bisaasi would have a good chance of beating them. They were trapped and would fight till the last man. Tempers were running high, and a good chest-pounding duel would help to cool them.

Bonaparte knew the rules. In his younger days, he had taken part in one of these painful duels. He couldn't back off now. He had to be *waiteri*. The men moved to the central courtyard, carrying their bows and weapons. They kept them upright now, the Bisaasi-Teri ones having lowered their arrows.

Bonaparte, in front, readied himself for the painful exercise. Bakotawa pointed to him. "Shaki, you go first. Against me."

A roar came from the crowd. Bakotawa offered his chest. Bonaparte knew that there was no backing off now.

He pulled his arm back and swung it around several times, in preparation for the blow. He measured his distance from Bakotawa as if he were a baseball batter, making the movement several times, in slow motion. Bakotawa stared at him proudly as he offered his chest. He was in his fifties, but still strong. Then, Bonaparte unleashed his punch with a loud scream. Bakotawa fell to the ground, but got up immediately. A "frog" grew on his pectoral muscles from the impact. Bonaparte unleashed two more strikes, and Bakotawa withstood them.

It was his turn now. Bakotawa walked around for a while, gathering his strength. Bonaparte stoically waited, concentrating on how he could absorb the blow without acting like a coward. Should he keep his body as firm as possible? Should he try to soften the blow? He opted for the former. In any case, it would be over soon. The duel would get worse later, and he was lucky to be the first. He offered his chest, and took the first blow standing. It was not so painful. The second one was much worse, and threw him momentarily on the ground. He jumped up immediately and adjusted his penis string. He knew that it would be improper to continue without rectifying this. This second blow had been much more painful, because it hit in exactly the same place as the first one.

Then, Bakatowa unleashed his third blow, incredibly hard. The crowd had been cheering him on, and he put all his strength into it. Bonaparte fell to the ground, tasting blood in his mouth. He could no longer breathe, and saw stars. Harnessing the last trickle of energy in his body, he tried to get up. He felt like a knocked out boxer hearing the ten second count. He had to be *waiteri;* he had to get up. So, he crawled first to his knees, then spit a mouthful of blood as he climbed back onto his legs. The crowd cheered. They had given and withstood three blows. They had proven their valor. Two younger warriors stepped into the center, eager to measure themselves.

They traded blows into the night, Kaobawa and Bakotawa keeping the event from escalating. At one point, the Haximu demanded a club fight. Kaobawa vetoed this. He also instructed his men to go easy. The Haximu were growing desperate, since they were falling behind in the contest. At the end, it was declared a draw. It was almost daylight when they went to sleep, and all that Bonaparte could hear now was the wailing of Koamashima's family. The next day, they would have the funeral. He hoped that the vaccine would take effect before the tribe was exposed to the live virus. He had demanded that the other sick children be isolated. Fortunately, they had the good sense to agree. They understood the disease better now. News of deadly outbreaks of measles had reached them in the past, and they were aware of how the disease was transmitted.

It had been a couple of weeks since the chest-pounding match. Bonaparte's group had stayed at the Haximu Village, waiting for his recovery, which was slow. He could still feel the lump from the cracked rib. The first days had been especially difficult, and he spent most of the time in the hammock. Even breathing was painful. His condition had been a great source of pleasure and pride for Bakotawa. It gave him the recognition that he was the victor. He would come by every day and, with great help from gestures, would tell the entire group how and where he unleashed the killer blow.

In the meantime, Bonaparte continued to gather information on surrounding villages. There were three villages within five days walk, and he had decided to visit them, as soon as he could walk without pain again. The Haximu village had an excess of women. This was due to a couple of raids by the Pakatanowa few years earlier. Several of the Haximu men had gotten killed. Hence, they were eager to offer them some of their women. This was a long and drawn out affair, and Kaobawa was in the midst of a complex and intricate negotiation.

Magnanimously, Bakotawa had sent one of the women to help the ailing Bonaparte. She was one of the raid widows, about twenty-five, quite attractive by Yanomami standards.

"Watch out, Shaki, "Kaobawa said. " They are trying to unload their women on us. Make sure she has a nice cunt."

Bonaparte was infuriated by the comment. "Try to get us some tobacco, Kaobawa. The last thing I need is cunt right now." At this, he held his ailing rib with his hand.

He had exhausted his supply of cigarettes and the Bisaasi no longer had any tobacco. This was a precious commodity and a constant source of worry for the Yanomami. Everyone was hooked on tobacco: men, women, and children. Kaobawa screamed a few words at his son, Rerebawa, and he soon came back with a young Haximu boy. After a heated argument, they struck a deal. A good-sized wad of tobacco leaves materialized, which was promptly transformed into a few small cylinders. Rerebawa and Kaobawa stuck them into their mouths, with great pleasure.

"Shaki, stick it like this," Rerebawa said, opening his mouth and showing the black leaf between the tongue and the teeth. His mouth salivated profusely and he sucked it with intense pleasure. Bonaparte improvised a cigarette and lit it, being able to take a few puffs before it went out.

He was familiar with the process and relighted it. He felt the wonderfully inebriating smoke coat his lungs with warmth, while his entire body was invaded by peace and absolute relaxation. They lay in their hammocks for a long time, enjoying the intense pleasure of tobacco. For a few moments, he engaged in a self-serving soliloquy. He had standards as an anthropologist. He could not explain to Kaobawa that it was considered anathema for anthropologists to have intimate relationships with the subject of their studies. He had a few slips in the past thirty years, but all in all he was able to maintain a professional relationship with the Yanomami. Nevertheless, he felt vulnerable.

His thoughts floated to Mahima, the girl that Bakotawa had assigned to help him. She was a pleasant person and always smiled at him in the most natural and appealing manner, showing her bright teeth. She looked particularly pretty this morning, having inserted long sticks in her cheeks and wearing her most beautiful bead necklace. She was of average build for a Yanomami and would be petite in the US. Her breasts were small but nicely shaped, and she had a shy grace that appealed to him. She had cooked for him in the past days and helped him with daily chores. Although completely naked, she always behaved with decorum. As she sat or got up from the hammock, she would always be careful not to expose her private parts. Bonaparte knew that this was part of Yanomami etiquette. They grew more and more familiar with each other and were starting to operate like a couple. Few words were necessary.

The first days had been especially painful. He had spit blood and the badly bruised lungs healed slowly. Mahima had helped him bathe and had rubbed his body with her able hands. Bonaparte tried to repress his feelings for her, but there was warmth, excitement emanating from her that he could not contain.

That evening, after she brought him a couple of manioc breads that she had baked, she sat in his hammock. The *shabono* was already surrounded by darkness and the night was moonless. He enjoyed her warm presence, and they chatted about trivial affairs, the day's hunt, the upcoming trip to the Auaretê village. Mahima asked how his rib was healing.

"The lump is smaller, and I breathe without pain."

"Be careful and do not lie here," she said, caressing his left side. Then, she turned her back to him as he lay on the hammock. He did not ask her to leave and could now feel her entire body against his. Slowly, a strange emotion rose in him. Feelings that he had thought long gone, far away in his youth, returned. A warm and strong passion gradually took hold of him, and he could no longer contain himself. He kissed her lightly on her neck. She turned her head, moving her hair away with a delicate gesture and exposed the side of her face, which he first caressed gently, and then kissed. "Mahima, you look so beautiful today," he whispered in her ear.

"Oh, Shaki, I made myself pretty for you." She pressed her derriere against his groin, and a wave of excitement ran through his body. His hands moved to her breasts, which he caressed first, then massaged vigorously. He could hear her breathing grow more rapid at each caress. She was also excited. She was warm and moist inside, ready to receive him.

On this darkest night of the year, Louis Bonaparte surrendered to his desire and made love to Mahima. With one thrust, he threw away all the stupid little rules of field research. Her rapid breathing became muffled moans that she could not, at the end, control. She moved with such dexterity and vigor that he soon was engulfed in pleasure. Their noises merged with the cries and many mysterious sounds of the jungle. The aging Berkeley professor and the young Yanomami were united on this moonless night. Afterward they lay there, and he knew that Mahima was smiling, although he could not see her face.

Over the next days, Bonaparte explored the surrounding areas. He felt reenergized and rejuvenated by Mahima. Every night she would climb into his hammock after dark and leave in the early hours of the morning, when he was sound asleep. Two days after she had first come to his hammock, he summoned Kaobawa. "Let's check on the miners' camp on the Vauapés River."

"First tell me how her cunt is, Shaki."

Yanomami took sex naturally and thought about it all the time. "She's fine, Kaobawa, very fine." He knew Kaobawa for many years and kept no secrets from him. "I don't know what will happen, but she's very good to me."

Kaobawa gave him an understanding and wise look. He had three wives and they all played vital roles in his life. Yarima was the oldest and was actually his first cousin. They resembled each other physically and she was his true companion. Kamaiha was a young second wife and was now pregnant. She was his favorite for sex. Once in a while, he let one of his younger brothers have sex with her, but only when she was really *beshi* (horny). The third one was a widower that he had taken as a wife in a trade. She was nothing but trouble and cheated on him all the time. He was wise and was getting rid of her, passing her on to one of his nephews.

"We'll take her with us, Shaki," he said with an understanding smile.

For a moment, Bonaparte thought of his old wife in Berkeley. She was probably shopping at Vons, or cleaning the house. In her sixties, she had been his loyal and patient companion. Her best days were behind her, but she kept the home clean and was in constant contact with the family. "There is an important place in society for post-menopausal women," his colleague Professor Beifuss used to say. Then, he would elaborate on the important social functions performed by older women, serving as a link between generations. But Kaobawa had three wives, each serving an important function.

At last he said, "I can't take Mahima with me like that stupid student, Ken Goodman did."

"We keep her for you in Bisaasi-Teri." Kaobawa grinned. "And when you are in your country we take good care of her."

"You bunch of howler monkeys," he said in a feigned fury. "I know that you raped Ken's wife several times when he left her here."

"And where is she now? She left Ken and is in Bisaasi-Teri with their two kids. She liked our treatment, Shaki."

"Let's visit the mining camp tomorrow. I want to see what kind of people brought measles to this village."

The next morning, they walked down the Auaretê River for a little over an hour. It was easy to find the camp. They had taken one of the Haximu children with them. The beach where they had set up camp was close to a mountain, which had uncharacteristically thin vegetation. They approached very carefully, but soon realized that the miners were already gone. The camp was a mess. They had built temporary palm thatch roof huts that they had abandoned. There were polyethylene bottles spread through the entire beach where they had camped. There was also a pile of garbage and a couple of empty oil drums. Bonaparte sifted through the beach, looking for clues. They were all over the place. He found some discarded shirts with the seal, SAMITRA MINERAÇÃO. He also found several mounds with rocks. Upon picking them up, he noticed their extraordinary weight. He had been a mining engineering student at Michigan Tech before switching to anthropology and always prided himself on his no nonsense engineering approach to science. None of that Lévi-Strauss theoretical stuff. He told it as it was, without filtering and adjusting facts to fit his theories.

It took him little time to figure out that this was a geological prospecting expedition, not a gold miners' camp. The mineral was probably laden with a heavy metal, lead, tin, or tantalum. Bonaparte knew that there was a lot of cassiterite in the western confines of the Amazon basin. So, that's what it was. He led his group to the closest peak of the Mavaca Mountains, which they climbed without problem. It was highly mineralized, with rocks everywhere. All of them were similar to the one in the camp. A mountain of cassiterite: this was a bad omen for the Yanomami. If he was right, they would soon receive more visitors. By the way the geologists had left the beach, he knew what to expect:

destruction of the environment and more disease for the Yanomami. He had to do something. But what?

The next day, he woke up in terrible pain. He had re-injured himself coming down the mountain. The cracked rib was now completely fractured. He knew that he had to lie there until healing was complete. *Mahima has to be very gentle,* he thought.

A few days later he was awakened from his midday siesta by a distant buzz and excited screams of the Yanomami. The buzz turned into a roar as he saw a Cessna fly over the village. The local Yanomami ran to the central courtyard with their bows and arrows, while the Bisaasi-Teri group laughed. The plane circled over their heads once at about one hundred feet. The Yanomami unleashed their arrows at the plane, in fury and despair. Bonaparte had warned them of the renewed danger of disease. The plane tilted its wings, giving the passenger a good look at the entire village. Bonaparte jumped off his hammock and was able to glance at the face in the plane. He stayed under the *shabono,* in the shade and out of sight. He saw the long-nosed man, wearing Ray Ban glasses, looking at them with a big smile, his teeth like those of a shark.

# CHAPTER SIX

Something bothered Clayton. He had wanted to see that mountain in person; to see if these Indians really existed. He flew from Rio de Janeiro to Manaus and from there to Auapés. In the airport, he arranged for a Cessna to take him to the Mavaca Mountains. A bush pilot finally agreed to take him there after charging him $500 extra for entering into the protected area. "In case I get caught by the Brazilian authorities," he had said.

They had left the next morning, shortly after daylight. They flew low, below the cloud cover, and followed the Auapés River, which at first flowed lazily toward the Negro River. Then came rapids, as the terrain became increasingly mountainous. "I'm here on a mission, Humberto," he said, a cynical grin on his face. "Hand me a cigarette."

"Smoking is prohibited on this airplane," Humberto replied. Nevertheless, he passed him his pack. "But hand me one of these beers. We need to celebrate. I can see the Mavaca Mountains out there."

The pilot was experienced at these types of operations; he transported gold diggers, drug smugglers, hookers, and other colorful frontier characters. The Dog's Head was one of the most remote places on the globe: a never-ending green carpet crisscrossed by rivers. The scenery was gorgeous, and the pilot would lower the right wing periodically so that Clayton could see bands of capybaras running and jumping into the water, scared by the plane's noise. They looked like giant guinea pigs. They also saw a tapir crossing the stream and hordes of alligators spread on the beaches. At the designated GPS coordinates provided by Clayton, the pilot left the Auapés River and followed a smaller *igarapé*, a side river. "We're on the Auaretê now," he said.

Clayton nodded. "The village should be off the river, on a creek."

Within a couple of minutes they saw the large circular house, with a central courtyard. As they approached the *shabono*, small figures filled the courtyard. They flew over and came back, even lower. Clayton could see the panic in the Indians' eyes. Several of them fired arrows from their bows, and Clayton laughed at their effort. Nevertheless, he felt a chill as they flew off. These were real people, not capybaras. At their left were the Mavaca Mountains; among them was a peak with scarce vegetation, which contrasted with the lush forest.

Two days later, Clayton arrived in Pasto, Colombia. As he looked out of the plane window, he recognized the green farmland and dramatic Andes *Cordillera* that he had visited ten years earlier. Pasto lay on the eastern foothills of the Andes and benefited from a much cooler climate than the Amazon. Three hundred miles west of there, the Pacific Ocean spread itself to the horizon, in infinite tranquility. How could such an idyllic country be so ravaged by war, he wondered. He felt a strange emotion as he stepped out of the plane, walked across the tarmac and into the small building. It was there, ten years ago, that he had seen Marco Aurelio for the last time. He had tried, in vain, to convince him to abandon the armed struggle. As they said good-bye Marco Aurelio had told him, with infinite sadness in his voice, "I have to spur Rocinante on, Clayton, and say like Don Quixote, *'Mis arreos son mis armas y muy descanso el pelear'* (My clothes are my weapons and my rest the struggle)."

Clayton felt the strong emotion of the moment, as he walked into the small white building that served as a terminal. He lit a cigarette and took a deep drag. There she was, dark flowing hair, beautiful and trim, in her early forties, waiting. She wore stylish jeans, a white shirt, and riding boots. Ana Maria gave him a strong hug and he felt her breasts against his chest. As he kissed her cheeks, he smelled the exotic cologne *–Ysatis?–* and felt a twitch in his groin. That familiar twitch that had guided his actions for so many years.

*By Odin, she is my brother's ex-wife; control yourself, Clayton,* he thought.

Marco Aurelio and he had seen the movie *The Vikings* as children and had learned the expression from its star, Kirk Douglas. They always used it in their war games. Now, thirty years later, the expression, buried deep in some hidden corner of his brain, came back to his mind.

"I am terribly sorry about Paulo," Ana Maria said.

"Thank you. I miss him more and more. In spite of our differences, he was my hero."

During the trip to the *hacienda*, they reminisced about Paulo. Ana Maria drove, and Clayton appreciated the scenery. He liked the vast expanse of land and the pastures where every now and then a group of *Zebu, Gyr,* or *Nelore* cattle grazed. Clayton tried to open the window of the SUV to better see through the dark glass.

"Don't try, the car is armored," she said. He realized that he could only open it a few inches.

"This is a necessity here," she continued. "I paid $20,000 to have the windows and sides armored."

"Karin wants to armor her Mercedes in Rio."

"This might be a fad there, but I don't want to die like my father. Every week we hear about kidnappings."

Clayton knew the danger under which everybody lived in Colombia.

Ana Maria's eyes darkened. "Natasha is right now in the middle of the Colombian jungle. She came to visit her father's tomb and has not yet returned. I'm very worried." Clayton knew that Ana Maria was distressed over the lack of news from her daughter. Perhaps he could help.

He remembered Natasha as a teenager. "Is she still as beautiful and fierce?"

"She has her father's temperament. I'm very worried and hope that she doesn't do anything foolish."

"Like her mother in her twenties?"

She smiled. "Yes, I was taken by the Left, but realized in time that the struggle had gone wrong. In those days we had a dream, a grand dream."

"And what's different today?"

She paused and reflected for a moment. "The world has changed. But, more importantly, *we've* changed."

Clayton told her that he would help to find Natasha. Somewhat reassured, Ana Maria took him to the corral when they arrived at the *hacienda*. A beautiful horse was waiting, held by a young boy. She climbed atop the animal and skillfully rode off, first loping, then at a full gallop. Clayton sat in the bleachers and watched the beautiful display of horsemanship by Ana Maria. She was showing him the various paces that the *Paso fino* was capable of.

"Do you want to ride him, Clayton?" she asked, smiling and challenging him.

Clayton waved no. After she finished the dressage, she showed him the stables. Behind them there was a second corral. She proudly showed him the bulls that she was raising.

"*Miuras*, pure *miuras*. I'm raising them for bullfights."

The splendid animals had been herded in and were being separated for the bullfighting season. Sitting on the fence and watching them was a slim and elegant man, in his early thirties. "Fernando Marques, a Portuguese bullfighter," she said, exchanging a warm glance with him.

With feline grace, Fernando jumped off the fence and shook his hand. "It's a pleasure meeting you, *señor. Doña* Ana has talked about you. You are the brother of Comandante Paulo." Then, he became serious. "My sincere condolences. Friends and enemies alike respected him. A hero, a Robin Hood."

"Yes, it was very tragic. My poor brother. So generous, so giving. But he found the end that he wanted, as a fighter."

Ana Maria took him by the arm and led him to the *hacienda*. She turned to Fernando, dismissing him casually. "We'll be having a private lunch today, Fernando. Don't take it personally."

The *hacienda* was decorated with exquisitely carved heavy Spanish furniture. Clayton felt that Cortez and Pizarro could have been there, sitting with them. Two large dogs lying by the fireplace completed the medieval look.

"*Fila Brasiliensis*," she said. "Your countrymen."

"Are they also here for personal protection?"

"I wouldn't walk around the garden in the middle of the night, Clayton. You'll have to behave." Her tone hardened. "You know the place. It has been in our family for two centuries. Did you know that FARC took over our other *hacienda* in Caguan, killed the five employees, and shot my father? It was horrible. They first asked for ransom. Then they decided to keep the *hacienda* anyway. My father was a proud man, and they simply killed him."

"These are like the fifties. Weren't they called the *Violencia* days?"

"Yes, but much worse. There's a lot of money in Colombia, a lot of drug money."

She said that FARC was actually the direct continuation of an anti-government struggle that had led to a civil war shortly after WWII. "FARC was founded in 1964 by Marulanda, who continues to be the elusive and legendary leader. A few years ago, the government and FARC had actually reached a truce. But the rightist paramilitary did everything they could and finally succeeded in breaking up the cease-fire."

After lunch, served by uniformed waiters, they went outside. It was already five in the afternoon and the scorching heat had receded. Clayton lighted a cigar and casually asked, "How about Mono Lopez, the fellow that Marco Aurelio knew? Is he still around?"

"That crook. He used to have a band of ruffians to kick squatters off ranches."

"Yes, I remember. And he was also a part-time arms dealer. Marco Aurelio needed him to get ammunition and those Brazilian rifles, the FAL. They were his favorites."

"The famous *Fusil Automatique Leger.* They were made under license from FN in Liège," she said. "I have a few here that I use for target practice. How about trying them out tomorrow?"

Clayton was impressed. *What a woman,* he thought. *And what an ass.*

"Well, this is not really my thing. I haven't shot a gun since my childhood days in Monlevade. Marco Aurelio was the star. So, what happened to Mono Lopez?"

"You wouldn't believe it, Clayton. He is now a senior officer, Colonel or Major, in the FARC."

"Quite a career. And where does he operate from?"

"Caguan." She rang for a servant.

"Bring me my phone, Alejandro."

She made a couple of calls and, a few minutes later, had the answer.

"He's in Caguan right now. Perhaps he can help find Natasha."

Clayton was elated. She would lead him to Mono. He would have to keep his mission a secret, though. He could not reveal that SAMITRA was behind this. If something went wrong he could not afford have an angry FARC colonel after him. "I'd be very glad to help you, Ana. But we must not tell him who I really am."

She looked at him. "You must have your reasons."

It had worked. There was another reason too. Breiterhof had authorized one million dollars for the operation. Clayton planned to pocket part of it.

"Yes. If they know I'm Marco Aurelio's brother, they could try to blackmail me and demand a hefty ransom. Natasha's safety is my primary concern."

"Always the gentleman, Clayton. It's nice of you to offer help. That's an excellent idea. But let's walk through the gardens." She gave him a hug and a kiss on the cheek.

He held her arm as they walked and felt the enveloping fragrance of Ysatis mixed with the garden aromas. Again, the twitch. It was already dark and a cool breeze had dissipated the searing heat of the day.

Overcome by her presence, he slowly pulled her closer. "Oh, this is so beautiful, Ana."

She backed away. "Clayton, don't be so forward."

*Slow down, you idiot*, he told himself.

At that moment, they saw the furtive profile of Fernando behind some trees. Then, he disappeared. Ana called, "Fernando, what are you doing here?"

"Oh, *Doña* Ana, I was taking an evening walk through your beautiful gardens."

Clayton understood. Fernando was jealously guarding her.

"Are you coming tomorrow for my practice?" Fernando asked. "I'm fighting some *novillas*."

"No, I'm taking Mr. Chauny to Pasto. He needs to leave right away."

In the morning, after breakfast and several phone calls, Ana told Clayton, "Everything is arranged. A trusted pilot will take you to Caguan. Here is a letter to Colonel Soto Mayor."

"Soto Mayor?"

"Yes, that's his new name and persona. But, under the skin, he is still the same old crook." She handed him the letter.

"I hope that you didn't reveal my identity, Ana. They could make mincemeat out of me."

"I wouldn't be so naïve. Actually, I'm worried and upset at the same time. It's possible that the FARC was involved in Paulo's assassination."

"Betrayed, after all he did," he said. Shaking his head, he picked up the letter and read:

> *Dear Colonel Soto Mayor:*
> *A personal and family friend from Brazil, Mr. Eugenio de Morais, will be carrying this letter. I am extremely concerned over the whereabouts of my daughter, Natasha Chauny de Betancourt y Hannaford. She arrived in Caguan ten days ago and I have not heard from her since. Mr. de Morais will personally hand you the sum of ten thousand dollars as a token of my concern. If you can ensure her well being, I will send you an additional ten thousand dollars.*
> *My best regards from Pasto.*
> *Ana Maria Betancourt y Hannaford*

She folded the letter neatly and placed it in the envelope that contained the coat-of-arms of the Betancourt family.

Colonel Soto Mayor read the letter intently, looking twice at Clayton with penetrating eyes. Will he recognize me? Clayton thought, as the eyes meticulously scrutinized him. But he looked quite different from his brother. He felt revulsion over negotiating a deal with the man that Ana Maria suspected of being involved in the death of his brother. He hoped that her suspicion was unfounded. Nevertheless, the callous expression of Soto Mayor clearly indicated that he was capable of such an act.

"We can try to find her," he said at last. "But I can't promise anything." He asked the Farquette acting as secretary to leave and close the door. Then, he said, "Do you have the money, Mr. de Morais?"

Clayton handed him the wad of $100 notes, which he counted, then put in his pocket. "Is there anything else I can do for you?"

"Actually, there is." He described the mountain on the Venezuelan border and its inhabitants, a few Indian families.

"Yanomami Indians," Soto Mayor said.

"Something like that."

Soto Mayor produced a bottle of scotch and some ice. He offered Clayton a cigarette and a drink.

"Look at these skinny legs. *Señor* Walker drank too much of his stuff," he said with a grin. They looked at the label, where an energetic English gentleman wearing a monocle walked at a brisk pace.

"I like him though, Colonel. He's been a good friend."

They understood each other. Clayton realized then that the answer was yes. All that was needed now was to negotiate. From the grin on Soto Mayor's face, he knew it would not be cheap.

"You know, Mr. de Morais, that this can be a costly and dangerous operation. Crossing the Colombia-Brazil border to displace an Indian tribe and destroy their village. Why would you want to do this?"

Clayton's face reddened. He was not prepared for that one. Would he want a cut of the profit?

"Gold, perhaps, Mr. de Morais?" he went on. "Or perhaps some other valuable mineral?"

"Let's say that I represent a company that needs the mountain. And let's say that the presence of Indians would be a ... nuisance. We need to go in there to prospect. We have some resources that are limited at present. Can this be done?"

"In principle, yes. We need funds to support our cause, our revolution," he said.

"You have the human resources and expertise to carry out the operation. Absolute secrecy would be required."

"And how could we do this?"

"I suggest opening an account in a neutral country, like Switzerland or Luxembourg, into which we would deposit the sum required for the operation."

"And how could I be sure that I would be paid?"

Clayton thought for a moment. This was a tough one. His mind churned, looking for a way out. "Ana Maria, in Pasto. If something goes wrong...."

He felt deeply ashamed... for one split second. Business was business.

"Mr. de Morais, you are very generous with other people's lives." He emitted a sly, hyena-like laugh, that was at the same time disquieting and annoying.

"How about holding you as a guarantee for the payment, Mr. Morais? Yes, this sounds perfect." He grinned and let go another hyena-like laughter, and took a long sip of the scotch.

Clayton nearly choked on his drink. This was getting dangerous. He offered a compromise. "I'll stay in *Doña* Ana's *hacienda* until the operation is successfully carried out. I'll order a transfer of money to your account "

"That's not good enough. You'll meet me at the Esperanza mining field and stay with us until the operation is finished. This is safer for both of us. You give the order to your representative to wire the money. In the meantime, I have a good drinking companion. You know, Mr. de Morais, I am starting to like you." He emitted another annoying laugh. "And then you are a free man."

Clayton had not bargained for this, but he realized that it was the only way. They needed to have each other by the balls for the duration. Soto Mayor would make sure that he was safe in Esperanza; otherwise he would not get paid. And Clayton could monitor the entire operation from there.

"How do I know that you've carried out the operation?"

"You'll be close by." He thought for a moment and pointed at his ear. "*Las orejas.*"

Clayton understood. He felt nauseated. For a fraction of a second, he saw the village. Those were people, not animals.

"How are you going to accomplish your mission?"

"That is our business."

"Now, about the price?"

Soto Mayor took a piece of paper and started writing down numbers.

| | |
|---|---|
| *Twelve men and weapons for ten days* | *$120,000* |

He looked up at Clayton, trying to decipher his expression. Then, he continued to write.

| | |
|---|---|
| *Four Cessna planes and pilots, two trips* | *30,000* |
| *Supplies, weapons, etc.* | *30,000* |
| *Management fee* | *300,000* |

He grabbed his calculator and totaled it.

| | |
|---|---|
| *Total* | *$480,000* |

"Isn't this too high?" Clayton said. "This *management fee* is excessive. How about $400,000?" He knew that Soto Mayor had inflated all the prices. He was taking the lion's share.

"$450,000, and this is my last word. The job will be done within thirty days after I receive an initial deposit of 20%. I want the first payment in cash, here in Caguan. I want a second payment of $100,000 before the operation begins."

Clayton gave in. He knew that there was no other way. Breiterhof had authorized one million for this operation. This would leave him $550,000. He had to find a way to hide his cut. Annick would help him. He extended his hand, which Soto Mayor shook vigorously. The colonel had become curious about the European bank account. This pleased Clayton, who proceeded to give him a lecture on the subject. Fortunately, he was familiar with Spanish and had mastered *Portuñol*, the Portuguese-Spanish mixture spoken by Brazilians in Spanish-American countries. He explained that he had a long-standing relationship with the Banque Générale du Luxembourg, where his cousin worked.

He concluded, "I highly recommend that someone in your line of business set up a corporation in Luxembourg. Your assets will be protected and anonymity is ensured. It can provide for a comfortable and safe retirement, which is not too far on the horizon for you."

Soto Mayor was intelligent and immediately saw the advantages of setting up a European account. This was also a safer alternative for Clayton. He abhorred the idea of traveling to Colombia with a large sum of cash. It was highly dangerous and, if searched, would lead to his arrest.

"About Natasha," Soto Mayor said, "I'll let you know as soon as my men discover her whereabouts. We'll make sure she is safe."

As he boarded the Cessna back to Pasto, Clayton was confident that he had been successful. He needed to report to Ana Maria about Natasha. He had some unfinished business at the *hacienda*: Ana's seduction. He would need an angle. He thought for a while. Yes, he had it.

Ana Maria finally could no longer put up with the jealous fits of Fernando and had to throw him off the ranch. She was still fuming over the bullfighter when Clayton returned. From the frying pan into the fire, she thought as the pilot called from the airstrip.

# CHAPTER SEVEN

Natasha's next few days were peaceful ones. Celeste and Antonio took her around and showed her the sites where Paulo spent his last days. Where he swam, rested, and wrote. There was a beautiful creek ten minutes away, with a waterfall. There, she and Celeste would bathe at midday, when the mosquitoes would give them respite. The women were growing closer. Celeste was in her fifth month of pregnancy and the stomach was already visibly distended.

"You know, Natasha, you probably think it's strange that your father and I were together," she said, looking at the water and playing with it. "But here in the Amazon, everything is strange. I cooked for him and took care of him and he took care of me. He was so much more intelligent than I, but in simple things I can do very well."

Natasha understood what she meant. That the differences between them were irrelevant. That they completed each other.

While bathing and giggling, they heard a scream. Antonio called for them to get dressed before he approached. They ran to the shore and wrapped themselves in their towels. Antonio, out of breath, exclaimed, "Eulogio just arrived at the house. He is wounded and needs help!"

"Celeste, walk back slowly, be careful. I'll run ahead," Natasha said, as she quickly pulled on her Dr. Martens boots. She jogged along the forest trail and within five minutes was back at the house. A young man sat at the entrance, leaning against a wall. Dried blood covered his shirt and he held a towel over the wound, in his upper chest. He looked pale and exhausted. Natasha helped him up and laid him in her hammock. She cut his fatigue shirt with scissors and examined the wound. It did not look good. The bullet had entered through the back and exited in front.

"An ambush," he said. "Leandro was ... killed. I ran into the forest and hid. They couldn't find me or they would've killed me. I heard them ... all around me."

"You need rest," she said. "We need to give you antibiotics." She noticed that the wound was starting to grow infected.

"I'm a dead man. They'll hunt me down ... wherever I am. They're here, I can see them."

Natasha realized that Eulogio was delirious. She soaked a towel and placed it on his forehead, telling him that everything was all right. Just then, Antonio and Celeste arrived. They also inspected the wound.

"If we don't give him antibiotics right away, he'll die," Celeste said.

She went to her box, took out a syringe and boiled some water, placing the needle in carefully. Then, she took a vial marked Streptomycin and shook it. She gave Eulogio the injection with obvious skill. "Every six hours one additional shot," she said with authority. "I'll put sulfur diazine powder on the wounds."

Since the bullet had exited the body, they did not need to worry about it. But there was a broken collarbone and torn flesh. It seemed that the lung had just been missed or only nicked. Natasha was surprised at Celeste's ability as she watched her in amazement. How could such a simple, poorly educated person know so much about medicine?

"I've learned over the past years," she said. "We don't have doctors here. Every now and then, one comes around. I've always watched. The important thing is to have good medicine. I think he has a good chance if we can treat the infection."

Natasha was gradually realizing that here, in the jungle, there was an entirely different set of skills needed. She felt unprepared for this type of life. Berkeley had taught her ideas, concepts, and theories. Celeste possessed practical skills. She could see that her father had taught her a lot. For one brief moment, she felt jealous that she did not have the chance to learn anything from him. She was also surprised at the medicine supply.

"Your father always kept a well-stocked infirmary. Antibiotics are our most important weapons here. Wounds infect quickly in this hot weather and this is what kills people in the end. Your father would always send one of his men to town to get medicines. Fortunately, we have a lot of them here, since we've not been fighting much in the past year."

Throughout the night, Eulogio remained feverish and delirious. He talked about the FARC, screaming names like Captain Mendoza and Colonel Soto Mayor.

Antonio had been quiet. Perhaps he was upset over the fact that Eulogio had been shot. The next morning he came to Celeste and Natasha, eyes to the ground. "The day after Comandante Paulo and you went to Caguan, I was waiting outside of town when Leandro and Eulogio came by on patrol. They asked me what I was doing there, since this was FARC territory. I told them that I had received orders to stay out of town. 'Orders from whom?' they asked. 'From Comandante Paulo, your boss?' I said yes. 'And he's in town?' Eulogio asked me. Not suspecting anything, I nodded."

"What did Leandro and Eulogio do in FARC?" Natasha asked.

"They patrolled the coca plantations and traveled through the jungle making sure that there were no government troops around. Then, they reported to Colonel Soto Mayor."

"This sounds very strange," Celeste said. "It would be a great coincidence."

They decided to question Eulogio as soon as his health improved. But they were afraid that he would clam up, for fear of retaliation. Celeste took the initiative of asking him while he lay in bed. Some cunning was necessary, and she commanded Antonio to interrogate Eulogio. She suggested a disguise. Antonio promptly donned a FARC uniform and approached the bed, imitating Mendoza.

"Captain Mendoza is here and wants to talk with you," Celeste said.

Eulogio shook when he saw the FARC uniform and the stern face, barely visible in the darkness. There was only a kerosene lamp burning in the distance and he could not distinguish the features.

"It's not my fault, Captain, I ... just told Colonel Soto Mayor what I knew!" he pleaded. "I had nothing to do with the death of Father Antoine and Comandante Paulo."

Antonio whispered the next question in Eulogio's ear. "Paulo is a traitor and Father Antoine is the representative of an exploitative organization. Have you told anyone else about this?"

"No Captain," came the weakened voice, "nobody else knows. Please spare my life! Where's Leandro?"

"Did you tell anyone about this?" Antonio said again.

"About *what*, Captain? About you ... shooting Comandante Paulo? We only know because we saw you in the jungle carrying the rifle with Sergeant Gomes."

They knew now. The FARC had assassinated Comandante Paulo. But why this betrayal? Natasha staggered away in shock, nauseous and dizzy. Celeste put an arm around her shoulders. Then, they cried, just cried for a long time. Like two sisters. They both loved Comandante Paulo, albeit in different ways. Nothing could bring him back. But each one knew that the other carried part of him. This united them.

"They resented his presence," Celeste said after a long time. "They resented the fact that he was abandoning the struggle and that one day soon he would denounce them."

"But how could Captain Mendoza have done it? He showed such admiration for my father," Natasha said. She could not deny the attraction that she had felt for him. Now, she felt disgusted. Betrayed again.

"Celeste, we have a saying: women give and forgive, men get and forget."

"Oh, Natasha, this is so cruel. Your father was different. He never betrayed anyone. I had told him not to trust the FARC."

"He was Mendoza's former commander. Why would Mendoza do this? And how could he face me and tell me all these lies?"

"Everybody knows that he is very ambitious. He wants to be the commander of FARC and later live a life of luxury. For money, he'll do anything. Haven't you observed him closely? He's a cocaine addict."

"He looks so ... robust."

"This is the danger of cocaine. People appear strong, healthy, and full of life. But their judgment is impaired and cocaine will slowly eat them away."

Natasha's rage toward Mendoza grew like a wave of blood in her head. Though loath to admit it, only revenge would quell this feeling.

Over the next days, Eulogio improved. The fever finally broke. He knew that he could not return to the FARC, but he was reluctant to share any information on the assassination of Comandante Paulo. Celeste offered for him to stay there. It was clear to her now that Mendoza had tried to kill him after the assassination, since he and Leandro were the only people that could trace the crime back to him. But he had not found his body and the doubt would always persist.

Natasha asked Celeste what they should do. She looked at Natasha with her inscrutable eyes, then stared at the ground. After a long silence, she whispered, "Let me show you something. Perhaps it will help."

Celeste led her to the back of the hut, where she asked Antonio to dig. He removed about ten inches of dirt, then hit something. Digging around, he unearthed a box, hermetically sealed. Within the box were plastic bags, several layers of them. She turned to Natasha.

"These are the diaries of the Comandante. He would write every day and they start many years ago, before you were born. I would always watch him," she said. Emotion filled her eyes with tears as she clutched the bag, stuffed with reams of his neat and methodical handwriting, line after line, page after page.

"These are for you, Natasha. Take them to the United States. I know that the Comandante wrote them with a purpose: so that the world would learn about the struggles of the Revolution."

Natasha was moved and accepted them, holding them close to her. The box contained his life, his dreams. She looked at the first cover: 1973. She turned to the first page, and the paper, yellowed by time and many travels, came to life with his words.

*Amazon, January 1973*
*Two months on the Purus River with the Rondon Project. Our government sent us here as propaganda. It is a wonderful experience, but an exhausting one. I have been coughing miserably, probably due to native cigarettes made from some strange tobacco. It is possibly full of strange*

*molds. We visited the Aporinan Indians and I had the op-portunity to see the sorrowful state of affairs in their decay-ing village. Many of them have mixed blood. The "civilized" man has left his mark. They no longer live in one village, but are spread along the Aporinan River. I understand bet-ter the primitive communism concept by our famous anthro-pologist Darcy Ribeiro. In an Indian village, a great deal of property is communally shared. This pattern is broken by the intrusion of the "civilized" man, bringing the concept of private property. Among the Aporinan, we see how this has led to the disruption of the village society and annihilation of their culture.*

*Pauiní, where we are stationed, is a little town with 600 inhabitants. It is a microcosm of Brazil, with a mayor, a priest, a wealthy merchant, a policeman and a majority of destitute people. The mayor, Mario Said, is the son of Lebanese immigrants. His father controls the entire Pauiní River, an affluent of the Purus. The Purus is one of the major rivers of the Amazon basin. The village sits at the mouth of the Pauiní River. All rubber tapers on the Pauiní River sell their products to the old Said. He is the only mer-chant allowed into the river. It's his territory. So, it is clear-ly a monopoly situation that subjects the rubber tappers to dehumanizing exploitation. They are virtual slaves. The boat comes up the river once a month from Manaus with essential supplies: alarm clocks, sugar, beans, rice, shells and gunpowder, rum. All tappers owe many months, even years, of wages to Said. If one of them tries to escape, he is blocked at the mouth of the river by Said's thugs. He becomes a fugitive of justice, since he did not fulfill his financial obligations.*

111

Natasha was mesmerized. She realized that her father's fascination with the Amazon came from his student days, before he was a Communist. The trip to the Purus River must have been the first event in a long chain. She realized that the diary contained the key to his soul. Personal experiences determined his destiny. "Have you ever read his diaries, Celeste?" she asked.

"No. I respected Comandante's wishes. He liked to write alone."

Natasha continued reading feverishly.

*Amazon, March 1973*

*Back to Porto Velho, close to the Bolivian border. We had two memorable flights on the old WW2 Catalinas. The Brazilian Air Force has a few vintage hydroplanes left. The screams and cusses of the mechanic that was working on the instrument panel of the plane as we were flying punctuated our flight to Pauiní. We had a scary experience on take-off. The plane was heavily loaded with medicine supplies and our team. It suddenly braked on the airfield when the pilot, the legendary Captain Boris, realized that the plane would not clear the treetops. We unloaded most of our supplies and were more successful on the second attempt, while Captain Boris took the opportunity to teach an inexperienced Lieutenant the intricacies of flying in the Amazon. He is a hero in the area, and was lost in the jungle for twenty-one days after crashing into the treetops. This left us in the village without the needed medicine.*

*On the way back to Porto Velho, the Catalina landed in the river, which was overflowing, carrying tree trunks that had been eroded from the margins at incredible speeds. We*

*approached by canoe, and the wind by the propeller pro-*
*duced such waves that the canoe started taking water as*
*we were climbing on board, holding a rope. I was the next*
*to last to jump in and the canoe sank under my foot, as I*
*stepped onto the Catalina. The impatient Boris just took*
*off. Behind me, the boat separated itself from the plane and*
*filled with water, as the plane started to rise. My buddy*
*Jaime dangled from the rope, bobbing in the water at an*
*increasing speed. I quickly retrieved him by pulling on the*
*rope and grabbing him by the seat of his pants when he was*
*sufficiently close. He was the proudest of the group and a*
*medical student, with all the superiority complexes associ-*
*ated with his profession. He felt deeply ashamed that I, an*
*economics student and a Leftist to bear, had rescued him. I*
*felt proud of my strength and quick reflexes. All I heard in*
*the plane were Captain Boris' screams about what a group*
*of jackasses we were, about how we endangered his mission.*

Natasha paused for a moment. She imagined her father as a
young man, courageously saving the live of his colleague from
the dangerous river. The scene unfolded in front of her as if
she were in a movie. For one moment, she saw him as Indiana
Jones. She again delved into the reading, seeking clues.

*We stopped at another village, Labrea, and picked up a*
*man that had been bitten by a snake. His leg was gangrened*
*and the smell was unbearable. All the guys, including our*
*two medical students, moved to the front of the plane, and*
*I was left there to console him.*
*We have been in Porto Velho for five days now waiting*
*for our flight back to São Paulo. We are stationed in the*

*local Military Police barracks. We got news that the snake-bitten fellow died after they amputated his leg. Poor fellow. An old sergeant tells us stories of the Madeira-Mamoré railway construction. He was there and fought the Cinta Larga Indians. He proudly told us that he killed dozens of them. This was built to connect Brazil to Bolivia, and was some kind of retribution for Brazil's aggressive conquest of the Acre territory from Bolivia. I am fascinated by the stories.*

*Decided to visit Bolivia and split from the Rondon Project group. We are now on the famous Madeira-Mamoré railway. They say that for each yard of the railway one person died. Thousands of Indians and workers died during the construction. Now it is almost abandoned. We are traveling in a converted bus: railroad wheels replaced the tires. Three days to Mamoré.*

*Bus broke down and the only way to move is by pouring gasoline onto the carburetor from a can. The fuel pump is shot. They put an Indian on top of the hood with a gas can. Not a great idea.*

*Indian threw can out as it caught fire, and it fell on top of somebody else walking by the rail. He burned to death in front of our eyes. I remember the horrible scenes of the self-immolated Buddhist monks in Vietnam. We took the burned man to his house. The mother cried copiously, but told us as consolation, perhaps, "He was no good anyway." It is a sad day.*

It was strange. Natasha understood now where this longing for travel and adventure came from. One of her friends in Berkeley had told her that the Germans had a name for it: *Wanderlust*. It was a particular feeling of the soul, searching for exotic places and people, in order to enrich oneself.

*On our way to La Paz, by bus now. We climb the Andes and enter into a magical world, totally different. We see snow-capped peaks for the first time. My first snow in South America. The people and scenery are as if from another planet. Quechua and Aymara Indians everywhere, with their typical hats and clothes. The Spanish-speaking people from the cities loathe them.*

*Today, March 15, another bizarre incident. Our bus was packed with people. I was standing in front. This gentleman, in his mid-fifties came to me and offered me a seat. Not his, but his neighbors. An Indian woman was sitting there with her husband. He orders her to get up, in Spanish. She refuses, and talks to her husband in Quechua. They both look at me as if I were from another world. The gentleman now addresses her in her own language. When no response is obtained, the gentleman slaps her in the face, screaming, "India sucia, levantate." She finally gets up and gives me the place. Cowardly, I sit down and smile to the gentleman, in a sign of appreciation. He apologizes profusely. I travel the rest of the road to La Paz, with the husband by my side. He smells bad and his face is totally expressionless, except for the constant chewing. Coca leaves, which numb his body and mind.*

Natasha was beginning to understand. "Celeste, let me read this to you."

She reread the last portion. "You see? He felt ashamed that he did not help the Indian woman."

"This is the way Indians are treated around here, Natasha. To this day."

"So, my father was responding to a deep need for justice."

She remembered *The Motorcycle Diaries* by Che, in which his early ideas take shape. She saw a commonality between the two accounts. Both Che and her father were guided by early experiences and vowed to bring justice to Latin America.

*Twenty kilometers from La Paz, in the middle of the night, the bus encounters an impassable barrier. A mudslide has blocked the road. We unload and walk in silence for several hours. The Indian gives me a wad of coca leaves, which I chew with him as we walk through the night. I feel energized and strong. I swear to myself that I will never be a coward again.*

*Crossed the Titicaca Lake into Peru. Cuzco and Machu Picchu are a wonderful experience. The Incas had developed an admirable civilization in the Andes. The poor Indians left behind are the result of centuries of exploitation and crushing by the Spanish conquistadors, and their descendents, the criollos and mestizos. In the street I buy Che Guevara's complete works. They are outlawed in Brazil. The reading is a true revelation and confirmation of my own observations, albeit in a much more advanced and eloquent manner. Only a revolution will change the status quo. The bourgeoisie and ruling aristocracy will never relinquish power freely. Che Guevara was killed not far from here, not too long ago. Allende was assassinated. Cuba is under siege. Bolivia's President Hugo Banzer is a puppet carrying out the orders of the Yankees. Operation Condor's goal is to stamp out any Leftist movements in Latin America. America is for Americans, said Monroe. He should have been more specific: Latin America is for Americans, i.e., the Yankees.*

Natasha read avidly, and then more slowly, savoring each word. Her father was coming to life before her eyes. His love of adventure, his sense of responsibility for the poor and destitute was tangible and strong. She understood then what led him to become a Marxist guerrilla leader. She could see something of herself in him, except that he was more articulate, more committed.

"Celeste, this is very precious to me. I'll cherish these diaries and protect them at all cost. But what will we do next?"

"We are at risk here. Mendoza probably knows that you are here and will come searching for you. As for me, he could even try to have me killed."

They spent several hours planning. The Berkeley graduate and a half-Indian that had spent her entire life in the forest, working together in harmony.

"You know, Natasha, you're like your father. Quiet and efficient. And you lead with the same natural grace that he had."

She blushed. "It's interesting that you say this. I have a bunch of crazy friends in the U.S., but it's true, they always turn to me. Except for Ernesto, that bully."

"Brothers want to be in charge all the time. Manuel was the same."

"Where's Manuel now?"

"With the old-timers, in the Dog's Head. He was wounded. A bullet entered through his right eye and bore through a small part of his brain."

"My God, that's terrible."

"We are all losers in this war, the dead ones and the survivors."

They told Antonio and Eulogio about their new plan. All but Natasha and Antonio would go on foot, through the forest, to the Dog's Head, and enter through the mouth, past Mitu. This would take about ten days, and had to be done right away. There, they would join the *compañeros*, at the Esperanza mine. But first, they would stop at the El Capitán airstrip and wait there for orders. The two girls living in the house with Celeste would also go with them. They were almost pure Indian, as was Eulogio. Long walks through the forest were not an unfamiliar custom to them. They would move slowly, at their own pace, stopping for fruit, fishing and rest.

The next morning, four days after Eulogio arrived delirious and half-dead, they left. Eulogio, far from recovered, could only walk with difficulty. But he knew that staying there would mean certain death. Natasha and Antonio departed for Caguan. She put the diaries in the backpack, fully aware of the danger she was exposing them to. But it was the only chance of getting them out of there.

# CHAPTER EIGHT

Clayton walked at a brisk pace down Grousgas Street and turned left on the Boulevard Royal. The meeting with Breiterhof had gone well and they had transferred one million dollars, through a *doleiro*, to his account at the Banque Générale du Luxembourg. He entered the bank through the unassuming door and took the elevator to the second floor. Upstairs, the luxury was in stark contrast to the Spartan first floor. Several offices, shaped like small bank vaults, lined the sides of a wide hallway. The receptionist led him into one of the offices, closing the door behind him. After a few minutes, Annick walked in. She was an energetic redhead in her mid-forties. She embraced Clayton, giving him two sonorous kisses on the cheeks. He felt the familiar twitch again and wondered if he should try to make a pass at her. So what if she was his cousin?

Annick sat down and asked him about his family. Clayton reached for a pack of cigarettes on the desk but she grabbed his wrist. "Not here, my darling. Wait until you're outside."

"All right, all right. You're becoming more anal than the Americans. But I forgive you, my little cousin. I've only one vice left." He winked. "Let me tell you about my family. My wife spends her days at the gym and country club. Little Karina is adorable. She is studying at a French school run by nuns. I hardly see her, with her active social life. Sabrina is in kindergarten and is glued to her nanny all the time. She even sleeps in her room. They are typical *Cariocas*, you know."

"I wish I could have your life, Clayton. Who does the cooking and cleaning?"

"The maids. Karin comes from a wealthy family. Her parents emigrated from Lebanon and made a fortune in Brazil. Smuggling precious stones, some other scams and a lot of other wheeling and dealing. She enjoys all the perks of the upper crust life in Brazil."

He sensed that Annick noticed the slight contempt and frustration in his voice.

"And you have to travel the world making all kinds of funny deals to guarantee this lifestyle."

"Yes, it seems to be the case. I fell in love with her body and her Mustang convertible in Belo Horizonte. You know, my parents were not wealthy."

"Your mother lost a lot of money in the stock market. You told me the story."

"But we had the aristocratic Chauny name. So, my mother was extremely supportive of my marriage to Karin. She figured that we needed some infusion of money in the family. Frankly, it appealed to me too. I loved driving through town in that brand new Mustang."

"And I bet you must have seduced some other ladies in it too."

"How would you know?"

"Pure female intuition, Clayton. So, what can I do for you?" she asked, with a twinkle in her eyes.

"I'll tell you over dinner tonight." Then, he turned serious. "Let's get down to business, Annick. I am taking your precious time."

He explained that he needed to set up a new company with a certain Mr. Soto Mayor as president and himself, Clayton Chauny, as silent partner. She gave him a list of names to choose from, of which he selected Portoluna. This would take ten days, she explained. The company was headquartered in the Bahamas and all operations would be carried out through the Banque Générale du Luxembourg. Annick gave Clayton a code for the company, in case Soto Mayor needed to make any future transactions by telephone. Otherwise, he would be able to withdraw money on presenting his passport. Clayton filled in the appropriate forms.

"Ah, there's something else. To keep this totally anonymous, my name has to be Eugenio de Morais."

"Clayton, you fox. One of these days we'll get in trouble."

"My little cousin, money has no color, and Luxembourg's banks are full of it."

She reluctantly agreed. They prepared a second document stating that Clayton Chauny had a second identity as Eugenio de Morais. He then told Annick to deposit $100,000 into the account and said that Soto Mayor would be calling in a few days to verify his account.

"Being a Bahamian company," Annick said, "the account won't be accessible from Brazil or Colombia. I hope your Mr. Soto Mayor is an honest man, Clayton."

"The best there is in Colombia," he said with a cynical grin, "and to make sure that he remains so, I want to retain the right to carry out transactions in the company."

"We can make you VP of Finance."

"That sounds great."

She told him that in three days the papers would be processed.

"We'll transfer $100,000 from Sidmar, your other company, to Portoluna as soon as it opens."

"I'll need $200,000 in cash now. Then, I'll need another transfer of $150,000 in a couple weeks. That will leave $550,000 in Sidmar."

"Just call me with the codes of the two companies and I'll take care of future transfers."

"You're the best, Annick."

Later, she took him to a quaint restaurant in the Glacis. They consumed a couple bottles of the best Luxembourg Silvaner with an exquisite meal of baked *heecht*, a local fish resembling a pike. When they parted, Clayton could no longer contain himself. He kissed her cheek, then let his lips slide to her mouth as he groped her. Annick put up a slight struggle but enjoyed the attention. They spent a long minute exploring each other before she broke away. "Nasty cousin," she said. Next time, he thought.

In the morning, Clayton left for Frankfurt and from there to Colombia. The next day, he landed in Caguan. Soto Mayor awaited him anxiously. He was tense.

"We know where Natasha is. She went to see her father's little girlfriend," he said with a snarl.

"I didn't know that Natasha has been found. That's wonderful."

"Wonderful for me too. If she is unharmed, I want to collect the second $10,000 before I even consider the other operation."

Clayton could not renege on his offer. However, he was not ready to pay. Not yet. "Patience, Colonel. Her mother wants her safely back in Pasto before I can make the payment. She's already given you $10,000 as a token of her concern."

He called Ana Maria and advised her of Natasha's whereabouts. She was elated. He was now ready to give Soto Mayor $90,000 in cash and told him that $100,000 would be deposited in his Bahaman Corporation as soon as it was established.

"You wait here until this corporation is set up," Soto Mayor demanded, "and then we will talk about your operation. But I still need additional cash. You know, I'll have all these expenses."

The following day they received news from Luxembourg that Portoluna was established. Soto Mayor also received faxes with account instructions and company registration numbers.

Soto Mayor next called the Bahamas, where he had an old acquaintance. The man told him he would check on the company. Within a couple of hours, the confirmation arrived.

"In any case, Mr. Soto Mayor, I would have no interest in trying to cheat you," Clayton said.

Soto Mayor took a deep drag from his cigarette and looked straight into Clayton's eyes. "I hope not. Our mutual guarantee is that we both accomplish our tasks. You'll stay with me until the end of this operation. Your job is to make sure that I get the money. And mine is that the Yanomami group is permanently ... displaced."

Clayton sighed with relief. Soto Mayor would keep his end of the bargain. And he was satisfied with the Banque Générale du Luxembourg arrangement. "What about Natasha?" he asked.

"I'll ensure her return. Once she is in Pasto, I'll expect the $10,000 delivered to my office."

Clayton offered his hand to Soto Mayor, who shook it vigorously.

"From this point on, Mr. de Morais, there is no going back. We have a deal."

"When will you begin?"

He consulted a wall calendar. "It's September 14. We'll meet at the Esperanza airstrip on October 14. This will give me a few weeks of preparation. I have some unfinished business here."

"What is the exact plan?"

"That's for me to know. I cannot reveal any details. All I can give you now is a date."

"And how will I know it's done?"

"Don't forget: you'll be there. Your company can send the geologist to verify this, after we're gone. We'll get you the..." He ran his hand over his small monkey-like right ear, uttering the hyena laughter. Clayton felt nauseated.

"There must be no trace of your presence."

"There won't be."

"Good. Then, let's get started."

Colonel Soto Mayor aimed a finger at Clayton. "Mr. de Morais, remember this well: from this point on, there is no going back. If there are any problems with the money being transferred to my company, you'll be a dead man. Don't forget that I need $100,000 in cash."

Clayton shuddered inside. Soto Mayor's dark eyes narrowed as they remained riveted on his.

"And I can get you wherever you are. Is that clear?"

As Clayton returned to Pasto, he could not remove the impression of Soto Mayor's eyes from his mind. Nevertheless, he enjoyed this dangerous game. The stakes were high and getting higher. Yes, life was a grand poker game, he thought. Soto Mayor's eyes were still stuck to him when the Cessna landed in Pasto.

# CHAPTER NINE

Natasha had been there less than an hour when a Jeep pulled up in front of the parish house and an angry Mendoza jumped out.

"So you are finally here, Miss Natasha. We thought you were lost in the forest. Ten days! You said that you would be back in five."

She looked at him and tried to conceal her rage. Here, right in front of her, was the man who had killed her father. She composed herself and remembered that she had to be in control at all times if Celeste's plan was to work. "I stayed there longer, trying to console myself. It was very soothing to spend a week in the house where my father lived his last days."

"We understand," he said, relenting, "but this is a dangerous place. We're always afraid of government incursions, and these regions are populated with all kinds of runaways.

Colonel Soto Mayor has been asking about you twice a day. He wants you safe and sound in Pasto. And I personally care for you very much, Miss Natasha."

He grabbed her around the waist and gave her a hug. She felt a mixture of fascination and revulsion, a deep nausea that she could hardly contain. *This Mendoza murdered my father.* She wanted to confront him right there. However, she had to stick to the plan. She pushed away slowly, feigning some interest in his advances. And struggling with herself. She had felt attracted to his virile presence before, when there was little doubt regarding his intention. Now, all she felt was rage. She forced a smile. "Captain, you're so aggressive," she murmured.

"It's your presence, my dear. I waited for your return and came here every day after touring the plantations."

There was something excessive in his voice. Now she knew that it was the cocaine.

"Miss Natasha, I've got strict orders from Colonel Soto Mayor. You have to leave tomorrow. We have already ordered the plane. Tomorrow at ten it will be here at the airfield."

Then, slowly, he backed off. The French cologne that he had splattered over his body filled the air. Natasha felt in control once more. His nostrils trembled like those of a bull and she knew that she could make him charge at will.

"This evening, I want to be with you," he said.

"In the parish house only," she replied with a smile.

"I want to come to America and visit you. Or perhaps we can meet again in Medellin."

"It's much too early for plans, Captain."

"Please, call me Raul."

"OK, Raul."

"Tonight at seven. My assistants will bring the food."

Back in the parish house, Pilar had prepared a bath for her. She scrubbed her body frantically, needing to get rid of every molecule of his perfume, his sweat. She finally broke into sobs. Was she ready for this? Betrayed by Aaron in Berkeley, here she was facing a murderer. Where would it all end? Exhausted from the walk and the encounter with Mendoza, she lay in Father Antoine's bed and fell into a deep sleep.

When she awoke, she saw a FARC truck with some *Farquettes* hard at work, setting up a barbecue and a table outside. A few minutes later, Mendoza arrived wearing white trousers and shirt, which contrasted with his tanned, muscular body. He flashed a smile as he jumped out of the Jeep. She wondered how he had driven through the dust in this outfit.

"Natasha, I brought an entire cow from one of the ranches and kept the best for us," he told her.

Natasha was now convinced that this new class of revolutionaries was totally corrupt. The *Farquettes* were nothing but disguised servants and entertainers, and the old Latin American tradition of class separation was evident: peons working for the élite.

The table and a stereo were set up under a large mango tree. Soon Ricky Martin was blaring through the town. Natasha was shocked at the lack of concern for the recent deaths. Less than three weeks had passed since the death of her father.

"Wine, my dear?" Mendoza offered her a glass of cold white wine. She had tasted better, but nodded her head in approval as they toasted to the revolution.

"As El Che said: '*Hasta la victoria siempre*'," Mendoza said. "You are seeing me now, Natasha, but I spent years in this horrible jungle participating in expeditions, fighting, and organizing the financial support of our cause."

"I believe you, Raul. Otherwise you would not have risen to your position."

"And I hope to rise much higher one day. Perhaps ambassador to the United States." He smiled. She tried hard to hide her disgust.

"Who knows?"

They sat down at the table, covered with a white cloth, and were served large portions of roasted meat. The smell had tempted the town kids, which surrounded the table. Mendoza got up and scared them off.

As the evening progressed, Mendoza's ebullience came out in waves. There was something fierce, a strange energy in him. Natasha struggled to remain focused. But memories of recent events made that difficult. *Stick to the plan, girl; stick to the plan.*

The town was engulfed in darkness. The *Farquettes* took the table and barbecue grill apart and loaded it into the truck. Mendoza's hunger was satiated and now he lusted for Natasha. The moment had come and she knew it. Give a little, not too much, she thought, as she planned her escape.

He walked her to the house, which was dark, since Pilar had been in bed for hours. He took her hand and faced her. "I hope you had a nice evening."

"It was wonderful, Raul. For a few moments, I forgot about the terrible loss."

"I did this for you, Natasha, to make you feel better."

Then he held her neck with one hand, caressing it. With the other, he pushed her to himself and kissed her. She felt his strong embrace and warm lips against hers and responded carefully. He became bolder and more excited. At this point, she pulled away.

"Raul, this is so fast. I am not ready yet..." She twisted herself from his embrace. "Tomorrow, at the plane, will you come and see me off?"

"Of course," he answered, breathing deeply and lunging forward.

She kissed him and backed into the house, quickly closing the door before he could enter. Turmoil grew within her. A physical attraction toward Raul on the one hand and a strong, visceral revulsion over the certain fact that he had killed her father, on the other. She lay in bed, restless, for a long time. Finally, she reached for her father's diary. She opened it and read randomly, trying to calm her emotions. She wanted to know what had led him to communism.

*Belo Horizonte, 4/1975*

*Now becoming more active in political affairs. Joined the DCE (Central Directory of Students). I started learning how to organize student demonstrations. The military have been in power for ten years and their leadership is increasingly corrupt. The dictator Garrastazu Medici is ruthless with our organization and many members are in prison. We are the historic vanguard and we shall overcome the reactionary forces of the bourgeoisie and military-industrial complex that* strangles and exploits Brazil. Many are being tortured in order to reveal our plans. We pass around books by Lenin, Marx, Che, and deepen our knowledge in Marxist dialectics. We also have more practical books, such as the Handbook of Explosives. Conditions are ripe for a Leftist revolution in Brazil, and this will occur through armed struggle, not through political means. The example of Chile, where Salvador Allende was democratically elected and then assassinated by a CIA directed coup comes to mind. We have to take over all levels of society; we have to cleanse it of its vices. Elimination of all capitalist elements is an absolute necessity. The Cuban example shall be followed. The armed struggle has to occur through rural, not urban guerrilla.

I rarely see Clayton, who is more preoccupied in chasing women and in his bourgeois pursuits than in anything else. I tried to talk to him a few times, but we cannot find a common language. This is indeed very sad, because we were inseparable companions in Monlevade. We would fish, hunt, and explore the forest. We shared everything: our lives and dreams. We planned on crossing the Amazon on foot with two 22LR rifles and a few fishhooks. Now, we have parted completely. Will we ever join again? Will we ever walk the forests of the Amazon, as we planned? Cross from the Purus to the Roosevelt River? He is completely taken by the US and does not see the selfish role that this nation is playing in Latin America. The goals of the Yankee are (1) to defeat the Soviet Union and communism and (2) to ensure markets for its products. Clayton has a Michigan State University sticker on his car and takes English at IBEU, an imperialist propaganda office. We are planning to bomb the building soon.

Natasha understood better now. Her father was led to Marxism by his own experiences of youth. Once he entered the Movement, he absorbed the entire dialectic of Marxism-Leninism and accepted this vision of events. He truly believed that he was going to reform the world. He was so different from Mendoza, who used FARC to further his own ambitions.

> *Belo Horizonte, 7/10/75*
>
> *Two policemen were killed during one of our demonstrations. We are testing our offensive capability, probing the weaknesses of the forces of oppression. We know that repression will be strong. We are prepared. The SNI (National Information Service) has launched an operation against us. If we are caught we will be tortured to reveal our future plans. I have no alternative but to leave the country.*
>
> *Father must have known something —perhaps Clayton snitched on me? He came to me yesterday and gave me a Luxembourg passport with my name slightly modified to Marc Chauny. He also gave me a ticket to Canada. I expect the worst in the next days. Two comrades were arrested and are probably being tortured right now. They have the names and addresses of all the members of our cell. Two of them hijacked a plane yesterday. Will try to leave tomorrow.*

This conflict with his brother bothered Natasha. However, she understood well that siblings could be very different. It was also her case with Ernesto. Some people become fascinated with wealth and power, and that consumes their lives. Others are drawn into the universe of ideas. This can also become their god. Where is truth? she thought. Is there a truth?

*Canada, 11/75*

*No problem exiting Brazil. Stupid police only checked Brazilian passports. I am sure that I am blacklisted. But it was my lucky day. Meeting a group of progressive Brazilians in Montreal. Plan to visit Cuba. Miss Father and Clayton very much. It is very sad that we wasted our days arguing over politics, I calling him an owner of latifundia and reactionary bourgeois, and he calling me all kinds of epithets. Mother is totally involved in her High Society life: parties, cocktails, luxury and ostentation. Can't she see the corruption, the exploitation, and the poverty in the streets? Why can't she? Her total alienation for the problems of Brazil has distanced her from me. My nanny Alaide, whom I remember living in a hut, is a nobler example of motherhood than my blood mother, who embraces all the trappings of bourgeois decadent values. I would run away from home and stay in her hut, enjoying the simple food prepared on a wooden stove, over the fine French crêpes that the maids prepared, on my mother's orders. I loved the dirt floor, the simple metal plates, the humble surroundings, and the three flowers in the garden. I started to hate our opulent surroundings then, the constant flow and subservience of our servants.*

*We meet every afternoon in Montreal, and I cannot wait for our next assignment. Officially joined the Communist Party and am reading Roger Garaudy now. It is very theoretical and complex. I prefer Che Guevara!*

*Joining the Party is a momentous decision, and I hope that I will find within myself the dedication and sense of sacrifice of my other Latin American predecessors. I solemnly vow to dedicate my entire life for the sake of humanity.*

Natasha finally fell asleep, but it was a restless night. Dawn came as a welcome reprieve from all the feelings that enveloped her in the folds of darkness. She had to be strong.

At 9:30, Mendoza's Jeep stopped in front of the parish house. He was less effusive than the previous night. It was only a five-minute drive to the airstrip. They sat in the Jeep on the side of the airfield, as the Cessna landed. Antonio waited for them there. He took the two small bags and jumped into the plane as soon as the pilot opened the door. The pilot did not even shut the engine off. Mendoza had not brought any of his assistants; he wanted to be alone with Natasha. In the Jeep, he held her hand and gazed into her eyes, with excitement and uncontrollable lust. Natasha noticed that they were bloodshot, and his state of excitement indicated that he had probably snorted some cocaine. She was familiar with the effects of the drug from Key Biscayne, where some of her wealthier friends indulged in it. He kissed her passionately, and she responded likewise. She could not overcome the feeling that she was prostituting herself.

"Come to Medellin soon, Natasha. I'll help you find the killers of your father," he said.

"When can you go there?"

"In three weeks. Why don't you meet me there? I'll call you and we can set the date. I have some powerful friends that can lodge us in an *estancia* ten minutes from town, a beautiful place."

"Can you get time off?"

"I have some work there. I'm now in charge of Business Relations. All I need is to make an official request to Colonel Soto Mayor. We need to be in touch with our clients."

Natasha climbed out of the Jeep and walked to the airplane. Antonio was already sitting in the back. He had asked for a ride to Pasto, to receive treatment for his malaria. Natasha held Mendoza's hand. She was nervous and excited as she led him to the plane. As she put one foot on the wing, ready to step in, he embraced her once more. He continued to kiss her as she leaned back into the plane. She pulled herself up and crawled into the plane; he followed. Oblivious to Antonio's and the pilot's presence, Mendoza pinned her to the seat, holding it with one hand, embracing her with the other, kissing her hard.

Natasha heard a click and saw the cold metal around his wrist. She slipped into the back seat. Antonio had slapped a handcuff on, attaching it to the seat, and was pointing a gun at the pilot.

"Take off right now, or I shoot," Antonio said.

"*¿Puta madre, que pasa?*" said Mendoza pulling on the handcuff.

Antonio slipped a second pistol to Natasha: her mother's Beretta 9 mm. She pointed it at Raul's head. "Pull your legs in!"

He was caught by surprise. The pilot received a second warning and started taxiing the plane. Natasha said, "You won't be harmed. We are changing course. I'll give your new GPS coordinates. All you do is drop us off there."

She pointed to her pack and Antonio promptly opened it, handing her a piece of paper that read:

# 0.5373 N
# 70.99W

"This is only forty kilometers from here. The El Capitán airstrip. Start right away," Antonio said.

Mendoza now pulled violently at the handcuff, looking at Natasha and the pilot in disbelief. The plane rushed along the airstrip. He stared at the ground, moving faster and faster below him. He jerked again at the handcuff, and Natasha could see blood on his wrist. He was firmly attached. His body still hung partially out of the plane as the open door flapped violently in the increasing wind.

"What is this, Natasha? Are you crazy!"

"You'll know soon. Jump in or you'll be dangling."

He obeyed and sat sideways in the front seat.

"We take off now, "Natasha told the pilot. "You'll be free as soon as we get there."

The pilot had been quiet till now. He knew that there were two guns in his back. "Another hijack." He shrugged. "I'll follow all your orders."

The Cessna finally rose at the end of the airstrip. Air gushed in through the open door. As soon as they were on their way, Natasha glared at Mendoza.

"We know that you killed my father. Eulogio escaped from your ambush and told us everything."

Antonio continued: "He and Leandro were the only people from outside who knew that Comandante Paulo was in Caguan. I told them by mistake."

Mendoza turned pale.

"You killed Comandante Paulo to wipe out all traces of your horrible crime. And to please your FARC bosses. You killed your own troops in Los Pozos!" Antonio accused.

"But Eulogio's dead!" Mendoza's face turned ashen and he started shaking.

"You'll meet him very soon," Antonio snapped.

"How could you have killed my father?" Natasha cried.

At this point, the pilot interrupted. "We have a law in this part of the country. Betrayal is paid with life. We all admired the Comandante." He turned to Mendoza, and spat at him.

Mendoza defended himself. "I...I received orders from Soto Mayor."

"But why, Raul, why?"

"His time was up and he was hurting us with his statements against our financial backers."

"The drug lords?"

"The people that are obtaining US dollars to support our fight for justice and independence."

"*And you killed him in the name of that?*" she screamed.

Mendoza suddenly grabbed for Natasha's gun. Before he could pull it out of her hand, Antonio fired. The noise was deafening, and the pilot momentarily lost control. The plane nose-dived. Mendoza's body slammed violently against the door, leaving the window covered in a mist of blood and brain. Natasha felt that she was going to faint, then shrugged it off.

"Get us up!" she commanded the pilot, amazed at her own cool in the face of this immense danger.

The pilot worked at regaining control of the plane. He could barely see through the blood on the front window. The plane's trajectory gradually stabilized. Looking down, they saw that they were only a few hundred yards above the jungle. The wind howled in, the noise was deafening. Mendoza now hung out of the door, grotesquely distorted.

The handcuff impeded his fall. The pilot had already logged in the coordinates given by Natasha. He slowed the plane, since they were near.

"We almost got killed," he said at length, trying to act calm. "I'll leave you at the airstrip."

Soon they saw a clearing in the jungle and the pilot circled it.

"You can land," Antonio said. "We've checked it out before. Somebody is down there."

Four small figures waited in the clearing. Natasha could not believe that the pilot could land safely there, but he circled once more, then came down over the strip.

"Celeste and the girls did a good job," Natasha said, after getting the OK from Antonio. It was only then that she started to cry and shake convulsively. She looked at the pieces of blood and brain spattered everywhere, and felt that she would vomit. Antonio's face was sprayed with blood. They landed without problems, although the ride was bumpy.

"Comandante Paulo used this airstrip a few times," said Antonio. "I knew it would work."

Celeste, the two girls, and Eulogio were already walking toward them. The plane stopped and Antonio tried to disengage the handcuff from the chair. It took some lifting of Mendoza, who had bled profusely. The 9mm bullet had done a lot of damage on the way out. The side window had a hole.

"You'll be compensated for this," Natasha said, regaining her composure. "Take $1,000 for the damage."

The pilot shook his head. "Don't worry, he killed your father. He deserved to die. We don't like traitors in Colombia.

I was never a communist, but always admired Comandante Paulo. He was something of a dreamer."

"Let's clean the plane," Celeste said. "My God, this wasn't in our plan."

She and the two girls got some rags, water, and entered the plane. They scrubbed off the pieces of brain and blood that were already drying on the instruments. The front seat was also soaked with blood. They did the best they could with the water they carried.

"He bled like a pig," Antonio said, after he dislodged Mendoza. They got him off and dragged him away into the forest.

"Can I go now?" asked the pilot. "How will you get back to Pasto, Miss..."

"Chauny," she said, turning pale again as she looked into the plane.

Then, she reflected for some time. She walked with Antonio and Celeste to the edge of the forest. They convinced her to stay. Pasto would not be safe. Bogotá would be even more dangerous. Soto Mayor would demand revenge.

She made her decision and informed the pilot, "For now, I'll stay with these people. They need me and I need them."

The pilot shook her hand. "All is well that ends well," he said, as he jumped back on the plane. "Don't worry. I won't say anything to incriminate you."

He reflected for a moment, then added, "I'll just tell them that I dropped you off in Medellin. Yes, how about that?"

"They'll think that I eloped with Mendoza. Not bad..."

After much insistence he accepted the $1,000 from Natasha. He would change the window in Medellin. Nobody there would think anything about a bullet hole. He reached into the cockpit and pulled out a card. "Here's my phone number. Call me when you want to get out. Send in the GPS coordinates and I'll take care of the rest."

"How can we trust you?"

"You can't. But then you can. Once, many years ago I was also a guerrilla. *Hasta la victoria siempre.*" An enigmatic smile lit his face. Natasha looked at him as he waved from the Cessna, which accelerated through the field, kicking up a cloud of leaves.

"He's had his adventure today," she said. "He's seen justice being done, in a harsh but fair way."

They were all proud. Revenge has a sweet taste and dulls some of the pain.

# CHAPTER TEN

As Clayton returned to Pasto, he looked out of the airplane window. The dense forest gradually gave way to pastures and more and more houses and roads appeared. The Cessna flew at a low altitude, approximately 8,000 feet. So, there was a lot to see, in contrast with the modern commercial jetliners. He was happy that he had accomplished his mission successfully. Getting the approval of his team at SAMITRA, setting up the corporation in Luxembourg, and convincing Soto Mayor that this arrangement was the best deal for him had not been a small feat. Everything had been accomplished in one week. He was anxious to see Ana Maria, and was looking forward to some payback. One hand washes the other, he thought, with a smile on his lips. He felt a twinge of remorse for having used Ana Maria as a security deposit in the transaction. However, there was nothing to worry about. He would keep his part of the bargain. Up to a point.

He reached for the cooler, in the back, and pulled out an ice-cold beer can. The pilot looked at him and said, "*Señor* Clayton, you shouldn't drink alone. I'll help you."

Clayton smiled and he passed him the beer. In the First World, people would be flabbergasted. But this was Latin America, this was Colombia. This is why he had returned to Brazil, after his MBA at Michigan State University. Rules, rules, rules, everything was rules in the U.S. They talked a lot about freedom, but it was he, Clayton, that knew real freedom. He had thought about staying in the U.S and Suzie, his gorgeous Oriental girlfriend, had begged him. He could still see her delicate body and porcelain complexion. It was only when she made love that she transformed herself into a vixen, simultaneously lascivious and energetic. Soon, she would return to her Oriental gentleness. But the true Suzie resided in those fleeting moments, when the doors to her soul were suddenly flung open. Where would she be today? Probably in Hong Kong, VP of her father's company. Would she be happy? Would she sometimes think of him, the wild Brazilian? He smiled as he took the last gulp and reached for a second Tecate. Yes, she was a hottie. The American women, on the other hand, were much freer than Oriental or Latin American women. And demanding. He was twenty-five then, and had plenty of power and money. He delivered pleasure and demanded satisfaction. It had been a good time. He and his Arab friends, Said and Arash, had set up an unbeatable system to attract, seduce and pass on girls. Their system had been perfected, just as the McDonald's franchises that they studied in Business School. They prided themselves on their efficient operation.

Clayton felt a burning in his lungs, an intense desire to smoke. He had kept his word to Ana Maria. Six days without one single cigarette. It was getting better but the temptation was almost impossible to bear after a couple sips of cold beer. Still, he felt healthier, more energetic. He breathed, inhaled deeply, and felt a new freshness in his lungs. When he had tried to kiss her, in the pergola, she had rejected him but left the door open. He would have a second chance on this visit. *Better not rush it, Clayton,* he thought. She attracted him in a strange, uncontrollable way. He couldn't put his finger on it, but there was something there. Just the thought of her, in the plane, was enough to arouse him. And yet he had all kinds of opportunity for sex in Rio. It wasn't just that. First, there was his wife, Karin, who had a beautifully kept body. She was a typical *Carioca*: small breasts, nicely shaped derriere, elegant demure. However, she had grown indifferent in the ten years of marriage, and was more and more interested with status, membership in clubs, redecoration of their Ipanema flat, than with romantic lovemaking. It was also perhaps his fault. He had developed a potbelly and his constant smoking and nightly drinking had given him the typical *Carioca* businessman shape, smell and mannerisms.

And then there were the semi-pros in Central Rio. He knew a couple and occasionally took them to motels. They worked as secretaries, assistants or hairdressers during the day. Many lived at home and had perfectly normal lives, including boyfriends or husbands. A couple of times a month they would moonlight with a discreet businessman.

Mauricio Nogueira, his good buddy, had become a million-aire in the construction business. He had what he called his 'harem.' And a discreet call to Mauricio was all he needed for a nightly escapade. He would just call Karin and tell her that he had an overnight business trip to São Paulo or Belo Horizonte. But lately, these small escapades had grown boring and predictable. He would have to spend the night in a motel, and invariably would sleep very poorly. So, it was ten-percent sex and ninety percent boredom. In the morning, he would drive back to the office sleepy, and the girl would be hiding in the back of the car. It had all grown too easy and predictable.

No, Ana Maria was different. Although in her forties, she had a firm body because of her constant exercise and riding. And she was the queen of that enormous expanse, her *hacienda*. What was it about her? Was it the fact that he always admired Marco Aurelio? Was it her proximity to nature, to the flowers, fruits, birds and animals of his child-hood? Or was it simply that he was tired of his life in Rio de Janeiro, of his demanding disciplinarian boss, of the empty luxury and corruption, of the filth that formed the under-belly of that immense city, where everything and everyone was for sale?

"*Estamos en Pasto,*" the pilot said, leaning the wing of the Cessna. "So, hand me another Tecate, *Señor.*"

Jarred from his thoughts, Clayton gave him the last Tecate. He also knew that a couple beers would not endan-ger the pilot's ability too much. The sky was clear, air traffic minimal. Just the occasional rancher or cocaine dealer.

They circled the airfield once and landed, as the sun was setting in the sky. Ana waited for them at the end. He noticed that she wore a short red dress that revealed her strong tan legs. Was it an invitation? He always analyzed how women dressed. There were hidden messages, secret desires expressed in them. Ana Maria gave him a hug and he felt her body touch his for one split second longer than usual. He pressed ever so slightly against her and felt a warm emotion inside, something he had not felt for the longest time, since adolescence in Monlevade. She pulled back and looked at him.

"How about the smoking?" She sniffed him. "Just a few bottles of beer. Not bad."

Clayton's lungs ached and he was tempted to run off and take a few puffs. The headiness from the beer had cut down on his willpower. But he knew he could not get away and just confessed, "Not a single cigarette this week." Then, in jest, "I can get a cigar this evening, as a reward?"

"No cigars, Clayton. They contain more nicotine than cigarettes."

*But I want to get you*, he thought. *You'll be my prize.* He felt the twitch again, this time stronger.

They jumped into the Landcruiser, and he rattled off his story as they drove to the ranch.

The next morning, Ana organized a cavalcade. When Clayton woke up, still exhausted from his travels, the breakfast table was already set. The servants brought trays with fruit – papaya, oranges, mangos, bananas – and assorted breads and cakes. As he gulped down the strong and aromatic coffee, Ana walked in wearing jeans, a white shirt, and cowboy boots.

"Clayton, we have a full day. We'll go to the Guaymas waterfalls on horseback."

Clayton had found a cigarette in the library and was planning to take a few puffs, just a few. Now, this was out of the question.

"Ana, I'd be delighted. But I'm so tired..."

"This will relax you." Her body exuded energy and enthusiasm and her strong legs and derrière bulged under the jeans. "I sent two servants ahead to prepare a barbecue at the falls. The plan is in action. You have ten minutes."

They hurried to the stables. As he entered the corral, Clayton's nostrils were assailed by the strong smell of horses. Instantly, he was transported to his childhood, when Marco Aurelio and he would lure horses with corn. Those beasts were left free by their owners in the pastures around Monlevade. They had fabricated a makeshift bridle with rope and leather strips. As the horse ate they would expertly pass the rope around its neck, throw the burlap sack on its back, and ride it. Not only ride it, but also literally bring the animal to exhaustion. Afterwards, they would let the tired horse go, and many an owner would be surprised to find such a sluggish animal.

It was a beautiful day and they loped along on dirt roads toward the river. "I remember my childhood in Monlevade," Clayton said. "Our father discovered that we liked horses and bought us two. Marco Aurelio and I would ride every Sunday. He on Cardão, an old white horse, and I on Pampa, a crazy paint. I always wanted to run but Paulo slowed us down, for fear of hurting his old horse. An old cowhand would come along and tell us stories of the cattle drives of his youth. It was a magical time."

He inhaled the air, still fresh from the morning. The burning urge in his lungs had decreased and he felt good.

"But why did you go such different ways?" she asked. "You used to be so close. Paulo always spoke lovingly of you. He used to call you Clayton *tretero*. What is this?"

He smiled. "This means 'sneaky' Clayton. People always said that I was tricky. And it must be true. Paulo was always courageous and truthful. That's why he always got the spankings from Dad. I somehow avoided them. But that's what big brothers are for."

"Now, you're the big brother."

"I know, Ana, and I'm changing. You see, I've stopped smoking."

"Then see if you can catch me!" She spurred her horse, a beautiful Arabian, and disappeared around the bend of the road in a cloud of dust.

Clayton followed, but could not keep up. Nevertheless, he was able to stay on the saddle as he continued to recall his childhood. The wind against the face invigorated him, and he screamed, "Run Pampinha, run Cardão." For an instant Marco Aurelio was there, running at his side. Yes, why had they gone such different ways?

The waterfall was beautiful, even in the summer when the flow of water had been reduced to a trickle. As they approached it, they could smell the burning wood from the barbecue pit.

Ana Maria jumped down from the horse nimbly and exchanged a few words with the cook and helper. They set up a table under the shade of a tree. Ana Maria reached for a bag and pulled out a pair of shorts and towel, which she passed on to Clayton.

"And now comes lesson number two, swimming."

"But can we, in these waters?"

"It's fine, Clayton. There's a large pool above the falls. Change behind these bushes. Then we ride up the trail."

On the way, Clayton could now see her entire body, barely covered in a bikini. The legs and butt: yes, they were magnificent. Ana Maria had a slim waist and small breasts. But there was something else that attracted him to her in a strong way, and he couldn't put his finger on it. Something beyond his understanding.

As they got in the water, he felt self-conscious. Although always on the beach in Rio, his main activity was to guzzle beers with his friends. His stomach protruded comically from his shorts, and his arms were flabby. Ana was already in, swimming with rapid strokes.

"Let's race, Clayton. You know, Paulo was a poor swimmer. It seems that Monlevade was not a hotbed for Olympians."

"No, we had only one swimming coach. *João Peixe*, John Fish. He would line us up in the pool and all we did, week after week, was to kick our legs. I couldn't take it and would fake an injury."

"Well, Clayton, this is your chance. Try to catch me."

He followed suit, splashing in the water and making some headway. Every time he was about the catch her, she would gracefully accelerate. Then, nearly exhausted, he grabbed her. Ana screamed, feigning terror. He felt her strong body in his arms, her legs moving in the water, and held tight. Excited, he pushed himself against her legs. Ana smiled and cried, "Help me, I'm being attacked!"

His manhood against her thighs, Clayton felt a *frisson* rushing through her entire body. For one moment she paused and looked into his eyes, now dark with passion. She opened her mouth slightly, and Clayton's kiss did not wait. He kissed her passionately. Her lips were hot, contrasting the cold water on their bodies. She whispered into his ear, "Clayton, what are we doing?" Then, she freed herself from his embrace and bolted for land. Disappointed, he followed. As they stepped out, he felt tired but rejuvenated. Yes, he would have her one day!

After lunch, they moved to the hammocks set up under the trees. Ana Maria told Clayton about Natasha's goal: to save the Yanomami.

"You've always been an enabler. This is what Paulo told me," she said. "Do what you can to help the girl."

"Let's first get her back." Images of terrified Yanomami, like scattered ants in the *shabono* courtyard, ran through his mind. No, he was not an enabler, but a destroyer.

"You always seem to know a little more than anyone else," she said, resting her hands on his for a moment. "At least this is what Paulo used to tell me."

He took a breath, then said, "Ana, the Koran says that when a married man dies, his brother has to espouse his widow."

"And when did you become a good Muslim?" She threw her head back and laughed loudly as she poured him a glass of Portuguese *vinho verde*. "I thought you were a committed hedonist."

"Don't judge the book by the cover. There are many things bothering me."

"I thought you were happy with your exciting Rio de Janeiro life. An important position, wife, daughters, lots of friends and..."

"I always admired Marco Aurelio's purity. Pardon me if I always use his real name. Somehow, we grew apart in Belo Horizonte. He pursued his dreams to the end and I got tangled up in the social web of the Brazilian upper class."

"I know. Paulo used to describe your dissolute lifestyle. The stories he told me, could they be true?"

"They can be, and this is what fueled our youth. We thought we were above the law. Everything was fun and games."

Clayton took a last sip of the *vinho verde*, feeling its delicate tingling on his palate. It was light and crisp, ideally suited for the afternoon. He felt slightly heady. He rested his head on the hammock and reminisced. Ana Maria listened attentively.

His parents expected more from him than just passing his classes at the engineering school. He had to mingle with the upper crust of Belo Horizonte, he had to look rich and date the girls from the best families, daughters of bankers, industrialists, and politicians. As long as he and his friends did this, they had free rein. Sports cars, wild parties with hookers and poor girls from humble families, racing through the city in the morning hours. Their tastes grew more and more demanding. He remembered the nights when they would drive through the city in search of some new adventure. One night, they invited some gays into their cars. After driving them out of town with promises of sex, they undressed them and left them naked on the highway. Back in the city, they distributed the clothes to the beggars. He'd had a good feeling in his heart, like Robin Hood. And other nights when they would pick up a couple of girls, probably maids, and take them out of town, where the whole group would rape them. It was all fun. His friend Austragesilo was not into sex. He would beat up the girls as the gang of satiated young males watched and laughed. Then, he burned them with a cigarette lighter.

"And do you know what Austragesilo does today?" he asked Ana Maria.

"He should be behind bars, but being in Brazil he's probably free..."

"Worse than that. He is the leading psychiatrist in Belo Horizonte."

"A pillar of society. And the police never caught you?" She could not keep from laughing.

"His father was the Secretary of Justice. It was all fun, at the expense of some poor souls. We spoiled brats became the terror of wayward women. At home and in the clubs that we frequented, we would transform ourselves into so-cial butterflies – charming, funny and lively."

"Quite dissolute, Clayton. This is why we have a vicious civil war in Colombia."

"Ana Maria, you call my youth dissolute. But this was the way we grew up, and my old buddies are now respectable citizens. They occupy important positions in society."

"And this is why Brazil is so corrupt. Paulo was right."

Ana Maria rose from the hammock. She looked splendid, and Clayton admired her anger.

"I don't condone guerrilla action any longer, but these timeless warriors have fought against corruption, exploitation and all the excesses that are the legacy of the Spaniard in Latin America. The *Criollo* always thought that he was the law, that he was above the law."

Clayton told her about how he and Paulo grew apart.

"I always admired his principles, his rectitude. But I disagreed with his chosen path, that of armed struggle."

"Yet he followed the dictates of Che Guevara, who he greatly admired. Che believed that you could only uproot the exploitative system of governance in Latin America by an armed struggle led by rural guerrillas. And this is what Paulo chose, to the end."

There was pride in Ana Maria's voice, pride and pain. This woman, who owned a large *hacienda* in southern Colombia, and yet was a former guerrilla fighter, fascinated Clayton. How could these two positions be reconciled?

He told her more about his and Paulo's childhood in Monlevade, about how they would fish, hunt, and explore the forest. They were inseparable, Paulo always full of new ideas, Clayton a little sneakier and shrewder. They made a perfect combination. At lunch, when the family assembled, frequent arguments would erupt between their father and Paulo. Marco Aurelio defended the Left, while his father represented the industrialists, owners of *latifundia*, and the military. There was no common ground, and Clayton usually did not take part in these diatribes. He planned his evening trysts and executed them to perfection. He had tried to involve Paulo, but his brother did not demonstrate interest and even reprimanded him for his irresponsible attitudes toward women.

Then, Paulo went to the Amazon on the Rondon Project for two months. When he returned, he appeared meeker, pale. He had visited Bolivia and had contracted malaria. At that time, he stopped arguing with his father but slowly distanced himself from his family, spending more time outside of the house, and becoming involved in the leftist student movements. He was now a student leader, organizing marches, coordinating activities, and mapping out the strengths and weaknesses of the military regime. He had moved from words to actions. This marked a definitive distancing from his family and from Clayton. Soon after, he would vanish.

As dusk approached, Clayton woke up, stretched, and looked for a long time at the sun that reddened the Western hills. Everything took on a magical spirit that enveloped the evening and his feelings. Then, his eyes rested on her. She was checking the saddles on the horses, giving firm and crisp orders to the helpers. "Fuck SAMITRA, fuck Breiterhof," he murmured as he jumped off the hammock with unexpected vigor.

# CHAPTER ELEVEN

O ver the next days Natasha, Celeste, and the rest of the group moved slowly through the forest, along a trail that only Antonio knew. They could have advanced much faster if they had chosen the highways of the jungle: the rivers. The Caguan River led to the Vauapés River. The Vauapés, in turn, led to the Papuri, which eventually ended in the Auaretê. All they would have to do was to find a good canoe and avoid the rapids. However, FARC controlled the rivers and they would inevitably encounter some of their troops. But Antonio knew the jungle trails from years of crisscrossing the Oriente provinces of Colombia and so they went by foot. The canopy in the forest is thick and only lets little light in, so the ground is clear and they advanced well.

In the evenings, Natasha would read excerpts from the diary. It was a fascinating experience to discover her father, as she discovered the jungle where he had lived.

*Cuba, 3/76*

*The Brazilian delegation arrived and was greeted by Raul Castro, Fidel's brother. It is with immense emotion that I meet the people and places that I have only known through readings. This is the magical island that freed itself from the imperialistic rule of the Yankee. We visited the University of Havana after a two-month preparation at Pinar Del Rio. The names resound through my mind: Camilo Cienfuegos, Che Guevara, Granma, and Sierra Maestra. We are receiving training in doctrine, conventional and guerrilla warfare. I often remember Clayton these days, as we crawl through mountains. It seems a kid's play, but one day, in the not too distant future, our skills will be put to use to liberate Latin America from the colonial oppression. It is curious that some of my comrades, and often the most eloquent ones, fade away in the difficult terrain. I, on the other hand, feel stronger and stronger as the hardship increases.*

*Next month, we visit Moscow as guests of the Soviet Union. We will all get new passports and identities. I chose the name Paulo Silva. Silva, because it is the most common Portuguese surname. And Paulo, because he was the indomitable propagator of the Christian faith. If not for him, Christianity would have remained an obscure cult within Judaism. He took it to the heart of the civilized world, to Greece and Rome. I want to be the Paul of the historical vanguard that communism represents. It is ironic that Father chose for me the name Marco Aurelio because he deeply admired the stoic philosopher who struggled much on the frontiers of the Roman Empire as its maximum leader. Mother named my brother, and she chose what she thought was a sophisticated English name: Clayton. I found out that it does not even exist in English. This shows the insecurity of Brazilians, a vestige of colonialism. It abounds with Emersons, Niltons, Hiltons, Clebersons, Claytons, Wilsons, Edilsons and all kinds of...sons. During Marcus Aurelius' reign some of the most brutal persecutions of Christianity took place. I, the one who has sworn to stamp out the Christian faith and replace it by a modern humanism that has a rational and scientific basis, trade it for the name of its apostle. The ironies of life.*

She understood now how he had chosen this name. On the one hand, he wanted a complete and total break with his Brazilian past. On the other, a total identification with the poor classes of Latin America.

In some places Antonio had to open the trail with a machete. Every now and then they crossed other trails, and Natasha realized that the forest had roads that had been used, perhaps, for centuries. The Indians knew them. They crossed small creeks and avoided larger rivers. The pace was leisurely, with frequent stops to collect fruit. Eulogio carried a shotgun and they were able to find some game. On the second day they shot a couple of *jaós*, ground birds the size of a small chicken. The rains had not yet arrived and they had plenty of dry firewood in the underbrush.

Celeste explained to Natasha that this was the way the Indians moved, in their semi-nomadic lifestyle. Each Yanomami group had a few villages. Every few months they would move from one village to the next, when game became more scarce and they had exhausted the reserves from their plantain and manioc plantations. Everyone moved on the trail. She also explained that they were following an old Indian trail that she had used before, with Comandante Paulo. Rather than being lost in the jungle, they were at home. At night they would hang up their hammocks and sleep comfortably under the mosquito nets. Natasha continued to read passages of the diary by the light of the fire. She was puzzled by her father's early fascination with the Soviet Union.

*Soviet Union, 6/76*

*We flew on a modern Soviet Ilyushin 62 of Cubana de Aviacion to Moscow, making a refueling stop in Shannon, Ireland. This modern aircraft is superior to the Yankee Boeing. The pilot informs us that it has autonomy of flight of 10,000 km. Arrive at Sheremetyevo Airport and are lodged in Ukraina Hotel. This is the nerve center of the Soviet world, and the majestic buildings along the Moskva River, the magnificent architecture, typified by the Moscow State University tower and our hotel, express the order and discipline of this society. Indeed, the New Man is coming, and he is here already. The entire population is focused on scientific progress, through which humanity will become a harmonious ensemble. Marx's dream is becoming reality through the splendid efforts of the Soviet people. Lenin, Stalin, Khrushchev and the other Leaders of the USSR had visionary intelligence.*

*We will spend six months at Patrice Lumumba and Moscow State Universities. We are being prepared for leadership roles in our countries, once the Revolution succeeds. It is fascinating to personally see how this enormous machine operates, how commands from the center reach the farthermost provinces, how the complex distribution of goods and services is regulated. In Brazil, we have a chaotic system of supply and demand, leading to inflation, social injustice, hoarding of products. It is a system that benefits the capitalist and exploits the proletariat. I can now see, in person, how all the concepts that we discussed in the Economics School operate in practice. The next ten-year plan of the Soviet Union was shown to us yesterday. It will put Yankee capitalism behind. The Yankees are fighting a losing war in Vietnam. Our comrades are being supplied with Soviet weapons and military advice. We are the vanguard of history. The reactionary forces of exploitative capitalism are retreating from Latin America, Asia, and Africa. The Italian and French communist parties are stronger every day. It is sad that Che is no longer here to witness the fruits of his sacrifices.*

She understood that his youthful enthusiasm had been stroked and nurtured by the Soviet propaganda machine. Many famous writers, politicians, and artists would come back from the Soviet Union convinced that Soviet socialism was indeed the vanguard of history. Her father had fallen for it, and she mentally compared this idealistic vision with the disillusionment he had expressed when he visited her twenty years later.

She continued to read, after pausing and reflecting for a moment.

*We visited the Kaliningrad Space Control Center and laid flowers on Gagarin's monument. It is entirely built of titanium, a metal used in advanced aircraft. It projects a haunting and futuristic image. It represents the New Man that Communism will bring us.*

*Fall is coming and we had the first snow. It is cold, very cold. I met a very beautiful Muscovite named Natasha. She is tall, blonde, and has the most beautiful blue eyes. She is a student at Moscow State University and is quite conversant in Spanish. We spent hours walking through Moscow, visiting museums and talking. She is preparing herself to go to Cuba, where she will organize a nursing school. Perhaps our paths will cross again, on my return.*

Now she knew the origin of her name. Her father had had a romantic encounter in Moscow. This had been always hidden from her. She had asked her mother and the answer given was that her father had chosen this name in honor of Russia and of the Soviet revolution. There was a deeper, more intimate explanation.

As they made their way deeper into the forest, Natasha soon became accustomed to the march. Her early fatigue was gone and she was adapting to the food. However, her light skin was sensitive to mosquito bites, and she had marks all over her body. They were initially large red areas, which soon shrank and became black spots.

"Your blood is sweeter than ours," Celeste told her. "In a month you will taste as bad to the mosquitoes as we do."

Antonio told her the names of trees and plants, as well as their uses. Minute differences in the trunks and leaves indicated different species. The variety of plants fascinated her. At night they would sometimes hear loud explosions, which initially scared her. Antonio explained that there were trees whose trunks had literally collapsed. The competition for light was fierce in the forest, and the new trees had to break through the canopy. The trees were extremely tall for their thickness, and every now and then one of them toppled, with a roaring noise. She began to recognize a few of the trees and vines of the forest among the seemingly infinite variety. Antonio taught her the names. The giant *Sumauma* tree, with its enormous webs holding up the trunk that could be several yards in diameter. The Brazil nut tree. The rubber tree. The noble and precious mahogany tree. Although she had taken several botany classes in college, she was at a loss in the deep recesses of the forest. Not all trees were large and tall. These were spaced fairly far apart, forming a high canopy. In between, smaller and slender trees filled the space. The light barely filtered through the leaves and the forest was dark, even during the day. By taking some basic precautions, they were safe and comfortable. Antonio explained that Comandante Paulo and his troops had adopted many of the customs of the Indians during their years in the forest. They carried their few belongings in backpacks.

Within a week, Natasha grew used to her new routine and Eulogio visibly recovered. The group moved at a steady pace, covering about twenty kilometers per day. Celeste carried a GPS, a concession to modern technology. It had proven immensely useful in the couple of years after they had obtained it. They knew exactly where they were as well as the distance to the target, the Esperanza camp, the last hideout of Comandante Paulo's old companions.

Eventually the terrain became less mountainous. They were descending into the Amazon basin. Soon, they encountered the cloud forest, between the mountains and the plains. The vegetation was unique. Every now and then, they would catch a glimpse of the immense jungle ahead of them. Natasha had run out of mosquito repellent, so they set up her hammock with the netting every afternoon, before the evening onslaught. She was able to avoid the brunt of mosquito attacks.

One night, they heard the roar of a jaguar. They lit a big fire and kept vigil. But most nights would dawn peacefully, and the group moved in harmony. Then one day, they saw a cobweb and threw a fly into it. From the edges came not one, but numerous spiders, and they quartered and consumed the fly in minutes.

Natasha was especially impressed by the efficient manner in which the group shared tasks. Everything went smoothly. She also noticed that they all deferred to her. After all, she was the daughter of Comandante Paulo. She would suggest rest stops, activities, often consulting with Celeste and Antonio. Eulogio was now well along in the healing process. On the days in which they did not find any fruit or birds, they would content themselves with manioc root that Celeste had roasted and mixed with some jerky. Their worst problem was crossing creeks. Each one posed a different challenge.

One morning, Celeste spotted a felled palm tree and ran toward it with the machete. She started to hack at the decomposing wood. With a triumphant cry she grabbed a white grub, the size of a mouse, and bit it behind the head. She pulled at the body, until it separated from the head and entrails that were left dangling from her mouth. Natasha watched in disbelief as she spat out the head and bit into the body with great pleasure. Antonio joined her. Then, they searched the wood, filling a basket with grubs and encouraging Natasha to share in their feast. Starved as she was for protein, she refused.

"Tonight you will eat one roasted," Celeste said. "They are even more delicious cooked."

That evening they made a small fire and wrapped the grubs in large leaves, laying them on the ashes. The shriveled white corpses exuded a buttery substance. Careful at first, Natasha tasted it.

"It's like butter," Celeste said.

"Not bad." Natasha tried to keep from gagging. The smoke had given the grubs a particular taste that was not disagreeable.

In the meantime the others were enthusiastically licking the fat from the leaves. It was indeed a treat.

A couple of days later, already on the plains, they crossed a river on foot and camped on the white beach. After nightfall, Antonio went out exploring and soon returned with an excited look in his eyes. "*Tracajá*," he said.

They grabbed a basket and followed him along the beach. By the light of the full moon they watched. Several turtles crawled out of the water and laboriously walked on the sand, leaving a long trail. A few dug holes. Antonio slowly approached one of them as it had finished digging a sand nest and grabbed it. Natasha followed them, remembering the Easter egg hunts in the US. The eggs had a soft shell and were round.

"They're all fresh. We're so lucky," Celeste exclaimed. "These we'll cook."

"Let's keep some for the rest of the trip," Antonio said. "But this little *tracajá*, we will have him now."

The fire was already lit. Antonio took the *tracajá* and placed it, shell down, on the embers. Natasha was repulsed by what she saw next. The poor animal stuck its legs into the shell, trying to hide them from the fire. A few seconds later it thrust them out, moving them frantically as the heat from the fire went through the shell. Celeste, Antonio, Eulogio, and Assucena danced with joy. Natasha could not comprehend this cruelty.

"Stop laughing. What's wrong with you people!" she snapped, but knew that she couldn't change anything. This was the way of life for a primeval group, in the midst of one of the most remote places on the planet. The hunt had been successful, and the hunter-gatherers were celebrating.

Within a few minutes the movement of the legs and head decreased to imperceptible twitches. Soon the shell cracked due to the expansion produced by the heat from the fire.

Antonio pulled the turtle out. He laughed, displaying all the few cracked and rotten teeth left in his mouth.

"No need for a cooking pot, *Señora*. This is *tracajá*, Indian style." He popped the chest and pulled out one of the legs, biting into it with delight.

Repulsed, Natasha left them to their savagery. Later, she ate a couple of eggs that Celeste had placed on the fire for her. They had a somewhat sandy texture but were otherwise delicious.

Antonio followed the progress of the group on the GPS. He knew, on the ninth day, that they were approaching the Esperanza camp. They increased their pace, and did not stop for foraging. They reached the Mavaca creek shortly before sunset, having announced their arrival by firing three shots in the air. Only when they heard the reply, two shots, and fired a second salvo of three shots did they proceed. This was their code of announcing that they were coming, an old tradition. People in the jungle did not appreciate surprise visits.

Comandante Paulo's group had rebuilt some huts by the creek. Like most huts on the Amazon basin, they were palafits built on stilts. A wooden floor about eight feet above the ground provided protection from floods and animals. They had used an abandoned gold mining camp and the soil around the creek had been moved and churned. Deep scars in the earth and mounds were visible everywhere. Antonio explained that there was an abandoned airstrip close by, and this helped to supply the group. They walked into the village and were effusively received by a group of middle-aged men. The poverty in the Esperanza camp was obvious. And the irony of the name did not escape Natasha. *Esperanza*, hope. *Desespero* would have been a better word. Natasha could see some furtive glances from the huts. Some women and children shyly watched from the inside.

Celeste ran to a hut in the back and tearfully hugged her brother. She saw the damage done to Manuel's face: a deep scar sliced through it. The bullet had ripped the eye and socket out.

The men then ran inside at the order of Caetano, their leader, returning a few minutes later in their combat fatigues and carrying their weapons. They formed a line in the front of the huts, and Caetano gave a short speech.

"*Compañeros*, we are honored to receive here the daughter of Comandante Paulo, who was cowardly assassinated in Caguan. They spent many days crossing the forest to meet us. In memory of Comandante Paulo, we will fire a salvo."

The troop was commanded to stand at attention Then, Caetano ordered the rifles raised. They fired, the report echoing through the forest. Natasha smelled the gunpowder mixed with burned oil and was moved to tears.

Caetano then presented the guerrillas to Natasha.

"These are the troops commanded by Comandante Paulo. At one time we were several thousand. We have left our blood in these lands, and our *compañeros* are buried in the mountains of Nicaragua, in the savannas of Angola, and in the forests of Colombia. I now present to you, one by one, our remaining soldiers, the old guard of Comandante Paulo."

He stopped by the first one, a slim fellow in his late 60s who stepped forward. The man was white, almost yellow, and did not have an ounce of fat on his body. The long hawkish nose denoted Spanish ancestry.

"Urbano Pombo, from Cuba, the oldest of us. He was with Fidel and Che in Cuba. Then, he went with Che to the Congo. Che took him to Bolivia, where the Rangers and CIA surrounded them. As you know, Che was killed there. Pombo escaped by walking through the jungle for one month, and crossing the border to Peru. He is the bravest of the brave, a man of undaunting strength and faith."

Natasha shook his long hand that was almost delicate. His aquiline features and slender body could hardly betray the immense strength of character. And yet, Che described him in his diary as a man of extraordinary fortitude. He grew tougher as the situation became more desperate. Natasha had read about him and was honored to have finally met him.

Caetano continued with the introductions. Each *guerrillero* stepped forward and shook her hand. She could see the high esteem in which they held her father through the respect that they paid her. Then, it was time for her to speak. She felt a knot in her throat but knew that she had to rise to the occasion.

"It is very sad for me to be here on this solemn occasion. But I am also happy to meet the old *campañeros* of my father, whom he loved so much. I know each one of you through his descriptions in the diary that I carry with me. I will have the opportunity, in the next days, to share his thoughts about the present and future with you all. His death has been partially vindicated. The Caguan FARC decided to eliminate him because of his constant criticism against the drug trade. I took him to the streets of San Francisco when he visited the United States and he saw with his own eyes the terrible destruction caused by cocaine. His mission in life was to improve the human condition, not to create new chains to enslave us."

Natasha felt exalted and the words came to her in a torrent. She was surprised at her strong delivery. "I was born among you where I lived my first years. I have traveled and seen other realities, other truths. But my short presence among you marked me forever, and your faces bring back my childhood. Over the next days, I want to share with you the last thoughts of Comandante Paulo."

She paused. Her blue eyes had gained the intensity that her father always demonstrated. She finished strongly with the words of Che, "*Hasta la victoria siempre.*"

She saw the tears running down the faces of the guerrillas and she understood these tears were for her father, for the little of him that they could see in her. She promised, at that moment, to honor this bond, forever.

That afternoon, as Natasha lay in her hammock, renewing the energy expended from the long march and the emotional encounter, she read from her father's diary. It described the Ocamo Mission visit, in October 2001. He discussed the meeting with Father Antoine and Professor Bonaparte. Comparing the different ideologies, he sought their commonalities rather than differences. She could glimpse into his evolving ideas, into the synthesis that his mind was forging and saw with clarity the common threads in Socialism, Christian Democracy, and Darwinian Capitalism.

Natasha continued to read, mesmerized. Her father described his personal revelation from the visit to the Yanomami village of Bisaasi-Teri. And here she was, one year later, retracing his steps. How would it turn out for her?

# CHAPTER TWELVE

A fter a few days with the *compañeros*, spent reading the diary and resting, Natasha arranged with Caetano to visit a Yanomami tribe nearby. Her father, always precise, had described the Bisaasi-teri and Kokorishi-teri villages in his diary. The Kokorishi had migrated south, but Caetano knew of another village, Haximu-Teri, within one day's trek. They were a splinter group from Kokorishi. The *compañeros* had scouted the surrounding areas and seen evidence of the village. However, they had refrained from contacting it, following Comandante Paulo's strict orders. He had warned them about the danger of infecting the Indians with diseases. They were fully aware of their low tolerance.

Paulo's diary contained a commentary on the customs of the Indians and even a small dictionary of one hundred words. Natasha was immensely curious. She had seen Yanomami villages in documentaries and in the class that she had taken with the controversial anthropologist, Louis Bonaparte. Natasha also knew that they had no immunity against our diseases. She had now been in the forest for two weeks and none of the group showed any signs of infectious disease. So, it was safe to contact the Yanomami.

They had to walk slowly because of Celeste's condition. Antonio and Gilmar, one of the younger guerrillas, came with them. Celeste would continue on, starting from the Auaretê River, down the Casiaquiari River, and from there to the Auapés until the village of Auapés. She would now be able to travel by canoe, because they were past FARC-controlled territory. She wanted to be with her mother. They took hammocks with them and stopped on the trail. By now Natasha had gotten used to these forest highways and even felt safe on them. It was dangerous to venture even a few yards off the trail. The jungle was unforgiving and looked identical in all directions. She knew how easy it was to get lost. Somewhere during the march they crossed the border into Brazil.

At mid-morning they approached the village. It was a small *shabono*, a circular building covered in palm leaves with a central courtyard. They entered the structure after passing through a wood palisade that served as protection against raiders. At the center of the yard, they announced themselves with loud screams. A group of warriors surrounded them, pointing arrows in strung-out bows at them. Natasha fought back panic. The chief approached them. Pointing at himself, he gave his name, "Bakotawa *Tushaua*."

"Bakotawa," Natasha repeated. She remembered the name *Tushaua*, chief, from her father's diary. She grabbed her backpack and pulled out three of the five machetes she carried. They had been brought as gifts for the Indians. The chief took them out of their sheaths and examined them methodically. He walked to the edge of the plaza and tested them on the wooden columns. He came back and, with a smile, thanked Natasha. The other Yanomami then dropped their bows and hugged the visitors.

"They do this every time," Gilmar said. "First they try to scare us. Then, they are overly friendly."

They sought cover from the grilling sun under the thatched roof. Natasha touched the heads of the children, then stroked their jet-black, silky hair.

Celeste said, "Natasha, you touch the children in the same manner as your father used to caress me."

She smiled. "It must be the genes."

It was then that Natasha saw a man approach slowly. He was short and had a beer belly. In contrast to the Indians he wore shorts, and had a scraggly beard and balding head. Natasha recognized him. By the way he held his ribs with his right hand and the rictus in his face, she could see that he was in pain.

"Dr. Bonaparte, I presume," she said, mimicking Stanley, who, upon meeting Livingston after a long search in Africa, had supposedly used this introduction.

"And you must be one of my Berkeley coeds." He smiled with satisfaction at being recognized, but the laughter disappeared, replaced by pain.

"Yes, and I'm also the daughter of Comandante Paulo, whom you met not too far from here."

"Sorry. Broken ribs," he said, holding his chest. He lifted an eyebrow. "He was an extraordinary man. Please accept my condolences. Yes, I met him and he became deeply troubled by the future of the Latin American Indians."

"I know, Professor Bonaparte. This was quite recent. I'm here retracing my father's last steps. May I ask what brings you to this village?"

"We're both outlaws here, as you know. This village is within Brazil and I have very few friends there."

"I've heard about the controversies."

Natasha had followed the debate in the news. Bonaparte had close ties with the Venezuelan government, and Brazil had time and again refused him entry into its country. The nationalistic Brazilians were fearful that the US was trying to create an international Yanomami nation between Venezuela, Colombia, and Brazil. There was a lot of gold on Yanomami land, and perhaps other precious minerals. Although the internationalization of the Amazon was clearly a phobia that had been fed by the media in Brazil, it had soured the relationship between Bonaparte and the Brazilian government. And to top things off, Brazilian anthropologists disagreed with Bonaparte's vision of the Yanomami as "fierce."

"I'm here trying to protect this village. At the same time, I'm studying this group. We're collecting blood samples for a genetic study."

Natasha excused herself reluctantly in order to explore the village. She could not believe that she had met the legendary Bonaparte.

"Come over for dinner, Natasha. I'll prepare a *tracajá* omelet," he said, as she left. "If you want to refresh yourself, the creek's down there." He handed her a bar of soap.

Natasha and Celeste walked out and found a discreet spot at the creek where they undressed and soaped up. When she turned around she saw a group of teenage boys and girls watching her and laughing. One boy approached her, touching the soap and caressing, in the process, her breasts. She acted upset and they exploded in laughter as she swam away. The water was refreshing and her aching body felt momentarily soothed.

She walked out and covered herself with a towel. Back in the *shabono*, she put on a pair of spare shorts and T-shirt. This time the adults watched her, some with curiosity, others desire. Bonaparte railed at them loudly. They turned around and went back to their duties.

"I told them that you were my wife and to let you alone," he said with a smile.

"Professor Bonaparte, I don't know how to thank you," she said in jest. "But I must decline the honor."

The afternoon was spent watching the women make baskets, visiting the plantain fields, watching the kids learning from their parents. When they returned to the village, Natasha saw Bonaparte holding a glass of scotch.

"Aha! Getting used to our local customs, Natasha? There is not much privacy in the village. You are surrounded by people all the time."

"I noticed."

She accepted a shot of scotch, and he put the bottle back into his box, locking it.

"All care is not enough," he said, looking around. "This is my last bottle."

He told her about his struggle to help the Indians, about the forty years that he had spent visiting the tribes, about the wars he had witnessed, and about the destruction that had occurred during these years. He shared with Natasha his deeper, sadder thoughts. He was hurt by the severe criticism he received, in the media, over the past few years. After years of adoration, the tide had turned. From hero to villain. The press was ruthless, and he had been variously accused of scientific dishonesty, causing the death of countless Indians by improper inoculations, and of other real or imaginary crimes. His mercurial personality contributed to this. The many enemies he had made in his long career had banded against him and were pursuing him like a pack of hounds. It had all started with a disgruntled graduate student that had married a Yanomami woman, taken her to the U.S., and written a critical book about him.

"I should never have brought him to this region. He back-stabbed me," was his bitter comment.

Then came the Brazilian anthropologist Alcida Ramos, who opposed his view of the Yanomami as an aggressive people.

"And yet it's true. I love the Yanomami, but have witnessed countless fights, skirmishes, even worse. Death by violent means is one of the major causes of adult male deaths," he added.

"Twenty-five percent of males have killed someone, Professor," she said, proudly regurgitating the material learned in his class.

Last came a French adventurer who crisscrossed Venezuela looking for dirt on Bonaparte and wrote a scathing book about him.

"Sebastien Tierny," Natasha said.

"A fucking French faggot," Bonaparte said.

"But you are half French Canadian yourself."

"But not a frigging faggot." His wide grin displayed his tobacco-stained teeth. "He is a pedantic pedestrian pederast. Is that better?"

Natasha could not contain her laughter at his raucous, yet poetic remarks. She had heard about the book and even browsed through it. It was a scathing account of the excesses of Bonaparte. Then, there was another, more controversial character.

"Professor Bonaparte, what about Jacques Lézard?"

Natasha had read Tierny's account of the activities of anthropologists, geneticists, and other assorted scientists and adventurers among the Yanomami. Among them was Jacques Lézard, the Caligula of the Orinoco. His homosexuality, directed at young boys, was legendary. He escaped prosecution only because of his stature as an anthropologist with the unique credentials of being a former student of Claude Lévi-Strauss, the brilliant French scholar and father of Structural Anthropology. The Yanomami nicknamed him *Bosinawarewa*, literally Ass Eater. In his twenty-five years among the Yanomami, he had survived several confrontations with missionaries, other anthropologists, and the Yanomami themselves.

"He is a bright and dedicated researcher," Bonaparte said, grinning again. "His sexual needs were somewhat unorthodox, even for Yanomami standards."

"Is it true that he exchanged sexual favors with young boys for tools?"

Bonaparte nodded. "The going rate was one machete for one session, one shotgun for six sessions."

He called Kaobawa and asked him about Bosinawarewa. Kaobawa replied with a hand gesture mimicking the actions that young Yanomami performed.

"Kaobawa was once deeply insulted by Lézard's boys," Bonaparte said, turning serious. "He then organized the largest war party in the recorded Yanomami history: over one hundred and fifty warriors from fifteen villages."

Natasha listened as Bonaparte translated what he had just said to Kaobawa. He nodded approvingly, and waved his bow and arrow, as he proffered, "Tayari-Teri, Bosinawarewa."

"They attacked the village of Tayari, killed seven of Lézard's boys, and took a considerable bounty of machetes, shotguns, and other goods."

Natasha vaguely remembered some of these accounts from her Berkeley readings for the anthropology classes. But being there, in the middle of the jungle and a thousand miles from the closest city filled her with emotion.

"Oh, I forgot to mention," he said after exchanging a couple of words with Kaobawa, "they burned their village down. Lézard escaped but was lucky. Kaobawa's band was afraid of government reprisals if they had killed him."

"I hope that cooled his heels. Didn't the missionaries report him to Caracas?"

"Actually, Father Antoine, the poor fellow that died with your father, was always protective of him. The Church is sometimes too forgiving..."

He became thoughtful for a few minutes. Natasha knew that he was thinking about Father Antoine. Why was he so understanding?

"I don't know, Natasha, I don't know. The fact is that he's no longer a problem. He returned to his intellectual circles in Paris."

Natasha tried to be supportive. "Professor, all famous people eventually collect enemies. People try to get their fifteen minutes of fame by dragging accomplished men, like you, through the dirt. Look at my father. A fellow guerrilla fighter killed him."

"It's indeed true. And since you mimicked the explorer Livingstone this morning, you might know that another British explorer, Burton, was practically robbed of his discovery of the source of the Nile."

"The Pinzón brothers tried to steal the discovery of America from Christopher Columbus."

"The list goes on and on. But let's eat the *tracajá* omelet."

Natasha noticed the beautiful and gentle Indian girl that was helping him. He pointed to her and said, "Mahima." She turned and smiled at Natasha, who saw with a mixture of alarm and curiosity the wood sticks hanging from her cheeks.

"Her cheeks are perforated, just like your ears. The sticks aren't painful at all," Bonaparte said. As she quickly prepared the meal, he explained that turtle eggs were richer than chicken eggs. Natasha was starved and wolfed down the omelet. Bonaparte showed her how to mix manioc flower with the eggs.

"It dilutes the strong oil and enhances the flavor."

After dinner, he settled in his hammock and continued talking. He revealed that a geologist had been snooping around the region.

"I'm sure he noticed the cassiterite ore that's on the mountain," he said. "And this means trouble for these poor people. They have lived here for thousands of years. Now, the company will find a way to kick them out."

"How do you know it's cassiterite, Professor?"

"I studied at the Michigan School of Mines, now Michigan Tech. I had to spend my freshman year identifying rocks."

"Is cassiterite valuable?"

"It's the tin mineral. Tin sells for $1,000 a ton. This mountain could be worth hundreds of million dollars."

"What can be done?"

"Stop the company. I got its name: SAMITRA."

"This might be too much of a coincidence, but my uncle works for a Brazilian mining company."

Bonaparte jumped off the hammock, his smallish frame in fighting position.

"Natasha, you have to help me. How can we find out? Can you call somebody?"

"We had some bad encounters with the FARC. I'm afraid they are after me."

Then, she told him about her father's assassination and her revenge. Bonaparte was impressed.

"Well done, Natasha. A Yanomami would have done the same. Wasn't it the old Kennedy who said, 'don't get mad, get even'?"

He showed her his satellite dish and global telephone. He would call his secretary first thing the next day.

"What is your uncle's name?"

"Clayton Chauny."

"Good. Tomorrow we'll know. Cathy can go to the Internet and check SAMITRA's website. What's his position?"

"He is in marketing and finance, pretty high up."

Bonaparte told Natasha that he would try to send a message to her mother on his satellite phone. They both knew that FARC could be monitoring her calls, so they felt it would be dangerous to call directly. They finally agreed that the safest way was to dictate a message to his Berkeley office and have it faxed to Ana Maria. In this manner, they would be able to bypass any bugging of her phone.

The next morning Antonio and Celeste departed. They had been able to fix a small canoe and make it water worthy. The small and barely navigable creek by the village led to the Auaretê. Their trip would take a few days down-river, but would be more comfortable than a long walk through the forest.

After seeing them off, Natasha had some time on her hands. Bonaparte worked on his phone. Eventually he called his Berkeley office and dictated the message. He also asked his secretary to inquire about SAMITRA and its Board of Directors.

Natasha wanted to experience the life of these Indians, a dream that she had nurtured for many years. Now, that dream had come true. Before walking back to Esperanza, she decided to go hunting with one of Kaobawa's sons, a teen-aged boy named Rerebawa. Kaobawa first patiently explained to her the arsenal of weapons. He knew some Spanish and she rapidly became acquainted with the various artifacts. He showed her his quiver, repeating the word *tora*. Then, Rerebawa pointed at the tips of the little arrows, while he mimicked a falling animal that slowly became paralyzed. "*Husu namo*," he exclaimed, as he continued his theatrics. She understood that they were dipped in curare.

They walked through the forest silently and Natasha wondered at the boy's stillness and concentration. His eyes were fixed on the canopy. Every now and then, he pointed in the direction of the village, whispering *teri*. He did this to reassure her that he was not lost. They encountered two or three groups of small monkeys that he ignored. Suddenly they heard a deep humming sound, like the chant of a Buddhist monk. Rerebawa instantly froze.

"*Paruri*," he said, as he advanced carefully, his eyes on the canopy. Again, the deep humming sound. He lifted his blowgun and pointed. At last, he fired silently. A few seconds later a large black bird, the size of a small turkey, fell through the branches. Natasha had seen several *curassows* in her trip, and she knew that they were good to eat.

They continued walking for about an hour. Rerebawa carried the bird on his shoulder. They heard the howler monkeys far away. Rerebawa knew that they were heading to the river and they positioned themselves in their path, waiting patiently. Suddenly, the first one appeared, then the entire group, making all kinds of noises, breaking branches. When they were on the tree above them, Rerebawa again lifted his blowgun and pointed. He had to fire several darts before he hit one. The other monkeys saw their wounded companion and started throwing branches and defecating on Natasha and Rerebawa. Their howls rose and Natasha was worried that they might come down from the tree and attack them. The monkey was now hanging from his prehensile tail. Rerebawa fired another arrow at him, and he finally came crashing down. He sliced his throat with an agouti-tooth knife and tied right foot and leg, then left foot and leg with lianas. He then took the monkey and, smiling, lifted it. He motioned for her to turn, then passed the loops formed by arms and legs around her shoulders. She was to carry the monkey in this fashion, like a backpack. She obliged grudgingly. He was already loaded with the *curassow*. As they walked back to the village, she could feel the monkey's head dangling from side to side and the long and hairy arms around her shoulder. Adventurous as she was, she could not hold back revulsion. There was something almost human in the dead monkey's expression, something hauntingly wrong in the act that they had committed.

As they approached the plantain plantation a few hundred yards from the village, Rerebawa again assumed his hunting mode, slowly slipping from tree trunk to tree trunk and staring ahead. Natasha hoped that they had completed the hunt. She just wanted to return to her hammock and, literally, get the monkey off her back. He turned around and made a gesture that she recognized. With a smile, he inserted his index finger into a circle that he made with the fingers of the other hand. He waved Natasha on, but she feared that the little teenager had lewd intentions. Then she saw, thirty yards away, a young Indian girl walking toward the plantain trees. Behind her came an adult man. The girl looked around and assured herself that she was not being watched, then crouched down. The man mounted her like a dog. Natasha felt a strange excitement in this voyeuristic experience. She watched in bewilderment as they copulated, in this simple and primitive manner. Rerebawa was visibly excited; there was no denying it, especially since he was naked. After a few strokes, the lovers were finished. They gave them a few minutes and then proceeded to the village.

After nightfall, they threw the dead monkey on the ashes until the hair was gone. The feeling of cannibalism grew stronger in Natasha's mind when she looked closer at the poor beast. Devoid of its fur, it looked even more human. Nevertheless, she forced herself to eat some pieces after it was roasted. She casually mentioned the encounter in the plantation to Bonaparte. He had a good laugh. "This is their lover's lane, dear. And we haven't taught them the missionary position yet!" Natasha blushed to a deep red.

Bonaparte's secretary had called back and confirmed that Clayton Chauny was the VP for Finance and Marketing of SAMITRA. She also confirmed that the fax had been sent and received by Natasha's mother. It contained a request for a plane. Natasha expected the plane to arrive at the Esperanza airstrip in, at most, a couple of days. She and Bonaparte agreed that she should return immediately and convince her uncle to leave the Yanomami Indians alone. Natasha was not convinced she could do anything, but she would try anyway.

That evening, she read some revealing passages about her father's Berkeley stay.

*Berkeley, 9/99*

*I come every morning to Bacci Café, at the entrance of campus. It is a couple of blocks away from Natasha's place on Durant Ave. I love the Berkeley atmosphere. Natasha takes classes and I take care of Tonto. He is a good communist: we share everything, even the bed. Here, I sip lattes (oh, divine decadence!) and watch the local literati. Visited Phoebe Hearst Anthropology Museum. It is indeed pathetic to see photographs of the last California Indian, ending his days as a guard in the Museum. His name was Ishi and he was the last descendant of the Yahi. The irony of life. This poor Indian was found in California, in 1912. His entire tribe of approximately four hundred had been hunted to this last man by government inspectors, ranchers, miners and other righteous citizens. He became the guard of the museum and one of its main attractions. He died of tuberculosis, after becoming somewhat of a celebrity in Berkeley.*

*As I sit here at Bacci Café, I realize that there is a new reality in the air. Having crossed the mid-mark my life, after all these battles, I discover that the struggle between rigid ideologies, between communism and capitalism, is contrived and nonsensical. There are much deeper realities, complex dynamic systems under these two structures. Somehow, it is with an enormous relief that I feel free of the strictures of Marxism, which guided my steps for twenty years. The real struggle in America is much more profound. It is a conflict between two visions of life: the Indian and the Conqueror. They are paradoxically opposite and the merger has only occurred in a few places: Mexico and Peru. The Yankees have solved the problem with their proverbial efficiency, by simply eliminating the Indians. The Argentineans have done the same. Everywhere else, the Church has acted as a mediator, as a buffer. Ishi represented the end of the road for Indians in California. And in the jungles of Colombia, Nicaragua, and Brazil, I saw many ends of the road. The Indian lady that was slapped by the gentleman in the bus, in Bolivia, many years ago, is still alive in my mind. The Spanish, English, and Portuguese colonizers arrived to destroy, to crush and to rebuild. Marxism tells us that society has to be modified in specific and predetermined ways. However, Pre-Columbian societies were rich in texture and variety, and developed their own ways.*

*How was the multitude of Mayan and Inca cities built? How was the intricate system of roads, connecting all American regions developed? It was not through Capitalism. Neither through Communism. An organic system of governance and division of labor evolved with its own characteristics, adapted to the local culture, topography, and climate. Importantly, civilization developed independently and simultaneously in the Americas and Eurasia. The ruins of Chico Norte, in Peru, are at least 5,000 years old. This is contemporary with Sumer, in the Middle east. How could thousands of Indians coordinate their effort and collaborate in the development of civilization?*

She kept reading, as if in a trance. Then came the outline of a play, which his restless mind had created. It had to keep probing all the time. There was a strange beauty in his writing, an inspired quality that attracted her immensely. He had called it *"Pasion y Muerte Del Che* (Passion and Death of Che)." He retraced the last two days of Che, drawing obvious parallels with Christ. The first scene presented Che riding a mule up a ravine, the *quebrada*. His group followed him. Natasha knew that this was historically correct, since his asthma impeded him from walking. Next he is a prisoner, with two dead comrades by his side. He spends his last night trussed on the floor of a miserable schoolhouse in the village of La Higuera. He is wounded in the leg. The next morning, the last day of his life, he watches as his future executioners await orders from La

Paz. Among them is the CIA agent Felix Rodríguez, who washes his hands as Pilate did. Che calls for the schoolteacher and tells her that the poor of Bolivia deserve more than that hut. He points to the blackboard and shows her a grammatical error. He tells her that he is dying so that others can have better opportunities.

He is prepared to die, just like Christ. At 12:30 PM, the order comes from La Paz. The Colonel sends a drunken sergeant, Mario Terán, to accomplish the task. Che tells him, "I know you've come to kill me. Shoot, coward, you are only going to kill a man." The soldier sprays his legs with bullets and Che bites his hand in order not to scream. Then, the bullets go through his chest and he drowns in his blood. In the last scene, he lies in the Vallegrande hospital morgue. His squalid shirtless body, beard, and long hair bear a strange resemblance to Christ. His eyes are wide open and the old matrons come and cut pieces of his hair, after lighting candles around him, kneeling down, and praying. In the last scene the image of the Che is splattered over posters, book covers, and movie screens throughout the Americas. The resurrection.

She closed the diary and held it close to her chest, falling into a deep sleep. When she woke up, dreading the idea of leaving Haximu-Teri, she saw a worried look on Bonaparte's face as he greeted her.

"We've got problems, big problems."

A group of children spoke excitedly to Bonaparte. All she recognized were the words *Shaki* and *shawara* (disease).

"There seems to be a measles outbreak in a small community about five kilometers inland."

"But you said that you inoculated the entire village, Professor. Could it be the vaccine?"

"This will never happen again, Natasha." For a brief moment, she saw grief and remorse in his face. "We used the Schwarz vaccine, much weaker than the Edmonston B that we used in '68."

"Everybody seems healthy here…"

"There's a small off-shoot of this village. Ushubiriwa, his four wives, with brothers and children. They had a big fight with the *tushaua*, Bakotawa," he said, pointing east, toward the Mavaca Mountains. "After a huge club fight, they left. Apparently, Bakotawa was having an affair with one of the wives."

"Could they've been infected?"

"I remember that they didn't want to obey Bakotawa's orders. They took off, screaming all kinds of insults."

"That's it, Professor. They probably carried the virus with them."

Natasha was aware of the disastrous consequences of measles infections among Yanomami. In some villages, over fifty percent of the population had been decimated.

"I can't go there because of my broken ribs." He pressed his hand against his ribcage and lifted himself painfully from the hammock.

"I'll help you, Professor," she said. Then, for a moment, she reflected. Was she up to it? Was she getting deeper and deeper into this journey?

"I have some antibiotics left, and a small supply of powdered milk. Pregnant women and children are at the greatest risk."

Natasha accepted the challenge. There was no time to waste. She unloaded her backpack and filled it with the medicine, while Bonaparte and Kaobawa instructed Rerebawa and a couple of other Bisaasi Yanomami to ready themselves. In less than an hour, they were packed. Natasha handed the package with the diaries to Bonaparte. She had also included a long letter to her mother, explaining some of their vicissitudes and the absolute need to stop SAMITRA from invading the region. At the end, she wrote:

> *My beloved mother, don't worry about me. I am doing what I love. I leave it in your hands to convince Uncle Clayton to protect the Yanomami. This was the last wish of my father, as you can see in the diary, Love, N.*

"Professor, these are precious to me. My father's life is contained in these pages. Could you make sure that Gilmar takes them to the airplane and that they get to my mother?"

Then, she turned to Gilmar and, in Spanish, explained to him the supreme importance of the diaries.

"I understand that this is his legacy, Natasha," Bonaparte said. "Kaobawa will personally go with Gilmar. The *compañeros* will guard them until the airplane arrives. They need to get out of FARC's reach."

"Thank you, Professor. I feel relieved now."

Soon they were on their way, rapidly advancing on a poorly marked trail. Natasha felt much stronger now. The urgency of the operation energized her. The Haximu boys carried baskets strapped to their foreheads filled with medicine, food, and hammocks. They had trouble keeping up with her.

# CHAPTER THIRTEEN

The diaries arrived with news from Natasha. Ana Maria was disappointed that she had chosen to stay among the Yanomami. The letter was puzzling. She implored her mother to investigate what SAMITRA's involvement was at the Auaretê River and she sounded accusatory about the measles outbreak.

Ana Maria confronted Clayton. Though evasive at first, his conscience had begun to weigh on him. The ramifications of the tragedy that he was about to cause did not escape him.

"So, the entire purpose of your trip here was not to get in touch with us, was not to mourn your lost brother," Ana Maria snapped.

He knew that he had disappointed her. "You don't understand. I had some professional dealings in Colombia, and I combined business with family."

"What business? Tell me what your intentions are in the Auaretê River. Pasto was only a convenient stop."

"We're in the mining business, that's true. But I really looked forward to this visit. This is transforming me."

"Don't you feel guilty about what your company is doing? Can't you see the harm?"

He looked in her eyes, which expressed pain and frustration. Selfish men had hurt her before. No, he wouldn't be another one. He had to redress his wrongs. But how?

"I'll have to ask you to leave, Clayton," she said with great sadness. "I was starting to ... fall in love with you. But I was just a convenient distraction, wasn't I?" She hurried from the room.

Clayton sat there for a long time. The two *Fila Brasiliensis* stared at him suspiciously, and he knew that they shared Ana Maria's distrust for him. If she only knew what his real plans were. He realized that he was endangering Natasha's life. He *had* to stop Soto Mayor. He went to the armoire, grabbed a bottle of Johnny Walker Red, and carried it to the garden. The dogs continued to watch him. He believed Ana Maria's accounts of how they had ripped smaller dogs into pieces.

He filled a glass and walked into the garden, looking at the rapidly fading colors of the sunset. The scotch burned his throat with a familiar sting, and he felt better. He could see more clearly now through the fog of alcohol, which dulled the shock of the revelation and of her rejection. He still felt the pained and accusatory eyes of Ana Maria. They reminded him of a scene from the past. Would he be a coward again? Love was indeed mysterious, and the more he delved into it, the more he surrendered to it, the less he understood it.

It had been in Brazil. He and his friend were on the prowl. It was during their ROTC days. They were future officers, the pride of the nation, and drove around town at night in search of adventure. The woman strode voluptuously down a deserted street. She wore a tight dress that accentuated her curvaceous body. For one moment, their eyes crossed. Was she a prostitute? A housewife returning from a fling? Women were not supposed to be out that late. Loureiro drove the car onto the sidewalk. She was summoned by the two officers and arrested for loitering. In the car, she was informed that she had to please them. They drove to a deserted area. Clayton waited outside while Loureiro raped her. Then came his turn, and he sat by her side while she cried. Her dress was half-open. He had to be a *macho*. Loureiro would demand it. After a while, almost shyly, he touched one of her white breasts. He placed it into her dress, caressing it. To his surprise, she responded with a faint moan. He kissed her gently on the neck. She offered him her mouth. He kissed her lips. Then, she grabbed him and kissed him with fury. Hungry with passion, she demanded him. They copulated furiously in the back of the VW bug. When done, they drove back in silence and dropped her off close to her house. As she walked away, she glared at Loureiro and spat, "Cowards!" Then, her eyes rested for a split second on him, and he felt that she was, in spite of everything, victorious.

They had both felt the sting of the insult. Ashamed at their action, they never talked about it. Now, twenty years later, Clayton remembered those eyes. They had the same flavor of pain, pride, and pleasure.

As he took one last sip of the scotch and felt its sweet sting on his throat, he felt two hands behind him. "Clayton, don't do this to me. Don't leave me. I need your strength."

He turned around and, in a sudden impulse, kissed Ana Maria. He felt that his entire body, his total soul, was surrendering. No, he would not be a coward again.

"Ana, I won't let you down. I can't tell you everything my company plans, but I will do everything in my power to help Natasha. You have my word."

His hand boldly moved under her dress. He caressed her buttocks, then her thighs and moved up. She was not wearing panties. His finger expertly slipped into her hot moistness.

"Not yet, Clayton, not yet," she said, escaping his embrace and running to her room. The two immense dogs rose when he tried to follow her, and growled. He stopped on his tracks.

Restless, Ana Maria took the diaries to her bed and caressed their covers as she composed herself. Her body burned with desire. She remembered Paulo always writing. The diaries were full of elaborate strategies and campaign details, military information, and she had never bothered to read them before. But on this night her feverish mind needed confirmation that she had been loved, and loved intensely. And she discovered, one by one, personal insights, as if Paulo every now and then opened his soul. She had left him because she had to choose between the revolution and her children. She saw her presence in his writing and was moved. She remembered well. It was in Nicaragua, where her fiancé Arnaldo had taken her twenty-five years ago, when she was barely eighteen.

*Nicaragua, 1977*

*We have been fighting in the mountains for over six months now. The Contras are growing more aggressive by the day. In the past weeks, they have been flying Apache helicopters and firing at us from the air. Our tactics have changed. Seek cover at all times. Our comrades in Managua tell us that the Yankees are stepping up support: weapons and training of the troops. Contras are supported by the CIA and have set up camp in Honduras. They attack us from there. The Miskito Indians are on their payroll, and have become our fierce enemies. The Sandinista Liberation Army is losing control of the Matagalpa area. Contras attacked several villages and the peasants are being terrorized. We are growing more isolated. Yesterday the* alcaide *of Matagalpa came in and told us that he can no longer help us. The village will be destroyed if they do.*

*The line between right and wrong, good and bad is becoming hard to define. The Contras have decimated several villages but we also commit excesses. What would Sandino have thought of these atrocities? He lost his life in Panama, fighting against the Gringos in the jungle. We are using his name, but the Fuerza Sandinista de Liberacion Nacional is becoming a bigger, global dispute. We are pawns in the global battle being waged between the Yankee and the Bear. The poor continue to be crushed.*

*Nicaragua, 1977*

*A beautiful and peaceful two months. My compañera Ana Maria has renewed my enthusiasm in this struggle.*

*She is a source of strength and inspiration. Although she comes from the aristocratic Colombian Betancourt clan, she has joined the struggle and has proven herself in the battles of Tegucigalpa and Tenuacan. In spite of the CIA and Comandante Marcos, we have had significant victories.*

Ana Maria remembered the sad loss of her fiancé Arnaldo in the ill-fated incursion into Honduras. She also remembered the comfort and support that Paulo had given her during the subsequent months. She admired his quiet leadership and his sense of fairness. They naturally gravitated toward each other and it was so easy to fall in love with him.

*Colombia, 1983*
*Ana Maria has been fighting on our side for five years now. She is a dedicated compañera and is still willing to take the responsibilities in spite of our two children. I ordered her to stay at the camp for the next two weeks. We foresee bitter fighting against the paramilitary militia. San Vicente del Caguan is a safe place and I cannot afford to have her join the fight. Natasha and Ernesto are healthy and energetic. I would like to spend more time with them. Made a formal request to Comandante Marulanda to have Ana transferred to the educational division of FARC.*

*Angola, 1984*
*We have been fighting with the forces of José Eduardo dos Santos for two months. The Cuban soldiers are valiant and disciplined. They have held back UNITA forces at the gates of Luanda. It is ironic that we are fighting a conventional*

*war, with artillery, APCs, and large troop movements, and that Jonas Savimbi is the guerrilla leader. South African troops are supporting UNITA, but our Cuban soldiers, well equipped by Soviet weaponry, are holding the ground. Africa is exciting and different, but my heart is in Latin America. I miss Ana Maria and the children immensely, but my revolutionary duty is more important than my personal feelings.*

That last sentence hurt Ana Maria deeply, once more. Therein lay the impossibility of their love, the conundrum of their existence. She silently closed the diary and clutched her pillow, tears running down her face and uncontrollable sobs shaking her body.

The next morning, they went on a long walk. Clayton opened up about his previous life.

"I was fascinated by the U.S. Not that I fell in love with the country," he said. "Far from it. The Americans were cold and distant, although they appeared warm and friendly at first. They are used to casual relationships, and people move in and out of their lives at a brisk pace, all the way from childhood. But, I learned to understand them, and to take advantage of them. I had a couple of great friends, from Recife, in the Brazilian Northeast. They were rich like me, and wild to boot. While Americans looked at sex with a maturity that came all the way from adolescence, we were South American predators. Love them and leave them was our motto. Actually, love them and pass them on."

He told her the story passed on by Maurício and Leonardo, both of whom belonged to the sugar cane

193

aristocracy. Their families owned large plantations where they were raised as little princes. Leonardo was unrelentingly anti-Communist, a fact that had been triggered by being shot in the leg by a group of laborers from the sugar plants during a strike.

"One night, when they were totally drunk, Leonardo became somber and told me a horrifying story," he said. "The Brazilian newspapers had reported for several months the barbaric assassination of Father Henriques, a leftist priest. The killers had never been found, but it was rumored that it was the CCC (Communist Hunting Commando), a para-military group that tried to stamp out communism in Brazil's backward northeast.

"Their CCC group was trying to scare Father Henriques, the communist. So, they caught him one day as he was leaving the church. They threw him into the pickup and drove beyond the city limits. They were already a little drunk. They pulled him out and gave him a good beating, telling him to mind his own business and stop haranguing the poor people against the sugar cane companies. But he was dead serious and even insolent. He told them that they could not scare him, that he had a mission to help these struggling masses. It was then that one of the group, Antonio Teixeira, much wilder than Leonardo, pulled out his knife and told him to shut up or he would cut his balls off. The priest did not back down. They felt then and there that things were going to get bad. They pulled his pants down, but the damn priest would not shut up. Teixeira was screaming, 'Men that wear skirts are fags and do not need balls.' He jumped on him while the rest of the gang held him tight. The priest did not beg, did not get on his knees and plead. So his balls were cut off in one zap. Teixeira, frenzied by his actions, stuck the knife into the priest's mouth, prying it open. Then, he stuffed the balls into his mouth, telling him to shut up.

"They soon realized that there was no going back. If they took him back to town, he would fill all the Leftist papers with his story, and eventually the government would come after Leonardo and his buddies. There was only one thing to do – kill him. He was a real macho, a man, this Father Henriques, Leonardo had to admit. So they blasted away, each one firing so that none could tell on the others.

"Ana, I was disturbed by the story," Clayton said. "Our little adventures were nothing compared with this. My admiration for Leonardo grew into fear on that day. He never mentioned this again, and when we woke up the next morning he just mentioned that we had finished the entire bottle of Johnny Walker Black. The two of us, like real *machos*."

Ana looked at Clayton in disgust. "This is also the attitude of the Colombian aristocracy. The hate that is perpetuated through these hideous crimes fuels the violence that has existed in Colombia all these years. So, I created this refuge, *El Farol*. I cannot solve all the problems of Colombia, let alone of Latin America. Here, at least, I try to create peace and harmony."

Clayton felt that this peace and harmony was also invading him. It came from nature, from the pure water and air, the physical exercise, and her presence.

As they walked back to the ranch house, Ana asked him again to help Natasha. "Please Clayton, do this for me. And I'll help you regain that purity lost."

When they arrived home, exhausted from the emotion and scotch, he took a short nap. That night, at dinner, he told Ana, "I'll help Natasha. It won't be easy, and people will get hurt, but I will help."

She turned to him and kissed him warmly. "Clayton, this is wonderful. Paulo's last wishes will be fulfilled."

"Paulo's? I thought they were Natasha's wishes."

"I'll show you the last entries of his diary, shortly before he was killed."

She brought out the diary to the living room and read the final entries. They expressed his gradual disillusionment with guerrilla warfare as the long fighting of Angola and Colombia took its toll on him, both physically and mentally.

"Can I borrow these, Ana?" Clayton asked. He was visibly moved by the sight of his brother's neat and methodical handwriting. She gave them to him and he turned to the Angola campaign, a stage in his life that had been kept secret. Clayton had heard rumors of these years. Now, he had the truth in front of him.

*Angola, February 1985*

*Have been here for well over a year. The fighting has reached a stalemate. Terrain very different from Nicaragua or Colombia--flat plains and savannah. The African officers have not yet absorbed the essence of Marxism-Leninism. Tribal differences are very strong and the leaders instill fear in their subordinates by using* mandinga, *their form of voodoo. We now have a front that cuts Angola in half. The south is occupied by UNITA and we cannot seem to make further progress. The Cubans, mostly blacks and mulattos, lead the fight and show incredible courage and discipline. Fidel Castro addresses us periodically over the radio, and his inspiring words are a source of strength. But the soldiers are growing tired. My battalion has over one hundred Cubans. We already buried eighteen in these interminable plains and my men are homesick. I hope that Fidel will replace them soon. As for me, the struggle shall continue.*

*Angola, August 1986*

*Jonas Savimbi is the real hero in Angola. Not Agostinho Neto, not José Eduardo dos Santos. The latter are Soviet-educated cadres that head the Movimento Popular de Liberação Nacional (MPLA-the Popular Movement for the Liberation of Angola). They represent the mulatto-dominated intelligentsia. Fifty thousand Cubans were needed to uphold this regime. We often receive visits from Soviet apparatchiki. They are all the same, reeking of vodka, pig's grease and sweating profusely from their overweight bodies. I am growing tired of them. Where has their revolutionary fervor gone? They are bureaucrats trained since childhood in the art of kissing the feet of their superiors while stepping ruthlessly on their subordinates. They start as Young Pioneers, join the Communist Party as teenagers. They become Komsomols, a term used for young professionals that want to claw their way up the ladder of the Communist Party. I much prefer the revolutionary ardor of Cuba. However, we need them for supplies and weapons. Fidel probably needs them too.*

*Jonas is the real fighter. He eats, sleeps, drinks, and suffers with his troops, just like Fidel and Che did. He is pure black, pure Ovidundu. His is the largest tribe of Angola, and they farm the fertile South. Jonas was Maoist, then*

197

*supported by South Africa. Now, he is backed by the US. He doesn't care who backs him as long as he can keep up the struggle. Deep down, he wants the freedom for his people. If it weren't for us, the Cubans, he would have taken over a long time ago. He has read Che's book. But so have I. I try to neutralize his ambushes, his hit-and-run attacks on the Benguela railway. I am now a Brigade General and have five thousand soldiers under my command.*

*There is an increasing lack of food in Luanda. The Soviet Antonov planes have to supply the front and Soviet cargo ships bring in food. I see a lot of corruption in the MPLA. The Soviet equipment finds its way to the other side: AK47 rifles, RPGs. The MPLA cadres are Soviet trained and therefore rather rigid in their response. Where did they learn to be so corrupt? Are we fighting on the wrong side?*

He put the diary down, exclaiming, "What an *epopée*, Ana. I had no idea that such large troops were committed to the region. My brother was a general!"

"I followed his exploits over the Cuban radio. That's about the time I came to Pasto."

Clayton continued, reading out loud.

*Atlantic Ocean, 6/1988*
*Here at sea, on the* Admiral Kuznetsov, *on our way back to Cuba. A Yankee submarine is trailing us, but they are afraid to fire torpedoes against us. The Soviet Union would take this action as a declaration of war. I miss Ana and the children immensely. It has been over two years. Will they recognize me? The wound on my face is healing slowly. Shrapnel that hit me in face and legs also destroyed several*

*teeth. The stalemate in Angola continues and Savimbi would have overrun the MPLA forces if it were not for our courageous soldiers. The Angolans don't want to fight and we were on the side of the weak hearted ones. I saw the most ferocious fighting of my military career. But this war is over for me. The malaria attacks continue, but the beauty and peace of the ocean are having a magical soothing power over my mind.*

Ana could no longer contain her tears. "I had already left for the *hacienda*, Clayton. What should I have done?'

"You did what you could."

"FARC had killed my father and I was deeply disillusioned with the guerrilla."

*Havana, 8/1988*

*We are received as heroes in Havana. Are we really? Fidel invited us all to Pinar del Rio to rest and train the new troops. Received a very sad letter from Ana Maria. She left Caguan and the FARC-controlled region. The welfare of our children was her principal concern. When will I see them again? I understand her decision. The health and safety of the children should be her first priority. But this does not dull the pain. The long and hopeful wait for them is over, leaving an emptiness that nothing, even the Revolution, can fill. I know that this is a weakness, and I have to overcome it. I have been a poor husband to Ana Maria, being married to the Revolution. Hopefully she will find peace and quiet in the family hacienda of Pasto. However, I am afraid that the government--or worse, the paras--will prosecute her. Natasha and Ernesto, when will I see you again? You look so grown in the photograph that Ana Maria kindly sent me.*

"My God, he must have suffered a lot. I want to understand my brother better. We were always so close."

"I see how much he loved all of us, Clayton. But his Communism was first."

"His generation of leaders always put the family second."

""Just like you businessmen."

"*Touché*," Clayton said in jest, feigning a sword wound to his heart.

Ana Maria asked him what they should do with the diaries. It was important to preserve them. Clayton immediately suggested photocopying all the volumes.

"That's a splendid idea. You're certainly the practical one in the family."

"Somebody needs to have some sense, Ana. All of you are bleeding heart liberals." He laughed. "I'll get everything typed and published."

"But we have to save the Yanomami first," she said.

"Absolutely yes! I am working on a plan."

That night, as he read Paulo's diary, he wondered what had led his brother to return to Colombia, after the exhausting Angola war, when he could have stayed in Cuba as a hero. He could have lived in dignity and comfort. Was it his love for Ana Maria and his children? Was it the hope of being, somehow, somewhere, reunited with them?

*San Vicente del Caguan, Colombia, 4/1993*
*Back in the jungle, strengthening the FARC. We walked for two days on a narrow trail. There is little fighting these days, and mostly verbal exchanges between*

*Comandante Marulanda and President Betancourt. The paramilitary organizations do most of the killing. They murdered hundreds of peasants that sympathized with our cause.*

*Nevertheless, I will continue my struggle. I will keep the sermon that I made in 1974, in the Bolivian bus. This is why I am still here, walking through this jungle. So that Indian women are no longer slapped by Spanish men. Never again. I remember with great admiration the last moments of Che Guevara, when he was taken prisoner in Bolivia. His rifle had been shot out of his hand and he was deeply weakened by asthma. He called for the schoolteacher. When she came, he told her that in the future, students would study in real schools, not in thatch huts. Then, he pointed out some spelling mistakes on the board. He knew his last hour was nearing but nevertheless had one bit of inspirational advice to give. She should teach the students so that they would become free.*

There it was again, his undaunting admiration for Che Guevara. Clayton remembered his student days in Belo Horizonte. He would find secret copies of Che's writings in Marco Aurelio's room, and often his brother would talk about his idol. His father had once ripped the Che poster from his room, shouting that he would not harbor any subversives in his house. He severely criticized Marco Aurelio for growing a curved mustache, calling him Mao Tse Tung. At which Marco Aurelio would answer in an insolent manner that Mao did not have a mustache, that he was actually emulating Ho Chi Min.

*Colombia, 4/2001*

*Thousands of members of the Patriotic Union, the po-*
*litical arm of the Colombian Left, have been killed in the*
*past years. The little hope that existed for a political solution*
*is gone. FARC was never a radical organization, but we*
*realize now that the right-wing paramilitary organizations*
*will never accept the Left. FARC will only survive through*
*armed struggle. We are hidden deep in the jungle and are to-*
*tally inaccessible to the government and paramilitary troops.*
*The landed gentry of Colombia and the bourgeoisie will nev-*
*er freely give up their corrupt and exploitative means. The*
*urban Left, which prided itself at being civilized, has been*
*decimated. However, I do not agree with Marulanda's ways*
*or with FARC's methods. Fidel Castro executed one of his top*
*generals, a revolutionary hero, for getting involved in the*
*drug trade. The winds of war are blowing the revolutionar-*
*ies and drug cartel too close together in Colombia.*

*We are formulating separate plans, and I will move to*
*the Oriente Province with a small cadre of companions that*
*remain loyal to the ideals of Che Guevara, Fidel Castro,*
*and the Cuban revolution. We will not compromise our*
*principles for political gains. Our victory would be tainted.*
*We have the support of Fidel Castro, who will be sending*
*us weapons, ammunition, and reinforcements. We plan to*
*establish a strong presence in Oriente and then march to-*
*wards Bogotá. FARC will continue operating from its head-*
*quarters in San Vicente del Caguan. We have one last joint*
*operation planned in the Guaiania region.*

His disillusionment with FARC was clear. Then, there was
a second-to-last entry in the diary. Clayton felt a strange

emotion in his heart, as if he was following his brother to his martyrdom.

> *San Vicente del Caguan, 7/2002*
> *The malaria monkeys are back and weaken me, and I have now spent two months under their influence, with a few intervals of relief from the fevers. My molar aches horribly, and I need to have it taken out. The compañeros moved to Esperanza, and need help. Cannot go to FARC. They want to forget that we ever existed. We are a reminder of how guerrilla fighters should be. The Yanomami need my help and protection. They are the embodiment of pure, primitive communism. Everything, except tobacco and wives, is shared. They have existed here for millennia and will be displaced by this terribly disorganized and destructive development. As soon as they discover gold or some other mineral deposit on their land, they will be dispossessed. The Yanomami in Brazil are already in total decadence, with rampant alcoholism, prostitution, venereal disease, and widespread malaria. It happened very rapidly, in the period of ten years. I need to do something for them. Perhaps the missionaries from Ocamo can help. I know that I can count on Bonaparte.*

Clayton finally had found the answer. This complex man was looking for new challenges, new mountains to climb, new lions to kill. Modern industrial communism was dead, he finally realized it. His family was gone, and he accepted this. But he had discovered, in the hidden folds of the jungle, a fascinating reality. Small Indian tribes that needed protection from predatory civilization. They needed a paladin.

The painful realization came to Clayton that his brother was searching for another dream. He had found it shortly before his death, in the vanishing Amazon Indians. The dream for which he had given his life was about to be destroyed through the actions of SAMITRA. He, Clayton, his own brother, was playing a key role in this. He remembered their childhood together in Monlevade and the bond of loyalty that they had created. Later, life had separated them as they followed different paths. While Paulo pursued his heart, Clayton followed his senses. Cars, women, posh hotels, first class airline flights, food, liquor, and all the other luxuries of life fascinated him. But, somehow, this pursuit had led to a dead end. He had a drawer full of all the watches he ever dreamed of: Girard-Perregeux, Patek Philippe, Jaeger Le Coutre, Beaume & Mercier, and Rolex. He had driven and wrecked numerous cars –the same with women. He had been pampered in adulation by countless stewardesses, maîtres, and bellmen. All the expensive clothes and cigarettes… And yet, here was a yearning to do something else. It was Ana and all that she represented. To win her, he had to be determined.

When he fell asleep, the sun was starting to rise in the sky. He had a plan. A workable plan.

It was already hot when he awakened, the sun burning his face. He rose and walked out onto the patio. The servants brought coffee, milk and took the covers off fruit trays. Clayton felt energized as Ana greeted him.

"You look good this morning, Clayton," she said. "Must be the exercise and good food."

As she kissed him on the cheeks, he pulled her toward him. "I have a plan. But I need your help."

"Where do we start?"

"Book me the Cessna. I'll see what I can do in Caguan."

"Caguan? But the Yanomami are past Mitu, in the mouth of the Dog's Head."

"I need to check on something. Can we get a Xerox machine? First, I want to make copies of the diary."

"My office in Pasto has a good machine. I'll make the copies," she said. "But first, one hour of calisthenics. We work on your chest today."

"How about my dancing? I want to perfect my salsa."

"Clayton, I know what's on your mind." She kissed him lightly on the lips. "We have some work first. A couple more weeks and you will be ready."

The Cessna was ordered for three o'clock. They spent the rest of the morning copying the four volumes of the diary. It was clearly written and legible. Paulo had made drawings of his many campaigns, and even in his darkest hours showed an admirable sense of organization. The diaries were soiled and crimped, but had withstood the passage of years. Paulo, being rather methodical, had chosen the same paper for all the volumes. This extra strength waterproof paper was favored by geologists. He'd likely had the premonition that his diary would one day serve a greater goal, such as Che's diaries, which were his legacy. Unlike Che, Paulo related the general disillusionment of the guerrilla movement, as the world changed with the crumbling of communism and the economic expansion of Latin America. He realized that, in the end, the revolution came from the right, through a mixture of economic development, technological innovation, and enhanced communication. In Colombia, the revolution led by FARC had spiraled down by getting entangled with drug production and trade.

Clayton proudly read aloud some of the later passages confirming Paulo's belief that Capitalism was the solution for all the evils of the world.

*Berkeley, 8/2000*

*Been convalescing from my latest wounds and illnesses in Berkeley. The constant support and love provided by Natasha has been admirable. She is a student at Berkeley but still finds time to take me to doctors and dentists. I have the opportunity to rest and to reflect on the struggles of the past twenty years. The years have gone by so fast, I hardly noticed them. I am now over forty, the same age Che was when he went into Bolivia. Like Che, I feel that my body cannot endure the guerrilla hardship for much longer. Nevertheless, I will return. My troops await me, and the years of struggle in Nicaragua, Angola, and Colombia forged a bond that nothing, not even disillusionment, can destroy. In the end, we fight for the ones close to us. They are like my children.*

*I cannot avoid reflecting on the recent changes in Latin America and in the world. Communism, or this strange form of government that called itself communism, has suffered a great defeat in the Soviet Union. The balance of power has undoubtedly changed toward the US. It is clear that the introduction of the computer into the mainstream of society has resulted in enormous changes. The Soviet Union and the US were in a race without clear indication of victory. Vietnam, Angola, Cuba, and Nicaragua were a seesaw of battles without a clear victor. Indeed, the race would* have eventually led to mutual annihilation. Twenty thousand nuclear warheads, ten thousand pointed at the US and Europe, the remaining ones at the Soviet Union, would have ensured the entire extermination of these two nations. The silicon chip broke the impasse, and propelled Western nations into an acceleration of technological development that could not be matched by the centralized economies. Capitalism was the fertile ground in which innovation took place and grew. Silicon Valley, a few miles from here, was the battleground in which the Soviet Union bled to death. Not one shot was fired, but the defeat was devastating, the annihilation staggering. The New Revolution was born from the Chip.

I have seen how youth is connected globally via Internet. Natasha talks to friends in the most remote places, exploring exotic regions: Machu Picchu, Nepal, Namibia. They have an immense thirst for knowledge, a desire of experiencing other cultures, of adventure. This was also, to a large extent, the driving force behind my love affair with the Left, I must confess. The need to identify, myself, as a child, with the poor and destitute, created in me the impulse to seek simplicity and stoicism in life. The stoicism of Marcus Aurelius. The rejection of luxury and ostentation, on my part, was met by a doctrine that I embraced too readily: Marxism-Leninism. Are there alternatives? Yes.

Went to Cody's yesterday. Natasha and Adalgisa arranged an afternoon session with readings and autographs. Met numerous Berkeley Leftists. Somehow, I feel that they are out of touch with reality. They are perhaps a mirror that reflects my own reality. I have changed while they are frozen into the ideological pattern, into the beliefs of *their youth. They were surprised and hurt when I defended Pope John Paul II and his crusade against Communism. The Revolution started in the Gdansk shipyards and spread, like wildfire, through the Warsaw Pact countries. Lech Walesa and Wostija were the heroes of this second revolution. The results were disastrous for our struggle in Colombia. Cuba is in economic shambles. Russia can no longer support itself, let alone finance revolutions throughout the world.*

"Look, Ana, here is the passage where he recognizes, finally, that Communism is not economically competitive with Capitalism."

"Not so quick," Ana said. "Let me continue here." She took the diary and went on.

*Fidel Castro received John Paul II a few weeks ago, and I watched on TV the moving reception to the old Pope. Fidel hands back his flock to the Roman Catholic Church after forty years of bitter feud with it. Does he realize that the seeds of a new age, of an alternative to predatory capitalism and uncontrolled materialism lie in the Church? He did not take the communion. This would be an act of surrender, an act of cowardice. John Paul used his pulpit to launch some virulent criticism at the US, at the culture of death. He offered an alternative, the culture of life. Indeed, it is interesting that Wostija took the name John Paul. Paul, like I.*

"He seemed to be gravitating toward the Church, Clayton."

"As a child, he was very devoted. His nanny, Alaide, instilled in him a deep faith."

"Marco Aurelio, why couldn't you just live? Did you have to take upon yourself the suffering of all the destitute?" Ana Maria exclaimed, her voice breaking in despair.

They were moved by this passage, and Ana Maria had tears in her eyes that Clayton kindly wiped, as he controlled his own emotion.

Paulo's clear mind went much beyond the travails of the jungle, the day-to-day grind of guerrilla warfare. This was evident in a 1998 Berkeley entry

> *I am also re-reading Teilhard de Chardin, the vision-ary Christian philosopher and anthropologist. As I do this, I revisit my early adulthood, before the virus of Marxism took over my body and soul. He was the first to feel and define " Complexity." We are in constant evolution, from simple to more complex systems. Caught in the whirlwind, we cannot escape this universal force. It is omnipresent and omniscient, and will drive us to Point Omega, Chardin's God. Marxism is dead, and we have to move on.*

At last, Ana prepared three packages. One was sent to an address in Rio de Janeiro, Brazil. Clayton addressed one to a trusted secretary that also served as part-time lawyer, Laura Couto, with instructions to type the manuscript, which was written in Portuguese. It also had instructions for her to translate it into English and Spanish, two languages in which Laura was fluent.

"I'd bet she has many skills," said Ana Maria.

"Don't remind me," he said, somewhat annoyed.

"And if anything happens to me, she will send the copies to a good publisher that I know, Editora Globo. I know its

VP for Finance very well. The proceeds of the royalties will go to a foundation to help the Yanomami."

"Clayton, you're becoming an admirable human being."

"The memory and inspiration of Marco Aurelio is having its effect."

They sent the second copy to Natasha's address in Berkeley.

"And you'll put the original in a tin box, seal it, and bury it in a well-protected place under your house," Clayton said. "Tell Felizmundo to burrow a hole in the floor in one of the rooms and reseal it."

"Why all this care?"

"The FARC would give everything to destroy this document. It incriminates them in a very bad manner."

"The third copy can be kept in the hacienda, so that I can finish reading it," Ana said. "We are the only two people here that know about this. The legacy of Paulo is safe now."

When Clayton arrived in Caguan that evening, it was raining heavily. The few roads were covered with mud. He was informed that Soto Mayor had left two days ago, and that he would be back in one month. Apparently, his mother was very ill in Cali and he needed to spend the last days with her. Clayton drove to the barracks the next day but could not get any further information. For security reasons, Soto Mayor's address could not be given. Clayton had expected this. But he needed to be sure. Now, there was only one possible solution.

# CHAPTER FOURTEEN

S oto Mayor walked the back streets of Cali, looking around in amazement. These were the same streets through which he ran as a teenager, bumping into people and robbing their wallets, twenty years ago. Except that, in those days he was not yet Colonel Soto Mayor but Mono, a street urchin with more smarts than his buddies. Every now and then he saw a familiar face, only twenty years older. He was home again, but did not miss the oppressive heat, pollution burning his eyes, and multitude of fetid smells of the street. He had made it out of this latrine, and would one day be Governor of the Province of Caquetá. Yes, he, Mono. They called him Mono because of his monkey-like features and small simian ears. But he had become Colonel Soto Mayor, an important commander of the FARC, trusted assistant of General Lopez. He had proven himself, and the supreme commander of FARC, the elusive Manuel Marulanda Velez, had plans for him.

He had graduated from small-time pickpocket to runner for the Cali cocaine cartel. His faithful and dedicated service had been rewarded by a promotion. He was sent to the Oriente to supervise production and refining. Infiltrating the FARC had been a natural and necessary move. FARC controlled the territory and wanted a cut in the deal.

Gradually, he became more FARC and less Cali. The Cali organization was responsible for exporting. General Lopez had promoted him to Captain first and then to Colonel. The years had passed and the organization had grown. Soto Mayor had proved his worth in the interminable dealings between FARC and the drug cartels. He had been in battle a few times, and had shown courage, although this was not his forte. It was a dangerous business, and Soto Mayor knew that the laws of probability were working against him. One day he would be killed. Either in battle against the government or paramilitary troops or by a disgruntled coke dealer. This was a good time to get out of the business.

Eugenio de Morais' proposition was a good one, and the four hundred and fifty thousand dollars, added to another five hundred thousand stashed away, would be enough to ensure a quiet retirement. Not in Colombia. Miami, perhaps. His cousins loved it there, and he would find peace on the white sands of Key Biscayne. With one million dollars he could get himself a good young woman, an apartment, a nice American car, and all the spoils that capitalism offers.

As he walked, he recognized Calle Veneto, where he turned. He stopped by a large colonial door with fine carvings. He ran his fingers through the iron buttons that resembled nipples. He remembered them. The door had the abandoned and decadent look of old faded glory. In his childhood, Servando and he would stop, admire the fine carvings of mermaids, run their hands over the iron nipples, and dream of beautiful women that they would have, one day. He rang the bell a few times until a black lady opened a small window.

"*¿Quien es?*"

"I am Mono Lopez. Does Servando Garcia still live here?"

"Let me see."

She returned after a few minutes. He could hear her feet shuffling along the floor.

"What was the name of your soccer team?"

"Cruz Azul, and Servando was the goalkeeper. I was right wing."

She left again in her slow shuffle and returned after what seemed to be an interminable time.

"Please come in, *Señor*. I have to check you out."

She searched him thoroughly then led him through a maze of hallways, and up a flight of stairs. In this old colonial house, the downstairs looked dilapidated. It was only upstairs that he saw the presence of people. He entered a dimly lit living room. A man sat in a dark corner. He slowly got up and walked toward him with a limp. For one moment they stared at each other, and then exchanged an effusive hug.

"Mono, where is your hair?" Garcia said, visibly moved.

"Cacorro, did you have a soccer accident?"

Garcia took another good look at Soto Mayor, and shook his head in dismay.

"Those were good times, Mono, our best times. We could've won the championship of Cali."

"If it weren't for your work at the goal."

"Don't remind me, Mono. But you guys didn't score any goals either!"

They sat down and reminisced. Garcia sent the maid to fetch a few beers, and they only slowed down after an hour. They were good friends, almost brothers. Soto Mayor had learned that Garcia had been wounded in a fight between the Cali and Cartagena cartels. He had been hit in the leg and intestines, and had almost lost his life.

"And what do you do now, Cacorro?"

"I just use my old connections and help people out. Odd jobs, you know. My days of fighting in the street are over. And then, I have a wife and two daughters. What about you, my friend?"

Soto Mayor confided in him about his new identity and responsibilities.

"A colonel, Mono, a colonel! Who would have ever thought? With your ugly monkey face. But you were always smart and determined. And you never enjoyed sniffing cocaine."

"It makes me too nervous, too jittery. It's like having too much coffee," he said. "But I don't argue with taste, and some people love it, especially the gringos."

"God bless them, Mono. If it weren't for them, we could only sell it to the Indians. And they have no money," he exclaimed, lifting his glass and making a toast.

"To the gringos, and may they sniff more and more cocaine."

They laughed. Then, Garcia asked, "But what brings you here, my friend? I doubt that it is my beautiful brown eyes."

Soto Mayor presented his plan. He needed fifteen determined men for one week. The pay was good. Each one would receive $10,000. He also needed weapons and ammunition. It was a quick job in the Oriente province.

"It can be arranged, Mono. But what will your good friend get?"

"How much do you need, Cacorro? I mean, your share? You need to bring me the best fifteen men, plus weapons and plenty of ammunition."

"How about $30,000?"

Soto Mayor wanted to negotiate, but knew that Cacorro needed the money. Honor among thieves, he thought, looking at his friend's tired face. They had been raised together in these dangerous streets. They had sniffed the same glue, buggered the same boys, fucked the same whores, and stolen the same wallets. Cacorro would bump the fellow and Mono would extract the wallet. They were a good team. He looked at his friend, a tired and wounded man, and offered his hand.

"OK, my friend, for old time's sake. I'll give you $40,000. But where are you going to get the guys?"

"Leave that to me," Garcia said, with pride in his voice. "I will give you the best and most reliable men. They all have their own weapons. Assault rifles and pistols. A couple of machine guns. I will also get you hand grenades, just in case. How big is the tribe?"

"About seventy, eight or ten families. They have a few shotguns. Other than that, bows and arrows."

For one moment, a cloud of suspicion came over Garcia.

"But why don't you use the FARC soldiers?"

"Because General Lopez would want a major cut in the deal and I just want to get the hell out of Cali and retire in Miami."

"Ah, Miami…"

Soto Mayor acquiesced, looking out through the dirty window over the roofs of the houses, full of antennas. The sky was gray with pollution and the city noise was not abated by the oncoming night. He looked at Garcia and could see that he also dreamed for one brief moment. Clean cities, wide highways, cold air conditioning, huge stores, peace and quiet. Some place where his daughters could grow up safe. Where he could bathe his tired and beaten body in warm ocean waters. But Soto Mayor knew that Miami was too lofty a dream for Garcia.

"Perhaps Santa Marta, Cacorro. You'll be happy there." Then, Soto Mayor told him that, if he cut out General Lopez from the deal and used FARC operatives, Lopez would eventually discover it. And he would be killed for it. But out of here, Cali, he could operate with impunity.

"And are you going with the guys?"

"Absolutely, I'll be their commander."

Garcia was impressed. "Mono, you can stay here until I assemble the force. It's safer than a hotel."

"How much money do you need, Cacorro? And how much time?"

"I'll let you know tomorrow. How about transportation?"

"Can you help with that too?"

"Of course. This is an important component of our business." He winked. "Maria, prepare a room for our guest and tell Leticia to get our dinner ready."

Old Maria walked down the hallway, dragging her tired legs.

# CHAPTER FIFTEEN

Natasha and Rerebawa took one of his cousins with them and Ruwahiwa, in addition to the Haximu boys that had just arrived from the settlement. The Indians carried baskets full of smoked meat and cassava bread. It took the group over two hours to arrive at what Ushubiriwa hoped would one day become Ushubiriwa-Teri. Natasha was by now used to these "short" jungle walks. As her physical condition improved, her Doc Martens boots looked more and more worn. Nevertheless, they were proving their worth in the Amazon, and she realized that they were more than funk rock attire; they were sturdy and comfortable boots. She knew that poor shoes would be disastrous in the Amazon.

As they approached an opening in the forest, they saw a plantain garden. Ushubiriwa's group had settled into one of the temporary Haximu camps and begun turning into their village. They had started to build a new *shabono*. Natasha could hear the coughing as they approached the hut. A fetid and squalid scene awaited them. The small group was, for the most part, lying in their hammocks. Walking into the hut, Natasha found a seven-year child. The girl's face was covered with pustules and her enormous eyes stared at her, full of pain and fear. As she looked around, she felt a welling of tears, which she controlled. The children, too weak to go to the garden, had simply defecated everywhere. She first went to an older man who had painfully risen from his hammock. Rerebawa served as interpreter. He had learned Spanish at the Ocama Mission and was a bright fellow. She turned to him, asking, "Ushubiriwa?" Rerebawa nodded.

"I am Shaki's wife and he sent me here to help you."

"Shaki is a good person, he is *waiteri*," the old man said.

Natasha instructed her helpers to clean up the place, while she quickly assessed the situation. She realized how terrible a disease the measles was. Most of the Ushubiriwa group had the characteristic rashes, with varying degrees of pestilence. Some of the children had blood in their stool as well as blood coming from their mouth. Bonaparte had told her that these pimple-like eruptions on the skin were only the tip of the iceberg. She went from hammock to hammock and assessed each case, peering inside the mouths. In many cases she clearly saw the sores, called *Koplik's* spots. She knew that they could spread to the throat and lungs, and the coughing she heard was an indication that in some cases the disease had already spread. She counted the total number of sick: six adults and five children. Two of the women, both Ushubiriwa's wives, were pregnant. She prepared a large jug of milk and started to feed the kids, after administering the first dose of antibiotic. She knew that they would not cure the measles virus, but would combat the secondary infections. Bonaparte had given her some specific instructions.

"Here in the Amazon, we quickly become doctors if we want to survive," he had said, only half in jest.

After feeding the group, she instructed her helpers to go to the garden, collect and roast plantains for the sick. They were so weak that they had neglected to eat. All this work consumed several hours. When nightfall came, she prepared several fires to keep the sick warm. It had rained in the afternoon: the first rains of the wet season were pouring down, drenching everything. This would not help matters. It was a difficult night, moist and cold. One of the children, the girl she had first seen, did not make it. Frustrated, she burst into tears as the wailing of the women announced that Yarima had died. Finally, a couple of hours before sunrise, she collapsed from exhaustion into the hammock that Rerebawa had prepared for her. The sun was already high when she woke up, guilty that she had slept. The pained eyes of Yarima haunted her. She had let her down. She had let her die.

"Tokibuti, we have to give the medicine," Rerebawa said, reminding her of her duties. She was surprised at her new nickname. Yanomami were famous for giving strange nicknames. Curious, she asked what it meant.

"Corn cob, because of your white hair."

She was relieved that they did not choose something scatological, like Lézard's or other infamous ones.

They went to work. The sick showed some improvement. She repeated the milk feeding to the children. The little faces were becoming individuals, as she gradually learned their names, one by one. There was a first smile and a first little hand touching her hair. After this, she busied herself preparing food for the entire group. She sent Ruwahiwa hunting and gathering peach palm fruits. Hopefully he would expand their food stocks.

She also noticed that, in spite of the terrible condition, their mouths were full of tobacco leaves. She ordered everyone to spit them out, especially the children. It shocked her to know that at Haximu-Teri all of them, even the children, were addicted to tobacco. She had seen Bonaparte smoking and thought that he approved of their vice. He had explained to her that they treasured their tobacco and that it was a constant source of worry and trades. She had also noticed how he took part in it. Since he had run out of packaged cigarettes, he now manufactured them with Yanomami tobacco, which he traded for hooks and other things.

Over the following days, Natasha and her helpers worked zealously in the village. Unfortunately one of the women, a pregnant wife of Ushubiriwa, also passed away. But the remainder of the group gradually improved as the antibiotics started to work. The skin and mouth infections decreased and the disease receded. Ruwahiwa had returned with a basket full of peach palm nuts and they cooked them, making a strong and oily potion that was highly nutritious. Natasha sent Rerebawa back to Haximu-Teri and he returned with a helper and two loads of food. The differences had been forgotten in view of the tragedy. Apparently the wife that had cheated on Ushubiriwa was the one that had died. They all felt vindicated and peace was on the way to being re-established.

Natasha finally had time to reflect on her actions over the past few days. She was fulfilled by her role and felt, correctly, that she had saved their lives. Ushubiriwa's clan was grateful to her and treated her with great deference given to a shaman. She also realized that the Yanomami had other serious medical problems: malaria, *onchocerciasis*, a debilitating infection of the eyes, and feet jiggers were among the most prominent. Many of the kids had distended bellies, a sign of malnutrition and parasites. Malaria was particularly dangerous, and Bonaparte had told her that it was endemic throughout the basins of the Orinoco and Negro rivers.

Ten days after she arrived, she received a visit from Bonaparte. His ribs had by now healed sufficiently for him to walk without too much discomfort. They had to brace against the afternoon rains, which now came with regularity and increased intensity.

"I've got good news for you, Natasha. Your mother received the diaries. And she knows that you are well." He paused for a moment. "Your uncle's in Colombia. He's trying to smooth out things with FARC."

"This means a lot to me, Professor."

"I've read the entries in the diary. It's difficult for me to say whether we anthropologists have triggered the wars among the Yanomami, or whether we were simply drawn into the melee. We got involved, willingly or not, into the whirlwind of events."

Natasha knew what he meant. As an anthropologist, he was only supposed to observe the unfolding of events. She vaguely remembered a physics course that she had taken where the professor described the uncertainty principle.

It stated that the measurement always modified the experiment. Bonaparte's situation was similar. His presence among the Yanomami changed their future. But how could this be controlled?

"We have hearts and emotions, Professor. These, in the end, determine our actions."

"I entered Brazil to help these people. And we have, by hook and crook, done the job. But you were my salvation. These people owe their lives to you."

# CHAPTER SIXTEEN

Clayton had a cozy feeling as they drove from Pasto to the hacienda. It felt like coming back home, and Ana Maria's enthusiasm when she hugged him at the airport filled his heart with warmth, his body with expectation. The twitchy feeling would not go away and he knew what he had to do: conquer her heart. But there were urgent matters to discuss and resolve. He had made up his mind and the plan was unfolding.

"We need to act quickly, Ana. We have only a couple of weeks," he said at last. "The Yanomami are in great danger."

"How do you know this?"

He reflected for a moment, and then decided to reveal the truth – at least the part that did not incriminate him.

"My company wants to exploit the mineral resources of the Macava Mountain, where the Yanomami live."

"And what does this have to do with their well being?"

"It's a long story, but I know that they have hired a group of people to get rid of them. Something to do with the title to the land."

"My God, that's horrible, Clayton," she said, turning to him in anger. "You know that Natasha is there. She is in danger and we have to do something right away!"

When they arrived at the *hacienda*, the table was already set. Clayton had a good feeling about the place. The two dogs looked at him with some contentment and one of them even wagged its tail.

"I have a plan that I want to discuss with you," Clayton said, at the end of dinner. " Send the servants away."

He told Ana Maria his plan. She discussed several aspects with him, using her experience. "I leave in three days," he finally said. "Do you think we can get the weapons and ammunition we need?"

"I'll see what I can do." She grabbed the bell and rang for the servants. "Eduardo, my foreman, takes care of our weapons. We have four FAL rifles and five AK47s. Enough to defend ourselves from small-armed groups. But I don't think we have a lot of ammunition. And no hand grenades, for sure."

Clayton gazed deeply into Ana Maria's eyes. She smiled. "You've come a long way, Clayton. I admire your determination and -- what should I say -- your sneakiness?"

" How about my business acumen?"

He laughed good-naturedly, caressed her hand and continued: "It's for a good cause. And my business background prepared me for this."

"This will be dangerous, Clayton. Are you sure that we'll come through it?"

"If the plan works, we'll be back in two weeks and Marco Aurelio's last wishes will have been fulfilled."

He knew that the moment was right. He felt in charge.

"Let's go for a walk in the garden," he said. " I am not ready to sleep."

He took her hand and they walked out, feeling the summer warmth penetrating their bodies. The jasmines exhaled a perfume that permeated the entire garden. He felt her shoulder rubbing his as they walked. Her hand was warm. He stopped and looked at her.

"I feel reborn, cleansed of my old weaknesses. And I owe this to you."

Ana was moved. Suddenly, she seemed like a young girl, on her first date. Clayton pressed himself against her as he held her shoulder with his other hand, his groin swelling. They kissed slowly and gently, then with passion. As he kissed her, his hand moved from the shoulder to her breasts, which he caressed. He could feel Ana surrendering to his advances and knew that she would be his this night.

"The servants... They'll see us, Clayton," she whispered.

"Can't we go to your room? I promise I will not force myself on you."

"I ... don't know. This is all so strange..."

Then, she kissed him once more, pressing herself against him.

"Come, let's go," she said.

They walked down the hallway separately and Ana checked for any stray servants. Then she motioned him in. She locked the door behind her as he grabbed her from behind, pressing himself against her derrière. Then, he gently removed her dress and bra. He did this in a smooth manner, like a skilled *Carioca* he was. Soon they were both naked. Tears ran down Ana's face as she embraced Clayton.

A couple of hours later, Clayton sat in the garden and watched the sky filled with millions of stars. He had never seen a sky like that. It was a virgin sky, free from any reflections, free to show its mantle of mystery to those that ventured to look up and dream. This sky was being offered to him now. Now and perhaps forever.

Then, two hands came from behind and gently caressed his chest.

"You have a wife and two kids, Clayton. I can't continue this."

"What do you mean?"

"You can be a good, a very good man. But I can't -- "

"I don't mean much to Karin," he interrupted. "She is wrapped up in her life of luxury. Right now, her greatest concern is remodeling our apartment. She's hired three architects. Her parents have been staying with her for four months."

"What about your daughters?"

"They are following in their mom's footsteps. Karina and Sabrina have their nannies. All they care about are their parties and their dolls."

"You shouldn't have let this happen."

"Fuck them, Ana, fuck them all. Fuck that rotten Rio." He felt suddenly free as he filled his lungs with the fresh air of the night.

# CHAPTER SEVENTEEN

Soto Mayor had grown bored, being locked up in Garcia's house. They had agreed that he would not wander around, in order not to arouse suspicion from the government police. The government was at war with FARC, and it was not wise to be parading around Cali. Worse than the government were the paramilitary organizations. They were more determined and less bureaucratic. They had killed thousands of Leftists. The term was applied in a broad sense and included anyone that they did not like.

He spent the time reading the newspapers that Maria brought and watching soccer and bullfights on TV. Leticia was a good cook, and wasn't bad looking either. He had put some moves on her, but with limited success. He had groped her a few times in the kitchen, but she had been able to extricate herself from his advances without appearing to be rude. She knew how to handle these horny men.

She had dealt with them all her life, while managing to keep her job. It was a tough balancing act.

After two days, Garcia returned with two men. They introduced themselves as Rigoberto and Julio Cesar. Rigoberto, a tall mulatto in his mid-thirties, had a charming smile that radiated warmth. Julio Cesar was short and pudgy, with strong Indian features. Serious, he always looked at the floor, avoiding eye contact, as if the truth came through the eyes, as if truth burned.

They sat at the table and presented their credentials. Rigoberto, a former Army sergeant, had been expelled for theft of weapons and now made a living as a bodyguard, messenger, and any other activity that required a strong and determined fighter. Julio Cesar was a former boxer who had turned to petty and not so petty crime; he had worked for the Cali cartel for several years. Soto Mayor gave a brief overview of his plan. Then, they discussed strategy and logistics.

"We need more than fifteen people, *Señor* Mono. Twenty."

Soto Mayor quickly calculated his loss of income: fifty thousand dollars more.

"And we need $20,000 each, because we are sergeants."

Seventy thousand dollars more. His profit was shrinking. He would take it out of de Morais' hide. Soto Mayor scratched his head. Rigoberto and Julio Cesar had a point. A large force would give them greater security. Seventy Indians was a big job. On top of it, they had to carry them away from the village and bury them all. This was an important part of the plan.

The two sergeants were put in charge of getting nine people each. They knew that they had to be reliable.

"They'll get $1,000 at sign up. Then $4,000 more before leaving, and the rest on return. Is that OK?" Soto Mayor asked.

"That seems OK." Garcia nodded. "I have arranged transportation for us. Two Cessna Caravans."

"Where do we leave from?"

"We'll meet at Escobar's *estancia*. It has a private airfield. The Colombian Air Force won't bother us because they think it's a regular drug run from the Medellin cartel."

He told Rigoberto and Julio Cesar, "We'll move our guys to the *estancia* over the next week."

"We'll need to train," Soto Mayor said.

"Our guys are well trained and competent, Mono," Rigoberto said.

Soto Mayor shook his head. "I command this operation and dictate the terms." He noticed that Rigoberto was clearly displeased. He was the type of soldier that didn't like to take bullshit from officers.

"OK, *Comandante*. As you wish," Julio Cesar said. He apparently noticed the rage building in Rigoberto.

Soto Mayor looked at Julio Cesar approvingly. Rigoberto seemed a little too feisty, too self-assured. But he had handled tougher cookies before.

"How about weapons?" Garcia asked.

"Each participant is responsible for his own weapons and ammunition. They need to have at least a rifle with two hundred bullets. I will check every gun at the *estancia*."

Rigoberto rolled his eyes, then shrugged. "You're the boss, you're paying the bill. I don't know why we need so many bullets."

"Have you ever fought in the jungle? It's quite different than the back streets of Cali. And another thing. Each soldier will need a backpack with food and other essentials. Mr. Garcia will purchase backpacks and plastic pouches."

Rigoberto scowled. "Are we going on an expedition or what? This is a small job, three days only. I could do this with a bottle of water and a baseball bat."

"If you're prepared for the worst, you have a much better chance. Remember, I am the commander of this expedition and I want to ensure that it's successful and that we all come back without any problems."

Soto Mayor knew that things could go terribly wrong in the jungle. They would be hundreds of miles from the closest town and had to be prepared for any surprises. He also knew that city folks had a rude adjustment in the jungle.

After the pair left, Soto Mayor expressed his concern to Garcia.

"Cacorro, this Rigoberto is a little too cocky."

"Don't worry, Mono. He's very courageous and self-assured. I'll talk to him. He is popular with the men. He'll settle down."

"When do we move to the *estancia?*"

"In another couple of days. We should be ready to fly to the *Oriente* in ten days. I have already ordered two Cessna Caravan 675s. They'll fit eleven passengers each. They want $10,000 each to take you there and pick you up."

Soto Mayor was not happy. However, he had no choice. He quickly calculated that the total cost was now up to $260,000. His initial plan had $180,000 allocated for expenses. This still left him with a profit of $190,000. He would talk to de Morais about jacking up the fee. He needed to net $400,000.

"Cacorro, I need twenty-five of each: backpacks, flashlights, water bottles, compasses, plastic ponchos, uniforms, pairs of boots. We need two pairs of thick socks for each soldier. Plus three GPS units. We also need two picks, three shovels, and two axes for the demolition work. Here is the food and the medical supplies list."

"My, my, you have grown organized at FARC."

"Don't forget that I am a colonel now. I recognize that organization leads to results."

"Mono, I can't argue with you. The future governor of the Caquetá Province has to practice his skills."

"The future Miami entrepreneur."

Garcia spent the next couple of days transporting the troops to the *estancia*. He had gathered all the equipment from camping stores throughout Cali, being careful not to buy everything at one store, in order not to arouse any suspicion. He had rented a Toyota Landcruiser for this, and Pablo had made available an entire wing of the house for the troops.

When all was in place, he picked up Soto Mayor and brought him to the *estancia*. During the drive up, he discussed the details of the training program with his old friend, who listened attentively.

"You know, Mono, this is why I always remain a small time operator. You have developed organizational skills."

"Cacorro, I've learned one lesson. The Roman Army conquered the entire civilized world through organization and discipline. So did the Mongols!"

"Becoming a historian, Mono? Who'd have thought? But you always liked to read. Remember the comic books we used to steal? I'd talk to the vendor and you'd snatch the books from under his nose. Perhaps they've taught you something useful."

"In the jungle we have lots of time. And, yes, I became somewhat of a historian. In the modern US Army training and doctrine are most important. The Yankees call it TRADOC."

Garcia smiled. "They'll come after you guys soon."

"I'll be in Miami."

"So, what's the plan?"

"I'll transform this group of twenty men into a disciplined fighting machine. I've only got three days, but I'll use them well."

"Just like our soccer days, when you coached us, Mono. But we lost the last game."

"Not this time, Cacorro. I'll make sure."

That evening, he summoned his two sergeants and gave them detailed instructions. "I want the men in uniform, lined up outside, at 7 a.m. sharp. Check their backpacks and guns."

Julio Cesar was puzzled and said, "I thought we were just going to shoot up an Indian village."

"That's where you're mistaken. You're going on a military operation that will last six days. The first goal is to completely eliminate the tribe: men, women, and children. Nobody can escape. The second goal is to bury the corpses, burn down the village and remove all traces. And remember your name: Julio Cesar, one of the greatest generals of all time."

"I see. But my men know how to shoot like nobody else."

"But they don't know how to get there, how to organize themselves, and how to get out. That is my responsibility, as commander of this operation."

He taped a large piece of paper to the wall and proceeded to describe the operation, using crayons with different colors.

"We'll penetrate their territory, surround the village at night, close the noose in the early hours, and start the clean-up operation at sunrise. By 8 a.m., we'll have concluded it. At 10 a.m. all the bodies will be collected, counted, and marked. Being the rainy season, we cannot burn them. It might be impossible to find dry firewood. We bury them some distance from the village. At 12 noon we start burning the village. If it's raining, we'll disassemble the large Indian hut to make it appear uninhabited for a long time. At 4 p.m. we start our return march. We walk for two hours of daylight and continue throughout the night. The Cessnas will arrive at the airfield in the morning, and we'll be back at the *estancia* by evening. Understood?"

Rigoberto and Julio Cesar nodded. Soto Mayor felt that he was gaining their confidence. He needed to know that they would only operate under his orders. He gave them walkie-talkies and demonstrated how to operate them. Then, he explained the GPS operation.

"Tomorrow morning, I'll train the soldiers in the use of the compass. The jungle is unforgiving. A few steps off the trail and you're lost. Your guys are city slickers and you'll feel totally lost in the forest."

"Captain," Rigoberto said, "aren't you taking this too seriously?"

"You can call me *Colonel.*" Soto Mayor glared at him.

"Yes, colonel."

"Dismissed."

When Soto Mayor walked out at 6:55 a.m., resplendent in his new uniform, he found the troop getting ready in the yard. They tried on their boots, adjusted their uniforms, and fixed their backpacks. They were obviously not familiar with the equipment. A group of recruits, no doubt. But dangerous and well schooled recruits.

"Good morning, soldiers. You can call me Colonel Mono. You've been recruited for a rapid operation. I demand perfect coordination and your full discipline for the next seven days. We'll have three days of training, three days of travel, and one day of work."

As he spoke, he saw this disorganized group of recruits, uncomfortable in their fatigues and backpacks, staring at him with a broad range of expressions, ranging from surprise to approval to utter disbelief.

"I'll take all steps necessary to get us there and bring us back without any losses. The jungle is difficult and dangerous, I have to warn you."

He looked at their expressions, which ranged from surprise to contempt. "You'll receive one thousand dollars now, four thousand in three days, and five thousand dollars in seven days. If we lose any of you, the money will go to a designated person. Please give the name and address of that person to your sergeant."

There was approval from all.

"I am taking all the necessary steps to bring us back alive and well. This can only be accomplished with discipline. First, I'll teach you to use the compass." The sergeants distributed the compasses and Soto Mayor began the training, methodically and diligently. He knew that he would gradually gain their confidence.

The afternoon was spent with weapons and equipment checks.

That evening, he organized a maneuver, simulating the formation of a semi-circle closing upon a point at the shore of the lagoon. There were several protests, but the operation was carried out in the woods surrounding the *estancia*. It was a total failure; half the soldiers got lost, flashlights were turned on, people fell into holes. Soto Mayor was furious. The next morning, he gathered the men and patiently discussed the various weaknesses. He made sure that each soldier understood where he had failed. He did not rail them, but explained that this was a learning process. They would repeat the operation again the second night.

"The Indian village is on the shore of a creek. We'll come from behind and form a semi-circle. Each one of us will move to within one hundred yards. At dawn we advance into shooting position and attack."

He introduced important changes in the plan. Rather than having the soldiers move separately, they would go in groups of five. Each group would position itself at a few hundred yards from the convergence point. At first light, they would fan out and form a semi-circle. Then they would converge.

The troop rested until two a.m. and then started the second maneuver. This time they were more successful and were able to surround a point on the nearby lagoon without much noise. Soto Mayor warned them about the danger of shooting into each other, especially since they were forming a semi-circle. He made sure that each soldier knew where his zone of fire was.

The plan took shape and Soto Mayor was satisfied. That afternoon he organized a three-hour march, to check the endurance of the troop. There were problems and complaints. Foot blisters, lacerations in soft shoulders unaccustomed to backpacks, and other problems were patiently taken care of by the Colonel, who now had the pulse of the troop.

"Be expected to march for *six* hours in the forest. We will separate the two groups and keep them one hundred yards apart."

"But why, Colonel?" a soldier asked.

"If for any reason one group is attacked, the other can react. This is standard procedure in military operations."

By now the troop respected his experience and wisdom. Somehow they felt safe under his command. Soto Mayor knew that this was essential to the success. He was not worried about the troop finishing off the Indians. They were all experienced fighters. They knew about death: how to inflict it, how to avoid it. But they were ignorant of jungle laws.

On the third evening they trained again, marching through the forest at night. This time the exercise was done from 7 to 11 p.m., in total darkness. Soto Mayor was satisfied with the results.

The troop assembled again at 7 a.m. He checked all the backpacks, making sure that all soldiers carried two liters of water and food.

"We'll have dry rations during the operation. There is no time to cook."

He checked their weapons and confirmed that they all had sufficient ammunition –two hundred bullets.

At 8 a.m. the two Cessna Caravans arrived. They were larger versions of the three-passenger Cessnas, each fitting ten passengers plus the pilot. The planes had to accommodate an extra passenger, since they were twenty-two. They carefully balanced the load on the planes. Before takeoff, Soto Mayor met with the pilots and gave them the exact coordinates of the airstrip, as well as the description of the route. They would take the four-hour flight without refueling. It was too risky to land. The airplanes would wait for them in Mitu and pick them up at the Esperanza mining camp on Day 3 at 8:00 a.m. If the troop were not back by Day 3, they would return on Day 4, then on Day 7. If one of the planes had mechanical problems, the other would make two trips.

He watched each soldier as he climbed onto the plane, shaking his hand and saying, "Operation Yamo has started. Good luck."

# CHAPTER EIGHTEEN

As he flew to the Esperanza gold mining camp three days before the meeting date of October 14, Clayton pondered his gamble. Would it work? Was he asking too much? He knew that Ana Maria was in a difficult financial situation. The *hacienda* would be lost if she did not pay the large loan on it. He had not been able to see Soto Mayor in Caguan to call off the entire operation. Now, he would meet him at the Esperanza airstrip, as agreed. Soto Mayor would not back off. He would demand full payment. Clayton had a better plan.

The plane approached the narrow strip in the forest, barely visible from above. One wheel touched down, then the second, and at last the tail. After a bumpy ride, it stopped. He jumped out, feeling the hot sticky air. He filled his lungs with it, and euphoria swept through him. This was the jungle. Why not? Go for it all.

He moved hastily toward the old mining camp. The pilot had passed over it. Paulo's old guard had been alerted and was waiting for him.

Before he reached the camp, he met Natasha on the trail. She had come to greet him. She looked tired with dark circles under her eyes. Her arms were covered with mosquito bites. She wore jeans and a long-sleeved camouflage shirt, the sleeves rolled up. On her shoulder she carried a holster with a pistol: the Beretta 9 mm that her mother had given her. Yet, Clayton could not keep from noticing that, under this military outfit, she was a woman. She reminded him so much of Ana Maria. She hugged him, and he noticed her blue eyes. Marco Aurelio's eyes. They had the same clear and intelligent expression. Eyes that looked at the world with pure intentions.

"Uncle Clayton, I waited so long for this moment," she said with emotion. "I'm so relieved that you came to help us."

He suggested that they return to the airstrip to make sure the supplies and weapons had been unloaded. As they walked he quickly appraised the situation.

"We have to do something right away, Uncle Clayton. We have to move the Haximu village immediately."

"I hadn't thought of this, but you're right. But where and how?"

"I'll return to Haximu -Teri and we'll get Dr. Bonaparte, Kaobawa, and Bakotawa involved. There are several camps within a day's walk."

"We'll take care of Soto Mayor from here."

"I'm sure the Yanomami can also help."

"They have, what, just a couple shotguns? What can they do?"

"They'd love to get in on the action," she said, and Clayton could see the fire in her eyes. He remembered Marco Aurelio in Monlevade. They were planning another attack through the woods, but this time everything was for real. People would die.

"Natasha, I never imagined that you could get involved in this mess."

"Nor did I, but I'll do everything to save these people. You don't know the hardship they just went through."

The pilot had unloaded the plane and was ready to leave. Now, they had to rally the *compañeros*.

Natasha led the way to the mining camp. When they arrived, she asked Caetano to gather the troops. Soon they stood in front of the shacks, in their usual formation. Natasha then spoke.

"*Compañeros* of my father, this is a solemn moment. As I told you last time, my father's last wishes were that the Indians, the true owners of this land, be protected. You have fought for justice in the jungles of Nicaragua, on the plains of Angola, and in these forests. I call upon you for one last mission: to defend the Yanomami. We know that an attack on them is being planned. This attack will begin in three days. I come to you to ask you to fight for my father one last time. Comandante Paulo's brother is here with us and will provide the details of the impending force that was hired to strike the Haximu village."

She gestured toward Clayton, who hesitated at first. It was not his nature to play a leadership role. He was better at scheming and contriving. Nevertheless, he addressed the group, in a mixture of Portuguese and Spanish.

"Natasha told me that you were my brother's *compañeros* of many campaigns. I just finished reading his diaries and have come to appreciate your heroism. The memory of my brother and of this group will stay alive. Natasha and I will make sure that his diary is published. But we are here for another reason. A valuable mineral has been discovered on the land of the Yanomami."

He described the impending attack on the Indian village to clear the mountain of any indigenous inhabitants. When he was done, Caetano addressed them.

"We are old and poor, and yet our hearts are young. We will go to battle one more time for Comandante Paulo. We share his dreams to the end and this is why we are here. The seed that we are planting in this treacherous land will one day sprout the tree of justice throughout all of America. We are with you."

He gave orders to the troops to ready themselves. Then, he invited Natasha and Clayton to his dwelling, a thatch-covered hut with open sides and hammocks stretched and tied to the roof. On a rough wood table he laid out a map of the area and they discussed a possible plan.

"We are very good at ambushes," he said. "Comandante Paulo was a genius at them. He learned this from Che's *Handbook of Guerrilla Warfare* and executed them well."

"But can we stop a force of fifteen men on the trail?" Clayton asked.

"A properly executed ambush can neutralize a troop of up to one hundred soldiers. And we can do this with a dozen men."

"How can you accomplish this?" Natasha asked.

"Leave the details to us. We know the trail very well. We will pick an area where there is a clearing, so that the enemy is exposed."

"We need to warn the Yanomami and Bonaparte," Natasha said.

Clayton nodded. "Actually, they can help us. We have to be absolutely sure not to let anyone escape. This group has to vanish in the jungle."

"In Angola, we once stopped a convoy of twelve trucks with only a dozen men," said Antonio proudly. "The UNITA forces took major casualties, over thirty dead and fifty wounded."

"I'll stay at the airstrip and communicate with your men," Clayton said. "I brought three walkie-talkies with me. We'll be able to stay in touch at all times."

They spent the next two hours discussing the details of their plan. In the meantime, the *compañeros* had gotten ready. The rag-tag group was assembled outside the headquarters. Though old and worn, there remained plenty of fire in their souls. Clayton went to the airstrip and took a couple of men with him. He gave the weapons and ammunition to Antonio, who was pleased.

"Good, four FAL rifles. Excellent for ambushes. These are precision guns with good medium range accuracy." He instructed his best shooters on the FAL and they spent the rest of the morning sighting the guns.

Antonio tried to dissuade Clayton from staying at the airstrip, but finally acceded. It was the best plan. If the group was forewarned of the arrival of the attacking troops, it would be much more effective in neutralizing them.

Natasha walked briskly along the narrow forest trail, preceded by Dinael. She had left immediately, ahead of the main group. She felt the adrenaline pushing through her veins, and some fear. The trail looked familiar now, like a well-traveled road. She remembered the creeks that they forded, the major hills, and the rivers. But it was not the emotion of travel, nor was it the fear of the forest that made her nervous. No, that wasn't it. She moved through the trail briskly and fearlessly, though retaining her almost feline elegance. She had to communicate the danger to Bonaparte and Kaobawa. They, in turn, had to convince Bakotawa to move the village. Clayton's plan seemed sound, and he was certain -- almost too certain -- that the troops would land at the Esperanza airstrip. And if they chose another route? She had visions of children being torn to pieces.

Would her father's *compañeros* have the firepower to stop the attackers? She looked at her watch. They would be there in three more hours, but not before sunset. She checked her flashlight, which had new batteries. Under the canopy, the full moon would not help that much. And if they walked off the trail, they would be lost. But the sure and fast pace imparted by Dinael gave her confidence. He moved with a rapid gait carrying his front-loading shotgun. He kept his gunpowder and bare essentials in a rubberized bag, strapped across his back.

As she considered this, a couple of distant thunderclaps and a few large raindrops reminded her that the afternoon showers were coming. This was the rainy season and the heavy rain came every afternoon, right on time. Dinael quickly stopped, took his shirt and trousers off, and just stuffed them into his rubberized bag. As he did this, he stared at Natasha, whose T-shirt was starting to get wet and revealed her firm breasts. After pulling her poncho over her head, she strapped the holster above the poncho and checked the pistol.

It was already night when they entered the village. Their presence was announced from a distance by Dinael's long howls. He cried "Iehhh" every few minutes, and eventually an answer came from the village. As they entered the central clearing, a dozen children ran toward them with big smiles, chanting, "Natasha, Tokibuti." She was touched by the reception and, after greeting Bakotawa, the chief, went straight to Bonaparte's hammock. She felt, somehow, at home.

Opening her backpack, she gave him the medicines he had asked for. The poncho had protected the load from the rain. Then, she took him aside and told him of the impending attack. Bonaparte sat on the hammock, his head between his hands, in distress. He jumped up and threw a fit that attracted the attention of the Indians, who surrounded him. He went to Kaobawa and explained the situation. Kaobawa was incredulous. How could the white man's greed reach such a level?

Natasha presented the facts to Bonaparte and Kaobawa. The *compañeros* had left the Esperanza Mine already and were going to prepare an ambush at the Sumauma Creek, about four hours from the mine and two hours from the village. They would need help from the Indians. Could Bonaparte convince them to take part?

"The Yanomami are fierce people and won't shy away from battle," he said, scratching his scraggly beard.

Bonaparte reflected for a moment. "How much time do we have?"

"One, perhaps two days. Uncle Clayton will call me as soon as Soto Mayor's troop arrives at the airstrip."

"We'll talk to Bakotawa right now," Bonaparte said. "You stay here in my hammock."

"Where will you sleep tonight, Professor Bonaparte?"

"I'll have to find a nice lady to take me into her hammock," he said, winking.

Natasha knew that he meant it. She had noticed Mahima's devotion. So the old professor had some fire in his heart after all.

"Good luck, Professor."

She lay in the hammock, pulled the mosquito netting over her, and fell into a deep sleep.

# CHAPTER NINETEEN

Clayton had been waiting for two days at the airstrip. It was mid-afternoon and he was dozing off in his hammock. He heard a noise, something like an annoyed mosquito. Then, it gradually increased. He realized it was an airplane approaching. The noise grew into a loud hum, then a roar. He saw the plane circling the airstrip. Jumping off the hammock, he reviewed the plan in his mind.

As the plane landed and taxied, a second one appeared. Another Cessna Caravan. The troops were coming. He took the walkie-talkie and called Natasha.

"How are you?"

"We're ready here," came the voice.

"They're landing. Two Cessna Caravans," he said quickly. "I'll call you at midnight." He hid the walkie-talkie in the woods.

The first Cessna taxied and approached the hut, then disgorged its passengers. Colonel Soto Mayor was the last of the uniformed men. He shook Clayton's hand. Two pairs of dark, deeply set eyes scrutinized each other. Clayton knew that Soto Mayor was a gambler, like him, and was trying to figure out his cards. But Clayton was always good at this, all the way from his teenage poker games and his many lies to his parents, teachers and girlfriends.

"Here we are, *Señor* de Morais, have you kept you part of the bargain?"

"I have."

He walked with him to the hut, separating himself from the troops, who were unloading the equipment.

"My *nom de guerre* for this operation is Colonel Mono," he said.

Clayton smiled. "Quite appropriate."

The second Cessna landed and taxied to the hut. "You have brought more troops than planned," Clayton said.

"Yes, I like to feel safe." Soto Mayor threw him a sly smile, followed by the hyena-like laugh. "And the expenses are higher now."

"Very good, Colonel," Clayton said. "Please follow me."

Inside the hut he opened his attaché case, where he had neatly packed $100,000.

"Do you mind if I count them, *Señor* de Morais?"

"Absolutely not. Good business makes good friends."

Soto Mayor pulled out a couple of wads of $100 bills and counted them. Nodding his approval, he said, "This operation is costing me more than expected. I will need another $150,000."

They argued for a minute, Clayton finally throwing up his hands. "You give me no choice, Colonel," he said. "But you should have let me know. I actually went back to Caguan, to make sure that everything was all right."

"I know," he said, and grinned.

Clayton had brought an additional $100,000 with him, which he passed on to Soto Mayor. The balance would be deposited in Luxembourg.

Soto Mayor went outside and ordered his troops into formation. Julio Cesar complied, then reported back.

"Colonel Mono, the troops are ready."

Soto Mayor then presented the plan. They would spend the night at the airstrip and would leave in the morning. As he spoke, the rain started, and they sought refuge under the shed.

They organized their sleeping bags in an orderly fashion and were able to fit tightly under the roof. The pilots waited for the rain to stop and then took off, after conferring with Soto Mayor. They knew the orders well. They were going to refuel and wait in Mitu. They were to return on the third day, then on the fifth and seventh if necessary.

The rain stopped in the same precise manner as it had started. It had lasted approximately two hours. There was a stove in the shed, and the troops prepared a warm meal of rice and roasted meat.

Soto Mayor told Clayton, "*Señor* de Morais, I hope you can come with us tomorrow. It will be a very pleasant excursion."

"I'm sorry, but I was planning to leave tomorrow morning," he said. "I have important business at home."

"More important than this?" Soto Mayor gazed into his eyes with suspicion.

"You think that I have the stamina to walk for eight hours, Colonel?"

Soto Mayor pondered for a moment, then nodded. "We need you here, on our return, to call the Banque Générale du Luxembourg and order the money transfer," he said. "I brought a satellite phone with me. We will contact *Señorita* Chauny right now. What time is it there?"

"Too early yet. We need to do this tomorrow morning, at 6 a.m.. It's a nine-hour difference."

"OK, we'll get everything prepared. But you stay here until we return."

Clayton shrugged his shoulders and agreed. Soto Mayor turned to Garcia. "Cacorro, you have a bum leg anyway. Stay here with *Señor* de Morais and make sure that he is well cared for until our return."

"It sounds like a good idea, Mono."

So, his name was indeed Mono. Clayton was impressed by his intelligence. This entire operation was being staged without involving his personnel at FARC. Colonel Soto Mayor would have no finger in the massacre. His political future was clean.

Clayton called his pilot on the cellular phone and asked him to postpone the return flight. They continued the discussion.

"And how will you know that we did the job?" Soto Mayor asked.

Clayton thought for a moment. "How about your idea, a string of ears?"

"You businessmen are more ruthless than us soldiers. But leave it at that. We'll bring the ears. You can take them to your boss in Brazil."

Garcia set up and tested the satellite phone. It would be ready for the morning call to Annick Chauny. Clayton hoped that she would not be on one of her frequent vacations.

Shortly before sunrise, they called Banque Générale. Annick was there. Colonel Soto Mayor spoke to her and understood her broken Spanish. They would wait for Clayton's order, hopefully in three days, to make the transfer to Soto Mayor's account in the Bahamas. The name of the company was confirmed. Everything was all right. After they were through, Soto Mayor glared at Clayton.

"If you try to double-cross me, Eugenio de Morais, I will follow you to the end of the world and finish you off. Not only you, but also Natasha and Ana Maria."

Clayton struggled to stay calm. "Don't worry, Colonel. This is strictly business. We're making a significant financial investment and we're not going to take any unnecessary risks."

Soto Mayor then went to the bushes with Clayton and placed the money in his backpack, away from the curious eyes of the soldiers. He set aside $80,000 to give the troops their down payment of $4,000 each.

"You're taking a risk, Colonel," Clayton said. "Are your troops reliable fellows?"

"There is only one person I trust here, and that is Mr. Garcia." He turned to him. "Cacorro, I entrust to you *Señor* de Morais and the backpack. Keep your eye on both."

"Don't worry, Mono," he said. "This is the best decision. You never know what the troops might do if they discover that their entire pay is coming along. They might just decide to take off."

"And go where?" Soto Mayor laughed, then looked at Clayton. "There's only one way out of this hell, and that's by plane. Cacorro will make sure than none come this way."

"I'll call you twice a day, Mono. Midday and evening."

The next morning the troops were assembled, and after one last check of weapons, ammunition and backpacks they were given their $4,000. This sent a wave of enthusiasm through the group. Shovels, axes, and picks were distributed. Cold food rations were apportioned. Soto Mayor instructed the two groups to stay one hundred yards apart. He walked with the lead group, at its rear. He was sufficiently experienced not to be the point man. That could be dangerous.

"I don't want any bullets in the chambers. No accidental shots. This will endanger the entire operation," he said, as they started out.

Rigoberto placed himself at the front of the lead group. "Let's go, *pendejos*," he said. "I want to screw an Indian girl and can hardly wait."

Laughter ensued and the column took off. It was already 9 a.m. They would walk until shortly after dark, bivouac on the trail, and then close in.

Natasha and Bonaparte had already met up with the *compañeros* when the walkie-talkie buzzed. "Hello, Clayton here.

They just left. Twenty-one, in fatigue uniforms. They're divided into two groups, one hundred yards apart."

"We're here at the Sumauma Creek. We'll be ready."

"Good luck and good-bye."

She immediately communicated the message to the *compañeros* and to Bonaparte, who was coordinating the Yanomami with Kaobawa.

They had chosen the spot judiciously. The experience of many unsuccessful and partially successful ambushes had been vital.

Antonio and Caetano had chosen the creek because it provided an open space about thirty yards wide. It was an ideal shooting ground.

"The *Comandante*'s methods," he told Natasha. "He had perfected ambushes much beyond the simple methods used by Fidel and Che in Sierra Maestra. He read a lot and had adopted ideas from WWI and WWII."

"You mean trench warfare? He described them in the diary."

"Yes, they're extremely effective. Soldiers hate them because of the hard work."

They dug foxholes for each *compañero*, after carefully analyzing the line of fire. They had brought short handled shovels, standard Soviet military equipment, and a pick. For several hours they were consumed by this task. Soil was put into burlap sacks that they either carried away or used as frontal protection. Then, they camouflaged every hole carefully, until it was invisible, using leaves and branches. The Yanomami watched them in disbelief.

"If fighting is so much hard work, it's almost no fun," said Kaobawa philosophically.

When the trenches were complete they carefully built a trap on the trail, by the creek. First, they dug a hole and removed all the soil. The hole was five feet deep and three feet wide. Then they foraged through the forest until they found a special hard bamboo. Using their machetes, they made pointed tips. They placed the sharp bamboo spears at the bottom, inserting them into smaller holes and fixing them firmly. They covered the hole with thin reeds and leaves. It was a perfect trap, intended for the point man. They hoped that it would throw the advancing group into disarray.

"We learned this from the Viet Cong," Antonio said.

This work took several hours. All Bisaasi-Teri and a few Haximu-Teri Yanomami had joined the group, and they numbered fifteen. Bakotawa had reluctantly agreed to move to a hunting camp one day's walk from Haximu. Bonaparte was coordinating the action with the *compañeros*. All they had to do now was to wait. The columns would be arriving between three and four p.m.

Natasha was fearful. She hated violence and thought the excitement of the men a dangerous, primeval expectation of pleasure. She did not share this feeling but hoped that this dangerous action would save the tribe. Even Bonaparte was transfigured, the impending fight energizing his aging body.

"I've been accused for years of starting fights between Yanomami only to study them," he said with a ferocious grin. "Well, now they will have a real Napoleonic war!"

When Natasha walked back to the forest from the creek, she saw the Yanomami happily applying body paint one another. Red *onato* paint and black charcoal powder were artfully applied to their bodies, and they appeared fierce. *The Fierce Yanomami,* she thought, remembering Bonaparte's textbook. She would experience this part of the Yanomami very soon.

Bonaparte lit up a cigar that he had made by rolling a tobacco leaf. He took some deep puffs, checking his old Colt 38 revolver. Then, he stripped his clothes while Kaobawa and Rerebawa helped to apply *onato* and charcoal to his body. He was not embarrassed in front of Natasha, who blushed watching him fix his penis string.

"Fifteen bullets. That's all I have," he muttered. "I have to use them sparingly."

Instinctively she reached for her Beretta, pulled it from the holster, and checked the clip. It was full: eight 9mm bullets. In her pocket she had a second clip. She had no plans to use the gun, but was prepared. Kaobawa came to her with the paint and applied it to her face and hair.

"Get some mud on you, Natasha," said Antonio, who supervised the entire operation with Caetano. "Go by the creek and put some mud on your body. Your blond hair and white face will be like a light in the dark forest."

He had stationed his *compañeros* along the left side of the trail, in groups of three. They all wore camouflage uniforms. Their faces were painted dark. Antonio and Caetano walked along the trail correcting mistakes, checking for footprints, and ensuring that the ambush was perfect. The Yanomami had received strict orders to stay on the right side of the trail and to hide in the webs of some enormous *Sumauma* trees lining the creek. They were instructed to stalk the ones that escaped the initial ambush.

Finally, Antonio walked up and down the trail one last time, pointing out visible *compañeros* and Yanomami, and ensuring that there was no trace of the ambushers. Absolute surprise was the key to success. It was also essential that they kill as many attackers as possible at first strike and completely terrorize the survivors.

Antonio had placed the three M23s with the best marksmen, at positions that had the highest visibility and clearance. The five ambush stations on the left of the trail were spaced approximately twenty yards apart and ten yards into the forest. The creek crossing was within their firing zone.

One of the Yanomami had been sent down the trail to warn the group of the advance of the attackers. It was Kaobawa's tenacious teenage son, Rerebawa. Possessed of a keen hearing and sight, he was ordered to station himself one kilometer down the trail. Now they lay in their respective hiding places. Natasha and Bonaparte had found a gigantic *Sumauma* tree and hid between its webs. Natasha felt the blood in her veins pumping a little faster than normal. *This is how my father felt before battle,* she thought. She knew that they were all resting and focusing on the upcoming battle.

Her thoughts flowed to the Haximu-Teri Yanomami. She hoped that nothing would happen to them. She would do everything she could. The forest grew darker and she heard a rolling, muted thunder. Rain fell on the trees. Her hiding place was like a nest. The three *Sumauma* trees each had five or six enormous webs, approximately six feet wide. These webs provided structural support for the large trunks like buttresses on medieval cathedrals. Two or three people could comfortably hide in each web. She snuggled herself in and waited.

# CHAPTER TWENTY

Colonel Soto Mayor felt the exhaustion gradually spreading through his legs. They had been walking since the morning and were making good progress, albeit slower than planned. The backpacks weighed down the troops, and they had made four ten-minute stops and taken one hour-long lunch break. They were not used to the jungle heat, quite a contrast to the cool *estancia* where they had practiced their marches. It was quite different in the forest, with humidity close to 90 percent and temperature in the low 100s, than the cool and dry *altiplano*, the highlands. The soldiers' shirts were dripping wet, and the complaints had started. Nevertheless, the group was disciplined, and a few hours of heat and sweat were not enough to kill their determination.

At three o'clock they heard two short rolls of thunder, followed by a few thick, warm drops. Soto Mayor ordered the column to stop.

"Put the ponchos on," he said, "and take a five-minute break."

The groups stopped and the soldiers reached into their backpacks. Soto Mayor could not keep from swearing when he saw them putting on the bright yellow and blue ponchos. Yellow for the lead group, blue for the rear group. Garcia had told him that there were no green ponchos available in Cali. Guerrillas and cocaine growers, who liked to move along the countryside undisturbed, had bought them all up. He had objected strongly, but they were already at the *estancia* and it would delay the departure.

At the airstrip, Clayton had been nervously waiting for any news through the walkie-talkie. Garcia had called Soto Mayor at lunchtime and told him that everything was all right. He would make a second call in the evening and something had to be done before then. The mid-afternoon heat was at its highest and Garcia lay on his hammock, sweating and fighting sleep. Clayton watched him, waiting for his opportunity, which he hoped would come soon.

"I hope they get back quickly. This heat is intolerable. The mosquitoes start at 5 p.m. and attack all night."

"This is a godforsaken place, *Señor* de Morais," he said. "What are you people doing here?"

"I don't know myself. It's the boss's orders, in Brazil."

Garcia's voice was sluggish and his eyelids weighed on him. He pulled the netting over his hammock and rested his head back. In a few minutes, Clayton could hear him snoring heavily. He did not have anything against the man. But he knew that he would be transformed after the next phone call.

The black beans and rice that Garcia had prepared for lunch weighed on his stomach, but Clayton could not, would not succumb to sleep. He slipped his hand into his bag and felt the Beretta, trying to remember whether he had a bullet in the barrel. He brought it into the hammock and lay there for a while, listening to the snores, pleased that Ana had given it to him. It had been hidden in the bushes with the walkie-talkie before Soto Mayor arrived and Clayton had retrieved it after Garcia fell asleep.

How would he shoot the man? When would he do it? Through the net, he eyed Garcia's hammock a few yards away. For a moment, he thought of Marco Aurelio. This one was for him. He lifted his knees inside the hammock, and placed his left hand on top of his right knee. He cocked the gun, and heard the click. Garcia's snoring continued unabated. He was not sure where to aim. He calculated the position of his chest, carefully lowered the top of the barrel until that area was in his line of sight, and slowly, delicately squeezed the trigger, hoping that there was a bullet in the barrel. The report of the gun was deafening. The shock waves reflected on the roof and he was stunned for an instant. He watched the hammock move and heard the agonizing sounds of pain. The snoring had changed into guttural, painful moans. Then, he squeezed again, and again.

The groans died. All he heard was blood dripping. The mosquito net was splattered with blood. Strangely, he felt no remorse. It was as if he had shot into a potato sack. He climbed out of the hammock and fired one last shot, aiming at the head.

A few minutes later, it felt as if the sky was coming down. In the darkness outside he walked in the rain and felt the water washing his face, his body, his soul. His hands shook uncontrollably and he dropped the Beretta. He thought of Marco Aurelio and Ana. How he missed them.

Soto Mayor's annoyance grew to a fury when he saw the column starting again.

"If this were a shooting gallery, they would be ideal targets," he muttered to himself. "Damn Cacorro!"

He had called punctually at twelve, telling him that everything was OK at the airstrip. He was doing a good job. Just a small-time thug, and sometimes careless. But he had good intentions and a pleasant disposition.

By the time they started again, the rain was pouring down as if the sky were full of holes. These jungle rains were intense, though short-lived. He instructed Rigoberto and Julio Cesar to have the troops take off the ponchos as soon as the rain abated. He knew they were easier targets like that. Hopefully, they would soon rid themselves of their colorful accoutrements and he would feel better again. His acute survival instincts had been honed by many years of guerrilla warfare in the *Oriente* provinces. They were sending him a warning signal.

An hour went by. Soto Mayor looked at the watch again. It was past four p.m. and the rain had not yet slowed. Another hour of this, he guessed. He judged that they were a little over two hours from the Yanomami village. Fortunately, with this heavy rain the Yanomami were probably huddled up there. No one ventured far during the height of the rain season. No one that wanted to be reasonably comfortable.

Shortly thereafter, they encountered the second creek. It had swelled from the rains but could still be forded.

Rigoberto forged ahead, after a short stop. Soto Mayor, at the rear of the first group, waved back to Julio Cesar, urging him to keep the one hundred yards distance. Because of the poor visibility he had kept marching, while Rigoberto had stopped. The two groups were now almost merged.

"Hold back," Soto Mayor called. "Wait until the first group is gone before you start."

"*Si*, Colonel," Julio Cesar said. "Do you want me to go back?"

"No need, but maintain the distance from now on."

Soto Mayor knew that these jungle rains stopped just as quickly as they started. In a matter of moments the clouds would be gone, and the afternoon sun would be back. At least the temperature had dropped a bit.

He was crossing the river when Rigoberto slipped and fell.

"*Hijos de una puta, saquenme de aqui*," the man screamed, as he disappeared on the trail. The group rushed to where he had fallen.

"*Dios mio*, Colonel, a trap!" one cried.

Soto Mayor ran to the hole and saw Rigoberto's contorted body at the bottom. Bamboo spikes perforated his thighs and arms, barely missing his torso. "These fucking Indians," he screamed. "Get me out!"

Soto Mayor immediately assessed the situation. Nothing major was perforated, but he could not go with them. They would have to leave him behind and pick him up on the way back. He knew that the entire operation could be compromised. They would have to advance carefully, avoiding the trail. The fucking Indians would pay for this.

"Let's get him out carefully," he said.

Then, he called for a man who carried the medical supplies. Looking back, he saw the second group crossing the creek. Then, he heard the first shot and felt a sharp pain in his shoulder. His body pivoted violently and he hit the ground.

"Ambush! Cover yourselves!"

The methodical mowing down of his troops ensued, as the firing grew in intensity. He recognized the rapid FALs, the zing of the M23s and the staccato of the AK47s. They were caught in an ambush, a perfect ambush. These were no Indians. They were experienced guerrilla fighters, jungle fighters.

He watched powerless from the ground, as his men struggled with their ponchos. One by one, they hit the ground in bursts of blood. Soto Mayor realized that the firing came from the left of the trail and screamed, "Into the forest, to the right! Return fire!"

He tried to remove his Colt .45 from the holster with his good arm. His other shoulder was crushed, and blood ran down his left arm. Finally, he pulled his pistol out but could not find a target. The shooting continued, deadly and precise. No unnecessary spraying, no screaming from the forest. They were professionals, the best.

Soto Mayor turned, careful not to move too briskly, and looked toward the river. He saw mounds of blue floating down and what was left of his soldiers running back into the forest.

Once more, he looked around and saw the remains of his group lying dead or wounded. Three feet from him lay the medic, his eyes rolled back, part of his head removed by the bullet that entered through his face. A few yards down was another yellow poncho covered in blood. A man, his black face gray now, still moaned, red foam spurting from his mouth.

Rigoberto had stopped screaming. Soto Mayor heard the command coming from the forest, and swore he could recognize the voice.

"Stop fire, stop fire!"

A middle-aged mulatto emerged, carefully looking at all the bodies and advancing step by step. Antonio, no doubt. He remembered Paulo's trusted lieutenant, a hero of four wars. He knew about his legendary exploits in Nicaragua, Angola, Cuba and Colombia. Here he was, within arm's reach.

"We're going down together, you *hijo de puta*," he muttered, as he raised the Colt and tried to take aim. Two more steps, he thought, as Antonio approached the hole.

Soto Mayor squeezed the trigger softly, almost with love. He felt, for a split second, a shade over his head, and then heard the crash. A thick *brauna* wood club crushed his head, breaking it like a coconut. The pistol fired reflexively in his hand. Blood and brains spewed from his head as his body jerked a few times.

"*Gracias*, Kaobawa," Antonio said, falling to the ground and holding his thigh. "Oh, this shit hurts bad." His face was a rictus of pain and laughter, the few teeth in his mouth squeezed between his lips and tongue.

Crossing the creek, Julio Cesar had had a bad premonition when he heard Rigoberto's screams. He lowered himself in the knee-high water and shrugged off his backpack and poncho. He had quickly reasoned that his life was more important than the load. He was turning around to order his group to do the same when he heard the first shot. He immersed himself in the water, holding his rifle. Survival was at stake, each one to himself. He let the current take him. The water was brown from the rains. He could not see or hear anything. He touched the bottom of the creek with his hands and the rifle helped to keep him from floating. His lungs burned and he felt he would faint when he lifted his head again. He heard firing from all sides and saw blue ponchos all around. Near the shore he dove again, resurfacing under some roots. He waited there, keeping only eyes and nose above water. He appraised the situation, then went under, after carefully planning his next resurfacing spot. When he came up, he was by the shore, among roots. He was saved — at least for now. He saw the remains of his group floating away. A couple ran to the forest. It was then that he decided to crawl out and make a dash for the trees. As he escaped, he heard muted steps and voices. He recognized Octavio and called to him. It was time to regroup what was left of the men.

Rigoberto lay impaled in the foxhole and listened to the gunfight. Gradually, he realized that he was lost, that they were all lost. Every movement of his body created intolerable pain. He felt his muscles ripped by the bamboo. Slowly, he extricated himself from one, then from a second bamboo stick. He knew he was losing his blood, and needed to give some payback: that was the law. Somebody had fucked them, fucked them bad. It wasn't Colonel Mono for sure. He lay there with the troops. Rigoberto finally was able to grab his rifle. He bolted a bullet into the barrel and waited patiently, until he saw the face peeking into the hole, and pulled the trigger. But the face had seen him too, and the two bullets fired at the same time. As his brains were blown out, his last thought was for the trigger that he had squeezed. He was sure he had given the payback. He had hit Gilmar in the neck.

The fire had now subsided. The *compañeros* slowly left their places of concealment and advanced carefully. Caetano assessed the situation rapidly. They had suffered two casualties but had defeated Soto Mayor's troops. They had to pursue the survivors.

"This one's for you, Comandante Paulo," he shouted in exultation, as the *compañeros* emitted a primeval victory roar.

Natasha had been hiding behind the *Sumauma* tree, wedged between the long webs that lifted themselves from the ground and up the trunk. It was a safe place, thirty yards from the trail. Bonaparte was in the next web, and she could hear his monologue while the gunfire raged. He could not keep from sticking his head out every few minutes and would jump down whenever the bullets zinged by his head. She saw two soldiers in fatigue uniforms running away from the trail. The first came by fast and she only had time to lift and cock the Beretta. The second was much slower and dragged his leg. She aimed carefully at his back and fired. Then, she fired a second shot, and saw his body jerk. He crouched down and melded with the background, rapidly disappearing in the foliage.

"Let's follow them, Natasha. We can get them."

"No, Professor, our orders are to stay put."

"Oh, fuck the orders." He was anxious to help.

"Let's wait," she said. "Our job is to save the Yanomami, don't forget."

When the mayhem stopped, they waited for a few minutes and then slowly walked toward the trail, announcing themselves with whistles. They found Antonio and Gilmar on the ground, being tended to. They had started to bandage Antonio's leg. The bullet had entered, making only a small, almost imperceptible hole. However, there were lacerations at the exit. The skin was ruptured, forming a petaled appearance, and sectioned pieces of muscle protruded. Antonio's *compañeros* pushed the muscle back into the hole.

"You'll need antibiotic ointment if you want to avoid infection," Bonaparte said as he lowered his backpack and looked inside. "Here, apply this to the wound."

He bandaged the wound by wrapping the gauze around the leg. Then, he proceeded to Gilmar. He was bleeding profusely from the wound and had lost consciousness. Somehow, they managed to stop the bleeding. Caetano gave him an adrenaline shot and he came back.

After the wounded men were tended to, they looked around and saw the results of the vicious fight. Antonio's *compañeros* were already counting the bodies and dragging them to the trail.

"Fourteen, Antonio," said one man. "And that does not include the two that floated down the creek."

They called Clayton and announced their victory. He was elated and told them that he had cleared the way at the airstrip. He confirmed that there were two groups of ten plus Soto Mayor.

"We got their leader and one of the sergeants, a big mulatto."

"Rigoberto."

"So, five got away," Caetano said. "We have to catch them, or they'll come back to haunt us."

Kaobawa had been proudly displaying his bloody club to the Yanomami. Bonaparte told him that there were some attackers in the woods.

"Two went in that direction, past the large *Sumauma* tree," he said.

"The remaining three must have gone downriver on the other side," Caetano said. "The Yanomami have to track them down."

Kaobawa nodded. "They will. Rerebawa, you go after these two." His son started toward the *Sumauma*.

"I'll come with you," Bonaparte said, putting his back-pack on and grabbing a FAL rifle from one of the fallen soldiers.

"Take a flashlight," Caetano said. "It'll get dark in two hours."

They noticed that the rain had stopped at some point during the firefight, and that the afternoon sun now shone on the creek.

The bloody bodies had shaken Natasha. The disjointed, discarded corpses had a nightmarish quality in the surreal atmosphere of the jungle. A light fog that rose by the creek accentuated this. She felt as if she was watching the entire scene in a movie.

Before she could stop them, Bonaparte and Rerebawa were gone, followed by four Bisaasi Yanomami. The group was already deep in the forest, on the tracks of the fugitives. They carried bows, arrows, and machetes.

Natasha joined the second group, led by Kaobawa. He proudly carried his club, soiled by blood and brains, and hoped to use it again, very soon. It would reaffirm him as the leader of the Bisaasi-Teri, as the fiercest of them all.

They had laid Antonio against a tree trunk and passed him a cigarette. As he took a few puffs and looked at the glowing tip, he thought for a moment.

"We'll wait here tonight," he told the *compañeros*. "*Señorita* Natasha, your father would have been proud of us."

Then, he took a drag and laughed, shaking his head.

"We had some bad ambushes, some really bad ones. Once in Nicaragua, we blasted away at a column for an hour. We killed one soldier and wounded three. Then they attacked us and routed us back into the jungle."

They all laughed and one said, "You've learned to shoot straight since then, Antonio."

"I've learned to plan every detail. But we had very old Mausers then, and half were not sighted properly."

"The FALs and M23s did the job on them, Antonio," said one of the younger fellows, who Natasha recognized as Celeste's brother, Manuel. "How is Celeste?" she asked.

"She was fine when I left her. She'll be giving birth soon."

Natasha's heart was encased in a deep feeling of warmth. She wanted to know the baby, to hug her little sister.

Antonio then turned to the Kaobawa. "We still have three of Soto Mayor's people on the other side of the creek. It will be dark in one hour."

The group, led by Kaobawa, crossed the creek and silently glided through the forest, looking for tracks, broken twigs, and other minute signs. Soon they found something. One of the Yanomami saw a few drops of blood. Natasha tried to keep up with them and remain as silent as possible. She was careful to let them walk about ten yards ahead of her. Every now and then they looked around and sniffed the air. Could they smell the men? Perhaps.

It was already dark when they stopped. They had advanced for over an hour and the direction was definitely the Esperanza airstrip. Natasha had taken her walkie-talkie and contacted Clayton. He was to move away from the strip, to the mining camp. They would try to meet him there, stalking the three fugitives. For this, they would stay on the blood track. They advanced, checking the ground, with the help of flashlights for a while, then stopped to eat. The food was Spartan but energizing: candy bars taken from the backpacks of Soto Mayor's men.

Soon they heard shots in the distance: AK47 rounds, then a flurry of FAL. Natasha could distinguish them now.

"Something happened there, and it doesn't sound good," she said at last.

Kaobawa's expression showed worry. His son and Shaki were in danger. But they had a job to do, and continued on.

At the Sumauma Creek, the *compañeros* also heard the shots. Caetano immediately organized a group and moved toward the direction from which the shots came. The moon had not yet risen. Darkness surrounded them and they were guided by Caetano's flashlight. He advanced carefully but with a sure foot. The entire jungle was one cacophonous symphony. Howls of monkeys, the buzz of cicadas, the screams of a thousand birds filled the air as darkness engulfed everything. Caetano was used to this nightly concert, which lasted about an hour. Nevertheless, here in the middle of the forest, it took on a frightening dimension. They had walked for over an hour in the direction of the shots when they heard muffled grunts in the distance. At first they thought it was an animal. Caetano turned off the flashlight and slowly moved in that direction. Then, they saw a faint light. It had to be Bonaparte's flashlight. He gave orders for the group to fan out and converge on the spot from different directions. The moon had come out, casting a silvery light through the forest. The groans grew louder and Caetano heard some words that he could not recognize. "*Merde, que ça fait mal.*" It had to be Bonaparte. They were now within twenty yards. Caetano waved to the others to stop and advanced, almost at a crawl. After a few minutes he stood and waved them in.

His flashlight illuminated the tragic scene. Bonaparte lay on his back, his shirt covered in blood. It looked like he had been hit in the stomach. By him lay Rerebawa, riddled by several bullets. Three had penetrated his chest. "Rerebawa ... was ahead of us," he said, shaking his head. "They waited in ... an ambush."

Caetano pointed the flashlight around, revealing the battle. Two bodies in green fatigues lay by a fallen tree trunk. One head appeared grotesquely deformed and swollen. The eyes had popped out from the sockets and brain matter had spewed out from a deep crack. One of the Yanomami's machetes, Caetano thought. The other had been shot in the chest and head.

"The other three Yanomami moved on," Bonaparte said. "I can't feel my legs. I'm … gone."

Caetano appraised the situation. "First, we need to take the Professor back," he said.

He ordered the other *compañeros* to cut two long wood poles. Then he took off the shirts of the dead attackers and buttoned them. He also took their belts. They passed the eight-foot poles through the shirts, making holes at the ends, and had an improvised stretcher. They carefully lifted Bonaparte onto it. Caetano noticed that the exit hole of the bullet was on the spine. Bonaparte was paralyzed from the waist down. The Yanomami carried Rerebawa.

They returned to the trail by the Sumauma Creek and joined up with the others. There, they discussed taking Bonaparte to the airstrip and calling in a plane.

"I'm staying here," he said. "I'm half dead. Let me go back to my people."

"We need four men to carry the Professor and Rerebawa back to the village. Caetano, you go with them," said Antonio, who, in spite of his condition, was lucid. Then, he turned to four of his *compañeros* and told them to get ready. "The others stay here. We return to the airstrip tomorrow morning. Gilmar and I need four people to carry us also."

They placed Rerebawa on a hammock and tied it to a long pole. The *compañeros* had by now made sturdier stretchers. Using bamboo, they fashioned a platform and padded it with a sleeping bag. Caetano inspected Bonaparte's wound and splashed some antibiotic on it.

"Don't bother with it," said Bonaparte.

Within an hour, they were gone. Before midnight, they had reached the village and were received by barking dogs.

As they entered the central courtyard, a few of the elders that had stayed behind were already up and running toward them. Their loud lamentations and screams followed suit, and continued after they placed Rerebawa on his hammock. The Yanomami that had come with them continued on to tell Bakotawa and the rest of the village that it was safe to return.

As soon as light appeared in the forest, Kaobawa, Natasha, and the five Yanomami were on their feet. They had rested for a few hours, sleeping in the moist soil. They continued to advance on the fleeing group. Every now and then they found broken twigs. The blood puddles were growing bigger. They saw other signs where they stopped to rest. They could tell that the fleeing group was having trouble with the wounded fellow. One of the Haximu Yanomami told Kaobawa that there was a large lagoon ahead. They either had to cross it or to go around. The Yanomami fanned out and advanced cautiously. They were close to the prey. Natasha maintained her distance. She knew that she was not as stealthy as they were. She admired their fluid movements. They froze every few steps, then advanced without any rapid movement. She saw them nocking arrows to their bowstrings. One of them carefully lifted the bow, pulled it in the Yanomami fashion, all the way behind the ear, and released the arrow. He repeated this two, three times. She heard a noise, like an animal rolling around. They ran forward. She followed them, pistol in hand. Her emotions ran a gamut. Suddenly, a rifle fired. She dropped to the ground.

The Yanomami had flushed the fugitives and they had only one way out: straight ahead. But the lagoon blocked their advance. Natasha slowly rose to her knees. The Yanomami hid behind trees and she could see them, twenty or thirty yards away. She looked around and tried hard to see the fugitives. For an instant, she saw a fleeting shadow between the trees. Then, there was additional fire. The Yanomami advanced boldly. One of them dropped to the ground, wounded. Kaobawa held his club, setting himself up for a run.

Natasha advanced a few more steps toward the lagoon behind the trees. She heard the splash, and the furious run of the Yanomami. They sped to the shore and she followed them.

"They jumped into the water and are swimming across," Kaobawa said, as the Yanomami fired salvos of arrows. She saw the three heads and splashing arms in the muddy water. The first one was close to one hundred yards ahead and swam steadily, while the last one trailed. They aimed their arrows at that one, soon hitting him. He continued to swim with difficulty, two arrows protruding from his neck. Then, suddenly, he emitted a horrible scream. He started to move frantically. The water around him roiled, and he raised his arms.

"Piranhas," Kaobawa said with a wide grin on his face. "His blood attracted them."

Within seconds the roiling became a feast and the water turned red around him. Piranhas were now jumping out of the water, biting his head and arms in their frenzy. Two sinister shadows glided toward him in the water. "Alligators," Natasha murmured in disbelief.

The two other men continued to swim. Kaobawa pointed at Natasha's pistol and urged her to shoot.

Natasha thought for a moment. This was a cowardly action. Like practice shooting. Then, she remembered the children of Haximu. They were going to kill them all. She calmly took the pistol out of the holster and aimed at the closest head, assessing the distance. Sixty yards perhaps. She fired a first shot, which splashed the water ten yards short. Then a second, long and to the left. She focused on technique, bringing the pistol slowly down, while she gently pulled the trigger. She fired a third shot. She gripped the pistol with two hands as the man was trying to dive. When he resurfaced, his entire body came out of the water. She kept firing. She emptied the first clip and put the second one into the pistol. Finally, she heard the thump after the shot. There was no bullet splash in the water this time. The piranhas hurried to feed again. The Yanomami danced around in exhilaration. They now demanded the last one, who was getting away.

She fired the rest of her rounds, but the head moved farther away. Soon, it disappeared in the distance. The man had escaped. They watched him disappear in the forest, two arrows buried deeply in his body.

Natasha felt like it had been target practice. Strangely, she was as if in a trance. There was no remorse, just a strange realization that she had crossed a dangerous boundary. Would she ever be the same? Would these hands, which had killed, be able to hold children?

The wounded Yanomami had a bullet hole in his shoulder. It had entered close to the collarbone and fragmented it, exiting through the shoulder blade. He was in a lot of pain, but sat there stoically. Nobody dared to enter the water and swim after the last fugitive. Circling around the lagoon would take a couple of hours. The wounded needed care. They had gotten two out of three. They had no choice but to return to the Sumauma Creek. Natasha radioed Clayton to be on the lookout.

At Haximu-teri, the *compañeros* carefully placed Bonaparte on his hammock and he noticed the grotesque rotation of his hip and legs as they moved him. His back was flexible, as if it had been severed.

"No feeling," he moaned, as Mahima tested his toes and legs.

They gave him scotch. The alcohol dulled the pain. Mahima sat by his side, holding his hand. She had cleansed his face, arms, and chest. In Berkeley, he had a white-haired grouchy lady in his house, telling him to wash dishes, cut the lawn, quit drinking and smoking. But here he was a Yanomami, and a fierce one. He had been in battle; he had killed in battle, and was back home now, cared for by his woman.

Natasha's group returned to Haximu-Teri that evening. They were exhausted, since they had shared the portage of the wounded Indian. He was from Haximu-Teri and his family immediately provided help for him. There, they received the news about Rerebawa's death and Bonaparte's condition. Kaobawa was stunned. He sat by his dead son, who had been placed in his hammock. In deep despair, he hugged the cold body already invaded by *rigor mortis*. Tears streamed from his eyes, and he chanted and cried all night. The other Bisaasi Yanomami sat by him in vigil. Rerebawa was his favorite son and he had taken him on this expedition. Natasha came to his side and tried to comfort him. He kept his head between his hands. Every so often, he stroked the young boy's hair.

Natasha lay in her hammock and fell into a restless sleep. She was awakened every now and then by Bonaparte, who screamed, moaned, or sang. She could also hear the chanting and crying of Kaobawa and his Bisaasi throughout the night. She noticed that blood flowed from Bonaparte's hammock. There was a puddle under it, and Mahima had to chase the dogs that came to lick it.

Several times during the night Natasha went to check on Bonaparte. He grew more pale, and his eyes were now glazed. His mouth still moved, and he muttered incomprehensible words. Shortly before dawn, the sharp lamentations from Mahima broke the silence and shook Natasha, who jumped up from the hammock. Bonaparte lay with his eyes rolled back. His arms dangled from the hammock. He was dead. Natasha cried, thinking that death carries a tragic irreversibility. She would never again experience his movements, moods, his raucous laughter, his confident arrogance. He would never again tantalize students with his heroic descriptions of village warfare among the Yanomami. Nevertheless, he had found, somehow, a fitting end, a *waiteri* end.

As the sun rose, the Yanomami village lay deep in mourning. The women brought wood from the forest and made a large pyre in the courtyard. Screams and lamentations continued throughout the day.

They placed the two bodies in the pyre and lit it. Natasha watched the strange ritual as if in a trance. The fire burned for hours. Then, the old women gathered the remains of the charred bodies and placed them in a large gourd. They crushed the bones with stones and ground them. They added water to the broken up remains of Rerebawa and Bonaparte. The entire tribe formed a circle and started a long, haunting chant. An old toothless woman took the gourd from person to person, filling a small cup. Each one drank the black and gooey substance. Natasha was moved by this primitive, yet hauntingly beautiful ritual.

The gourd was passed to her and the old lady said, "Tokibuti." She looked into the gourd, then raised it to her lips, smelling the acrid soup. She lifted the cup and filled her mouth with it, feeling the bitter taste. The spirit of Bonaparte and Rerebawa had entered her; Comandante Paulo's soul inhabited her. Through this primeval communion, Tokibuti was now a Yanomami.

They drank and chanted the entire night. Shaki and Rerebawa had died in battle, bringing honor to their tribe. Now, they had returned. Their souls would inhabit them forever.

# CHAPTER TWENTY-ONE

Clayton and Natasha had arrived that morning with good news. Ana Maria could not believe it when she hugged her daughter. She was thinner and appeared sick. Dark circles gave her eyes a sad and tired look.

"Natasha, my poor child, what happened to you?" she exclaimed, looking at her. "Your entire body is bitten by mosquitoes."

"Mom, I was in the forest for two months! This is normal. Have you forgotten your days in the guerrilla fight?"

"Yes, Natasha, I remember now. It looks worse than it feels. And your light skin is the favorite of those jungle mosquitoes. I hope you didn't catch malaria. Your father and I had it. In his case, it stayed with him until the end. I'll get you some pills."

"I'm fine. It's too late now. I guess I caught it. Don't worry. I've only had one single incident of fever. I think I'm free and clear. At least, for now."

"Oh, my poor child. Let me get you right to bed. Let's hope so, Natasha. There have been some deadly malarias in the *llanos orientales*."

Relaxed from a bath, Natasha borrowed some jeans and a shirt from her mother. They were a little wide in the hips and back, but otherwise were fine. Her only set of spare clothes was in shambles. But her Doc Martens had weathered the adventure well. The servant came back with them, having polished them to a perfect shine. She called Adalgisa in Berkeley and heard reassuring news about Tonto.

Ana Maria had already called the doctor, and he was on his way. In spite of her weakened state, Natasha was enthusiastic about the Yanomami. First, she had to return to Berkeley to organize a memorial for Bonaparte. She had already informed Cathy, his secretary. She was thinking about getting her Ph.D. in Anthropology and looked forward to doing her fieldwork with the Yanomami. Ana Maria told her that Ernesto was coming for Christmas. "Stay here until then, Natasha. It's already November."

Natasha needed rest. She needed to reflect on the past months that had so dramatically changed her life.

"Sure, Mom, I'll stay. I need some peace inside, after all this slaughter."

Finally, Natasha fell asleep, still weak from her bout with malaria.

In the garden, Clayton watched the moon rising over the mountains, as he sipped on a scotch. He felt light headed and relaxed. The night was fresh and inviting. A long bath had cleansed him of days in the jungle and the breeze coming from the mountains soothed his bruised soul. He felt that he had redeemed himself. He had left his selfish ways behind and acted with altruism and courage. Ana Maria stood by his side, and together they gazed at the sky, trying to find the Southern Cross. The Milky Way formed an enormous white cloud, almost excessive. Pointing at the sky, he said, "We are really insignificant when faced with the immensity of the universe, Ana."

"But yet, the center is here." She pointed at her heart. "So, we are not so insignificant, after all. We are a part of this immensity."

She looked at him for a long time. "You know, Clayton, you performed bravely. Wherever Paulo is, he must be proud of his brother."

He took her hand and gently stroked it. Then, instinctively, it slipped, to her breast, caressing it. They had made love, but in a hungry and rushed fashion, earlier that evening. "What should we do, Clayton? Will you leave, now that your job is done?"

A smile came to his face. Karin had a fat savings account in Switzerland. The daughters would not miss him much. As long as they had their status guaranteed.

"Actually, Clayton died mysteriously in the Amazon. But there is another fellow, Eugenio de Morais, who is fairly well off. He has an account at the Banque Générale du Luxembourg and..."

"Oh, you sneak."

"Perhaps you'd be interested in meeting him. Yes, Morais is the Financial Director of Portoluna. He would love to invest in a good ranch."

Ana flung her arms around him, kissing him repeatedly. He kissed her neck and felt her body writhe with pleasure. Yes, he would stay there for a long, long time.

# AFTERWORD

When Columbus arrived in Hispaniola (1492), the local inhabitants were described as handsome and healthy. The average height of Amerindians exceeded that of the Spaniards of that time. Twenty years later, the population of the island had been reduced to twenty percent. The Amerindians did not have any antibodies against the maladies brought from Europe, and a large number succumbed to simple diseases, such as influenza, measles, or smallpox. This sad cycle is about to complete itself, in the most remote regions of the Amazon. Recent studies suggest that the population of the Americas equaled that of Europe west of the Urals at the time of discovery. Up to 90% died of diseases brought by the Europeans and Africans.

There are approximately 20,000 Yanomami living in three hundred *shabonos* (villages) spread out over a territory the size of 70,000 square miles (roughly, the size of Minnesota) in the North Central Amazon. This remains the most remote and least populated part of the Amazon basin. The villages are primarily in Venezuela and Brazil, in the Orinoco and Negro river basins. For the necessity of this novel, one of them, Haximu-teri, was moved west, to the Dog's Head. These remote villages have resisted as-similation because of their inaccessibility; the Yanomami are land people and do not use rivers extensively. Their source of food is plantain, corn, manioc, and cassava, from gardens that they plant in the forest and from hunting and gathering. Rivers are the main thoroughfares in the Amazon, and most of the larger Amerindian groups living on them have completely disappeared or dissolved in the mass of the population. The remoteness, loose structure and relative independence of these villages have so far ensured their survival. That is, until thirty years ago, when massive logging and mining operations penetrated deeper and deeper into the forest, displacing the Yanomami, infecting them with disease, and disrupting their culture.

Two critical events initiated a massive invasion of Yanomami lands in Brazil and contributed significantly to their tragic demise.

1974: Construction of Perimetral Norte highway, crossing the Northern Amazon.

RADAM Project, which surveyed the mineral potential of the Amazon. The study suggested the existence of large deposits of gold, tin, diamonds, and uranium. In 1975, 500 miners invaded the Surucucus Mountains. In 1978 the Brazilian government authorized CVRD to exploit tin in Yanomami lands. In 1981, 2,000 *garimpeiros* (miners) invaded Yanomami lands, and successive waves have increased their numbers to 40,000.

They brought with them disease. Malaria, which was rather infrequent, is now endemic. It is estimated that 80% of Yanomami are currently infected. This has increased mortality rates and decreased birth rates. It is estimated

that the diseases introduced by the miners have extermi-
nated 15% of the Yanomami population.

There are efforts at preserving the Yanomami. In 1992,
President Collor of Brazil created the Yanomami Reservation,
with an area of a little over 1,000 square miles. Although this
covers only a small fraction of their territory, it was an aus-
picious beginning. In Venezuela, a similar but much more
generous effort has been taking place and President Carlos
Andrés Peres established a 32, 000 square mile reserve.

I became personally interested in the Yanomami over
two decades ago. In 1992, my son and I visited the legendary anthropologist Napoleon Chagnon, at the University
of California, Santa Barbara. My impression, upon meeting this middle aged man, whose book *Yanomamo: The Fierce
People* I had read with great interest and fascination, was
extremely positive. He talked about the Yanomami with
unbounded enthusiasm, and his concern for their well being was genuine. I had promised him to try to arrange for
visits to the Brazil Yanomami, which he had never studied.
He warned me, though, "You will find some very negative
things written about me."

I have a letter from Prof. Chagnon, dated 24 January
1992, in which he enthusiastically enlists my support for the
cause of the Yanomami. He starts by warning me against his
many detractors:

> *"I need all the help I can get in this struggle and would
> be very pleased to include you in my efforts. You must first
> decide if you want to be associated with me: just about ev-
> eryone, especially radical anthropologists consider me to be
> a controversial and evil person...especially a number of
> Brazilian anthropologists."*

Then, at the end, his true nature comes out, vibrant and determined:

> *"But, my ultimate objective is to do what I can to pro-tect these people and their environment, and that sometimes means pointing the finger at those who are doing things that jeopardize this."*

And indeed he was right, beyond all expectations. In reading the literature, I discovered a plethora of denigrators. Nevertheless, my first impression was so strong that I must deplore the chorus of mudslingers. Many great men have been controversial. And many smaller men have built a reputation by trying to pull down greater men. Chagnon is no exception. He spent close to six years among the Yanomami and has struggled, since 1964, for their survival. He is keenly aware of the rate at which their culture is vanishing and has done everything in his power to protect it. One might not agree with his stark and Darwinian vision of Neolithic Man in constant conflict, the objects being maximization and optimization of reproduction. He told me himself that the idyllic savage of Rousseau is a fallacy. But one has to respect his original and seminal contributions, which are part of the foundations of modern Sociobiology.

Attempts were made by colleagues to obtain permission for my visit the Brazil Yanomami, all unsuccessful. We wrote an extensive proposal and submitted it to FUNAI and CNPq. Unfortunately it was declined. Thus, I could not continue this effort.

The creation of a Yanomamiland between Brazil and Venezuela was a key element in this presumed US plan. This would ensure US access to all the riches of the Amazon. This concept still permeates, to a considerable extent, the Brazilian government. The best manner in which the territorial integrity of Brazil can be ensured is by minimizing the Yanomami presence and by integrating them rapidly into society. This approach has an undeniable genocidal flavor. This book represents an effort at exposing the reality and perils that Yanomami are experiencing. The royalties will be used toward their survival.

This book is dedicated to Professor Napoleon Chagnon, a hero and paladin of the Yanomamö, as he calls them. The latest edition of his famous book, "The Last Days of Eden," is a stark reminder about this vanishing nation.

To this day, I have done little for the survival of the Yanomami, but seek inspiration and strength from Prof. Chagnon. This book will hopefully sensitize the reader of the impending dangers faced by them.

I thank Mike Sirota for the splendid editing of this manuscript and for teaching me the rudiments of fiction writing. My gratitude is extended to Maria Cristina Alexandra Windsor for typing it, Carlos Henrique Meyers for providing the cover photograph, and Suzanne Meyers for her tireless work of translating it.

Comments by **Jaime Concha**, Distinguished Professor of Literature, University of California, San Diego

In the cultural landscape of Latin America, Marc Meyers is certainly a *rara avis*. Brazilian and Luxembourger -- a rare combination in itself -- he is a distinguished scientist who at the same time has authored several literary texts: fictional biographies, travel-books and a good number of novels. In the present narrative he explores a deep corner of Amazonia in connection with international events and the dark deeds of traffic against the life of people. Local and global, *Yanomami* will stimulate the reader to better understand situations and experiences taking place today in the first, third and fourth worlds of our planet.

Cover picture: Courtesy of Carlos Meyers
Back cover picture: Courtesy of Jeffrey Lehmann